MY UNUSUAL TALENT

JENNA MARCUS

CONTENTS

PROLOGUE

"Amber, help these people. Get them out as fast as you can," I commanded her, breaking her out of her shock.

"S-sure. But, what about you?" Amber asked, pulling one of the victims, Samuel Murdoch, to his feet.

Shaking my head slightly, I couldn't even believe what I was going to tell my sister. In my worst nightmares, I never imagined we'd be having this conversation. But here we were, trying to save people who had been kidnapped by a demented scientist.

"I need to stop him," I said, stepping out of the room and into the shadows of the third-floor hall, where I knew I'd have to stop the Parkway kidnapper from experimenting on anyone else ever again. When I entered the hall, the former doctor was staring at the wood boarding up the windows. Then, as if it was glass, the wood shattered into tiny daggers, falling to the dirt-coated floor. Rays of light poured into the warehouse.

"Turn yourself in, and there will be no fight," I said, keeping my hands firmly planted to my sides.

"Now, now. If I turned myself in, how would I take your powers?" he asserted, pulling a large syringe from his sleeve.

"Why did you kidnap people when you already have powers?" I inquired.

"When I was younger, I hardly had any powers," he stated, holding the syringe at his side.

I could tell he was itching to thrust the needle into me by the way his eyes kept shifting toward the device he grasped tightly in his right hand. Nervously clenching and unclenching my fists, I anticipated an attack, especially an invisible one.

1

IF I WERE JUST NORMAL

Sometimes I wondered what life would have been like if I were just normal. No gifts, no talents, no curses. I'm not saying I would have been an average, everyday teenager; however, life would have been much easier.

Some people would say that normalcy is overrated, especially my sister, Amber. She, unlike me, wanted to have something that set her apart. I suppose most people want that—a sense of the unique to hold onto, something that makes an individual truly *feel* like an individual. However, for those who were already ostracized, we wanted to find our place somewhere in that sea of sameness.

Do not get me wrong, I wasn't in favor of conformity; I didn't want everyone to be exactly alike. I just wanted to know what it was like to fit in. Sure, no one could tell that I was unique by just looking at me, but I could feel their eyes on the back of my head, trying to see where all of my secrets were stored. Perhaps I was just being paranoid, but then again, who wouldn't be?

I got through each day by knowing that this strange ability I had didn't control my life. It was a part of me, but it was not my core. It couldn't control me because I controlled it, for the most part. But that didn't stop the staring. It didn't stop me from wondering if those stares would peel away every other part of me.

"Watch the road!" Amber shouted.

Shaking my head, I swerved to avoid the curb and felt my wheels screech to a halt as my foot pressed down on the break.

"And you're the one who Mom and Dad trust to drive?" Amber joked, her hands splayed on the dashboard, bracing herself for a crash. Rolling my eyes, I shifted my white Honda Civic into park, unbuckled my seatbelt, and stepped out of the car to make sure there were no dents.

"You know, if you didn't take fifteen million years to deplete the ozone layer with your hairspray and try on about thirty different outfits, then maybe I wouldn't have to race to school," I said, getting back into my car and shifting the gear into drive.

Smirking, Amber twisted a strand of her curly red hair with her index finger, her emerald-green eyes sparkling with a suggestion.

"You know, if only you'd fly us to school, then being late wouldn't be a problem," Amber sang.

And there it was: flying. If I was a pilot, then Amber's suggestion would be plausible to any human being. Why not fly an airplane, helicopter, or even a hot-air balloon to school? Unfortunately, my sister knew I could fly us to school without a transportation device. She also knew I didn't need to hit the brake to stop my car.

"Cooper, I'm sure no one would see us. You could hold us up really high, even high enough so airplanes wouldn't see us," Amber suggested as she turned on the radio, quickly flipping through FM stations, listening to the menagerie of notes and lyrics melt into one another.

"Oh yeah, and the lack of oxygen wouldn't be a problem, would it?"

We had this discussion almost every morning.

Sometimes I wished she had the ability, so she would know what it was like have to control it. Not that I hated being able to raise anything without lifting a finger, it's just that I'd rather have been normal. I'd rather fight with my sister over who gets the remote than about why I wouldn't fly her around town.

Although she understood the consequences of letting her have a little fun with my powers, Amber tended to ignore them. She lived more in the present, whereas I anticipated the future, one in which I would have to explain how I could levitate a human being without any invisible strings. TV crews would come from all over the world to see the amazing teenager who could hold his sister in midair without even touching her. Perhaps I could convince them

I was Houdini's protege. However, repeatedly stating, "A magician never reveals his tricks" would lose its persuasiveness after a while.

Amber had a penchant for explaining how lucky I was to be "gifted," that being different made me special. When I was younger, I would agree with her, but now I was not so sure.

"You know, Cooper, you have telekinesis for a reason," she said, turning off the radio. "You could have a great destiny before you, but you'll never fulfill it if you're so worried about who's going to find out." "Destiny or no destiny, I'm not letting anyone else know I'm telekinetic except for you, Dad, and Mom," I said, pulling into a spot near our high school's front entrance. "It's too risky. Who knows what governmental experiments would be in store for me?"

"You have been watching too many sci-fi movies," Amber asserted. "I mean, you won't even let Sally know.

Don't you trust her?" Amber asked, unbuckling her seatbelt.

"That's not it. Let's just drop it," I said, trying to evade the truth.

I could never tell Sally my secret. She would think I was a freak. I couldn't even count how many times I'd wished I could tell Sally I have powers. Shouldn't a girlfriend know that?

She might sympathize if I told her about how I tried to fit in the crowd as best as I could, when I truly stood out. I didn't know how she would react. Would she still love me?

Sally had been my girlfriend for a year now, but she had been my best friend for a lifetime. I wondered if she'd ever suspected anything, especially that time at Rocker's Lake.

Sally and I had been sitting near the old willow tree, both our backs fit evenly against the bark. I remember that her glistening flaxen hair was draped over her thin, tan shoulders. Her shimmering, sapphire eyes looked at the tiny pebbles in the lake.

"I love this place," she said, easing her head onto my shoulder. "It makes me feel like I'm home."

I shivered, feeling her hand rest on my bare thigh. "Sally, I—" I began.

She gently placed her fingertip over my lips. Then, placing her finger under my chin, she turned my head to face her. It seemed as if her eyes grew larger. A glimpse of hunger flashed over them.

She pressed her lips hard against mine. I could taste her strawberry kiwi–lip gloss as we kissed. My hands made their way up her shirt. I could feel the underlining of her bra as my hands slid to the front.

Her tongue intertwined with mine, her hands pulling at my shirt. We broke our kiss so I could pull my shirt over my head. I never saw that shirt again.

We continued to kiss, our mouths becoming one. My heart raced as she unhooked her bra and flung it where my shirt had landed, in the lake.

She pinned her breasts against my chest. We lay under the cool shade of the willow tree.

I could feel beads of sweat begin to form all over my body. My heart practically ripped its way out of my chest.

Her hands fumbled over the zipper of my shorts.

She arched her back as we continued to kiss, trying to take off my shorts.

The world seemed lighter, as if I could feel every molecule. It was as if my body reached out for miles, levitating everything and everyone so they would know the sensation of truly being lighter than air.

That's when I realized I couldn't feel the grass on my back. I felt nothingness under me, hoping it was an illusion.

Opening my eyes, I was terrified of what I saw. Not only were Sally and I in midair, but the water in the lake hovered over the deep hole where it used to lay, the pebbles underneath the thick circle of water as if they were holding it up. The willow tree had ripped from the ground, it's roots clinging to large particles of dirt. Even the blades of grass were standing up more than usual.

I tried to ease everything into its place, but I couldn't. Nothing would move, not even Sally and me. It was as if everything around me refused to lay back on the ground. They were finally uprooted, free, and wanted to stay that way.

Again, I concentrated on the objects around me and tried to pull them down, but to no avail.

Sally continued to kiss me. Her body rested on mine, so she had no idea we were ten feet above the ground. My heart rate sped up as she began to slide my shorts off.

I wished everything would fall. The sky could even fall for all I cared. I just wanted to feel the ground underneath me.

I tried to slow my heart down. With Sally's body resting on mine, it was impossible to decelerate it to anything less than a hummingbird's heart rate.

Her kissing grew more intense as I tried to think of something mundane; however, the only thought that entered my head was that moment.

I knew then that the only way for everything to fall into place was if I broke our kiss. Quickly, I placed my hands over Sally's eyes. Her eyelashes fluttered under my palms.

She withdrew her lips from mine and exclaimed, "Cooper, what are you doing?"

Without a word, I concentrated on my heart rate, slowing it down enough so I could at least ease Sally and myself onto the ground. The blades of grass on my back felt good. Even the sticky dew was comforting. "Cooper, why are you covering my eyes?" Sally asked, removing her hands from my shorts.

I kept my heart rate down long enough to concentrate on the willow tree and the lake. Anything else that floated in midair seemed to ease its way onto the ground. The willow tree took its place in the gaping hole in the ground, and the water and pebbles set into the deep, wide hole. I couldn't see what else floated while Sally and I kissed, but I knew that everything found its place on the earth's surface once again.

After taking my hands from Sally's eyes, I quickly slid out from under her and pulled up my shorts.

"Cooper, what's going on?" she asked, as I began to slowly slink away from her.

"Nothing. I—um—just have to get home, you know? My parents will wake up soon, and it's my turn to serve breakfast."

Her eyes were soft and wanting. I, too, desired to be with her, but I couldn't risk exposure.

"Is it me?" she asked, lowering her head. "I thought you wanted me, too."

I did want her. I wanted her more than anything.

What really killed me was that I couldn't have her.

"No, Sally. It's me," I said, walking closer to her. "I'm—um—I'm just not ready yet. We should wait...until we're both ready."

I drew her into my arms. As she rested her head on my shoulder, I could smell the dawn's dew on her smooth hair.

"You're right, Cooper. That way, when it happens, it will be more special than we could imagine."

Oh, if she only knew how special that morning was.

I always wondered if she felt us floating. We were in midair for a while. Time seemed to stand still forever.

I'm surprised that we started dating after that morning. I still couldn't comprehend why she would want to date someone like me. She almost gave her entire self to me, and I pulled away from her. You would think she would be furious with me.

Ever since that day, I haven't been able to get too close with Sally. Sure, we kissed, but we never got any further than that. I knew she wanted more. She was ready to move to the next level, but I couldn't risk it. I would need to be sure that nothing would happen. Perhaps I could nail everything and everyone to the floor when it happened.

When I came home that morning, Amber told me she felt lighter, everything did. She said it was as if everything and everyone on the earth jumped in midair. It was even on the news that night. Good thing they described it as a minor earthquake, which was rare in New York.

I'm not sure if the entire world jumped, but what Amber told me still haunted my dreams.

"Cooper, are you getting out of the car?" Amber asked.

I shook my head, releasing the memory, and removed my seatbelt. The bell was just about to ring. "Don't forget we have to go home right after school today," I reminded Amber. "Mom asked us to clean out the attic."

"Correction, Mom asked you to clean out the attic," Amber said.

"So, where's your boyfriend?" I asked.

Amber rolled her eyes and began to walk toward the entrance. For the life of me, I didn't know why Amber seemed to have a different boyfriend each week. She had a menagerie of them. I think you could fill a stadium with all the boys she'd dated.

Granted, Amber was very beautiful, but guys seemed to flock to her. I was probably the only one who hasn't dated her. In fact, one of her ex-boyfriends asked me why we haven't gone out. Hopefully, he hadn't realized she was my little sister. Either that, or he was in favor of incest.

"Hey, Cooper," Sally whispered in my ear.

I felt the hairs on the back of my neck stand up.

She slowly ran her long fingernail up my spine, and I couldn't help but shiver. Her jasmine fragrance filled the air solely around us.

"We have to get to class, Sally," I said, turning to kiss her.

My fingers ran through her soft hair, seemingly never finding their way out. As her soft, luscious lips caressed mine, the first bell rang.

I withdrew from her and began to walk up the cobblestone stairs.

"I don't want to go in," Sally said, pouting.

I linked her hand in mine and pushed open the door.

"Save me a seat at lunch," I said, slowly sliding out of her grasp.

The day seemed to pass slowly. I wasn't sure why; it seemed like any other day at Erikson High. Bells rang, teachers gave out assignments, and the halls overflowed with students walking slower than snails to their next class.

I sat in my usual seat in AP Physics. Unfortunately, Sally's best friend, Michelle Gibson, sat right behind me. She thought Sally was too good for me. Everything that happened between Sally and me always made its way back to Michelle, who just happened to be the biggest gossip in school—another reason why I could never tell Sally my secret.

"Hey, Cooper," Michelle said, turning away from her horde of friends.

"Hi, Michelle," I said, hoping Mr. Nelson would hurry up and start the lesson.

Physics was one of my favorite subjects. Unfortunately, Michelle had to be in the same period, where she found every opportunity to reiterate the events of my latest dates with Sally.

Inevitably, Michelle tapped my shoulder before class begun. I sighed, preparing to be criticized. "So, Sally told me that you two are getting together tonight, which is ironic considering the disastrous date you had the night before," she teased.

Michelle had this uncanny ability to humiliate anyone at the drop of a hat. If she wasn't Sally's friend, I'd would have ignored her. I realized she was just trying to look out for Sally, but she hadn't known Sally for as long as I had. She didn't know half the things that I knew, like how Sally was petrified of needles. When she had to go for her hepatitis shots, she practically broke my fingers as she squeezed my hand while the doctor injected her with the vaccine.

"That's none of your business," I said, turning back in my seat, opening my textbook.

"It's more my business than you know," she whispered in my ear.

Before I could respond, Mr. Nelson entered the room just as the bell rang. Luckily, that was the one thing that could keep Michelle quiet. She might be a pest, but I had to hand it to her, she cared about her studies.

"Mr. O'Neil, why is the sky blue and not, let's say, indigo?" Mr. Nelson asked.

Ah, one of the questions of life inquisitive children seem to always ask.

"Simply put, blue has the highest frequency out of the color spectrum. If indigo's frequency were higher, then perhaps our skies would have a purple hue," I said.

Mr. Nelson chuckled and pointed to the color spectrum poster over the green blackboard.

"ROYGBIV. Excellent, Mr. O'Neil. Maybe that's why you were the only one who got an A on last week's test," he said, addressing the class.

I could feel the same, scowling students' eyes burning into the back of my head. Being the kid who sets the grade curve isn't a highly appreciated trait in our class. Kids were already stressed out about the AP exams.

I didn't blame them for disliking me. They probably thought I was the teacher's pet because I answered all his questions correctly and had a 4.0 GPA. It wasn't not my fault I was intelligent. It came naturally. Sometimes, I believed being telekinetic somehow affected my cognitive capacity.

After three periods of Einstein's theory of relativity, the Pythagorean theorem, and Fahrenheit 451, lunch finally came.

Sally waited for me at our usual table, away from the hundreds of kids yelling at the top of their lungs and the spattered traces of what the lunch ladies considered food all over the cafeteria.

"God, they're animals," I said, sitting next to Sally. "I know," she agreed, pulling out her bagged lunch.

Her eyes were cast downward as she unwrapped her usual tomato and bay leaf on whole-wheat toast sandwich. Sally's mother is a health nut and refuses to let her daughter eat anything that has fat or sugar in it.

"So, are you still coming over?" Sally asked, looking pensively at her sandwich.

I was surprised Michelle hadn't drilled my consistent unreliability into Sally's head already. I had cancelled a few dates, especially lately. I knew I could never tell Sally about my abilities, and yet when I was with her, I felt compelled to abandon my fears. Like Amber, I was tempted to release my inhibitions and just let the moment happen. However, sanity always pulled me back from this inevitable mistake.

If I told her my secret, who knew how she'd react? Who knew how fast the news would get to Michelle, which meant, how fast would it get to the entire school? My life would literally be a sci-fi movie experiment scene.

"Cooper, are you listening to me?" Sally asked, giving my arm a nudge.

"Um, yeah…could you repeat it one more time, just for clarification?"

Sally rolled her eyes and wrapped the rest of her sandwich in plastic wrap.

"I said my parents aren't going to be home, so we could have the house to ourselves. Not that you seem to care."

I playfully brushed a strand of hair behind her ear and caressed her cheek with my thumb.

"I do care. I said I'd come, and I'll come."

The corners of her mouth slowly curved upward into a seductive, content smile.

"Okay, just checking. You would never believe what Michelle was telling me—"

"I bet," I said, rolling my eyes.

"I know she can be a bit noisy, Cooper, but she's my best friend."

"Okay, she just blabs about us all over the school, but she's the greatest best friend in the world," is what I wanted to say, but I held my tongue. One rule I've learned about having a girlfriend is that you never insult her friends, especially her best friend.

I was just about to ask Sally if she wanted a frozen yogurt when, suddenly, I heard a shrill cry coming from outside.

"What was that?" Sally asked, trying to see past the leaves coating the outside of the window.

"I don't know," I said, walking toward the door facing the street.

Apparently, we weren't the only ones who heard the scream because almost every student crowded around the open doorway.

I held Sally's hand, trying to make my way through the crowd to see what happened. Students' feet seemed to be plastered to the ground by the way they refused to move.

It seemed to take forever, but Sally and I squeezed through the crowd just enough to see a battered woman sitting on the sidewalk. She looked disheveled and panicked. One of her eyes was swollen shut, as if someone had punched her with brass knuckles, and her pink jumpsuit was torn on the left arm.

"Oh my God," Sally said, pushing us to the front of the crowd until we were mere feet away from this woman.

Kids who'd made their way through the cafeteria doors first surrounded the woman, no one bothering to ask her what happened. How is it that when someone is hurt the only thing we can do is stand in a circle and gawk?

"Miss, are you okay?" Sally asked, helping the woman to her feet.

The woman brushed back strands of black hair that stuck to her tearstained cheeks. It took her a second to get her footing, but she finally stood up. Sally tried to brush away pieces of dirt that had clung to her clothing, but to no avail.

"I think so," the woman said, touching her eye.

New tears spilled over the old ones as she lightly dabbed her swollen eye.

"We have to get you to a—" Before Sally could finish her sentence, security guards made their way through the crowd.

"Ma'am are you okay?" one of the guards asked.

The woman nodded as she fumbled for something in her pocket.

"Oh God!" the woman shrieked. "He took my inhaler!"

The guards looked around, only seeing the hundreds of students standing around the woman.

"What'd he look like?" I asked, trying to see over the heads of the students.

"Th-this man who was wearing some type of ski mask took it. He took my inhaler," she gasped, trying to control her breathing. "He took my purse, too. It's my bright pink one that my husband gave me. My whole life's in that purse. I don't know what I'll do without it."

She began panting when she realized this. The woman leaned on Sally, trying to catch her breath.

While the guards were preoccupied with the woman, I tried to make my way through the crowd, but it was no use; I was stuck.

I concentrated on my feet, slowly balancing myself on my toes. Holding my balance, I once again tried to see over the sea of heads.

Even though I didn't have some type of super- vision, I could still see quite far. As far as I could tell, the mugger was probably blocks away from the school by now, but it couldn't hurt to check.

I slowly lowered myself onto the balls of my feet.

"I'll take her to the hospital. My car's right there," Sally said to one of the guards.

As Sally and the guard argued, the crowd began to break up.

"An ambulance is faster," the guard debated. "My car's just as fast," Sally countered.

I lightly placed my hand on Sally's shoulder. "Come on. She'll be fine," I said, gently moving her back into the cafeteria.

Just as Sally and I began to walk back, a kid came running from around the corner. He practically skidded into a guard as he tried to stop.

"I think I saw the mugger," the kid said, trying to catch his breath.

How could he have heard what she said? He must have been in the inner circle of the crowd.

"What way did he go?" I yelled over the buzzing crowd.

"Near the front of the school," he said.

A couple of the guards and I ran toward the front of the school. One of the guards said something about staying behind, but I ran right past him. When we reached the front of the school, the mugger was nowhere in sight.

Plus, even if he were, what made me think I could recognize him? The woman said he was wearing a ski mask at the time. I highly doubted that he'd still be wearing it unless he was a complete idiot.

I surveyed the area, irrationally thinking that somehow, I might be able to identify him without ever seeing him. That's when I saw a man holding a gaudy pink purse underneath his arm, briskly walking around the corner.

Without thinking, I ran after him. He must have sensed my pace, as his walk quickly turned into a run.

It's times like these when I wished I had paid attention in gym class because I was losing speed quick. This guy could be a track star by the way he was running. Either that, or he was an experienced mugger.

Realizing there was no way I could catch up with him, I concentrated on his feet. Even though he was moving quickly and more than twenty feet in front of me, I still managed to trip him.

He must not have hit the ground hard enough, because he quickly bounced back up and began to run again.

It was going to take a little more effort than I thought to stop this guy.

I concentrated on his feet once again, this time making sure I had a strong hold on him. Swiftly sliding his feet out from under him, I dragged him across the pavement about a foot or two.

Despite the countless scraps he must have had, he still tried to get up and escape.

Once again, my intangible hold gripped his legs, and I pulled him back a couple of inches and then firmly pressed him into the pavement.

"He's not going anywhere," I mumbled to myself. I called the guards over, and they apprehended the mugger. A crowd of students followed the guards as they surrounded and arrested the mugger.

"What happened?" Sally asked, interlocking her hand in mine.

"He tripped," I said. "Come on, let's go back inside."

I could hear sirens growing louder as an ambulance rushed by.

As we walked toward the cafeteria, I couldn't shake the feeling that something was wrong. The mugger should have been at least blocks away from the woman by the time I tried to look for him. Although, he did seem to put a lot of effort into trying to get away.

Maybe I was just being paranoid, as I'd been prone to be at times.

"It was odd. I could have sworn I saw him slide backward," Sally said, resting her head on my shoulder.

"I—I didn't see that," I stammered.

If she saw him slip backward, how many other people saw? Why did I drag him like that? Sure, seeing that poor woman did set me off, but that was no reason to use my powers the way I did. It was just that when I saw helpless, abused people, I felt the need to do something about it.

There was a reason I had these powers; why shouldn't I use my telekinesis to help others?

However, by doing so, I risked exposure. Thousands of reporters and scientists would come from all over the world to see the amazing telekinetic teen. Experimentation would become my existence. Needles would be part of the drudgery of daily life for me. I couldn't deal with that life. Conducting experiments was my dream, not becoming the lab rat.

Hopefully, the mugger didn't realize what happened; however, even if he told the police the situation, they wouldn't believe him...hopefully.

I had to learn to control the temptation to stop injustices by using my powers. That wasn't the first time something like this has happened. Some were insignificant acts. If I saw a kid stealing, I'd pull the items out of his hand. Or if I happened to see a bully beating up some defenseless kid, I'd pull his feet out from under him and hold him down long enough for the kid could run. Although, there have been times when I used my abilities to stop greater crimes, like felonies.

For example, when I was about ten years old, my mother, Amber, and I went into the city to pick out a birthday present for my dad. I could still remember my mom repeatedly telling me that I had to hold my sister's hand; she made me promise to always look after my sister. Amber tended to run away when she was let loose. Not much had changed now that she was fourteen, but at least she'd stopped running into oncoming traffic.

Instead of taking the subway, my mother had insisted on driving into the city. She told me the present she was buying my father was too large to bring onto a subway. In retrospect, she was right. There was no way we were going to fit a desk that was longer than me into a crowded subway.

My mother had just purchased the van. With my mother's promotion at the real estate agency, she decided that a van would be a perfect celebratory gift. That new car smell still lingered in the interior. Dents and minor scratches were a fear and not a reality. The driver's side door opened without a familiar, yet irritating screech.

The store had a strong cedar musk, which overpowered my senses. I told my mother I had to go outside because I couldn't take the smell.

"Take your sister with you and don't let go of her hand. I'll be out there in a minute," she said, turning her attention back to the store clerk.

Now, I knew I was from a small town and in the city they did things a bit differently, but I also believed that no matter where you went, you could easily recognize larceny, especially when the thieves were stealing your mom's new van.

Two guys had broken into our van and begun to drive off. I assumed it wasn't the first time they'd stolen a car, considering they broke in so quickly.

"Cooper, where are they going with Mommy's car?" Amber asked, trying to wiggle out of my grasp.

"Quit it, Amber," I said, squeezing her hand a bit tighter. "They're stealing it, but they won't get far."

I focused on the tires, slowing their rotation. Gently, I pulled the van backward, making sure it was exactly where my mother parked it.

Holding the doors locked, I told Amber to run into the store and tell our mother to call the police. For once, Amber listened to me.

Even though I stopped two criminals from stealing my mother's brand-new van, she still punished me because I let go of Amber's hand. She told me it was a good thing Amber listened to me instead of disregarding my instructions and running out into the busy street.

I think the main reason she punished me was because I used my ability without thinking about the consequences. There were many tourists with cameras in their hands. It was a possibility that one of them could have recorded my paranormal heroism.

My parents constantly warned me that I had to be careful. They didn't want my powers exposed any more than I did. I could tell they worried about me and wished they could keep tabs on me almost every second of the day, but I thought they trusted me. They knew I cleaned up my own messes and that I was mature enough now to weigh the risks before using my powers.

The rest of the day seemed to crawl by. The news of the mugger buzzed throughout the halls. Some even labeled me a hero, saying I attacked the mugger and threw him to the ground. Others said I pointed the mugger out to the guards, and they all piled on top of him like linebackers on the opposing team's quarterback. Luckily, no one mentioned that the mugger looked as if he was dragged backward by some invisible force. Well, at least not yet.

If Sally told Michelle she thought she saw the mugger being pulled backward, she'd tell the entire school that some ghostly entity did it. Knowing that I was there, Michelle would somehow pin the whole ordeal on me.

That's all I needed, Michelle spreading rumors about me that were secretly true. Well, almost. However, although I was responsible for dragging and holding the mugger down, there was no way that she could know or prove it.

When school finally ended, Sally and Michelle were waiting for me by my car.

"Damn," I mumbled as I walked toward them. "Hey, hero," Michelle said, grinning as I walked around her. "Sally told me about your good deed of the day. Intriguing."

Intriguing? Oh God, how much did Sally tell her?

"I didn't do anything," I said, fumbling for my keys. "Cooper, what are you talking about?" Sally asked, running her fingers through her smooth, flaxen hair. "You chased after that creep. Even though you didn't physically catch him, you still tried to stop him."

I wished everyone would stop making the incident into such a big deal. The mugger was caught, and the woman got her purse and inhaler back. What more was there to discuss? This was one of the many annoyances I faced as a high school student; kids wouldn't stop talking about one unusual occurrence. Hopefully, someone would come in tomorrow wearing last year's jeans or something, and students would cling onto that topic instead.

"Aren't you going to ask Sally if she needs a ride home?" Michelle inquired, nudging my shoulder.

I almost lost my footing and pressed my palm against the driver's side door to keep my balance.

"I'd be happy to take you home. But didn't you drive your car to school today?" I asked, narrowing my eyes at Michelle.

"Yes. Michelle and I came to school together today."

"Yeah, lover boy," Michelle teased. "Well, we better be going. Watch your step, hero."

I swore, one day I'd lose control of my powers and accidentally trip her. For now, I had to keep that temptation in check.

"Cooper!" I heard my sister call to me from across the courtyard.

She clung to her new boyfriend as if their skin had been fused together.

"Great, the new boyfriend of the week," I mumbled to myself.

"Hey, bro," Steve said.

With his varsity jacket draped over my sister's shoulders and her looking up at him adoringly, they looked like the clichéd, hopelessly-in-puppy-love couple.

"Hey, Steve," I said, opening the driver's side door. "Amber, we have to get home early today, remember?"

Amber narrowed her eyes at me. I knew she wanted me to like her new boyfriend, but I just couldn't; she only seemed to develop superficial relationships. There was no point in trying to get to know her boyfriends because they would be replaced with a replica.

"Fine," Amber hissed. "I'll see you tomorrow, okay."

She playfully tussled Steve's long, curly blonde hair. After giving him a quick peck on the lips, she reluctantly walked around to the passenger door and got in. "Why do you always do that?" Amber asked, as I pulled out of the parking spot.

"What? Mom asked me to clean out the attic as soon as possible, and I want to clean it out in time to go to Sally's house before—" I cut myself off. Amber didn't need to know all the details about tonight.

"Before what?" Amber asked, turning on the radio. "Oh, I get it."

She sheepishly grinned at me. Was it just me or did all girls have a particular grin that made guys feel like they were being mentally probed?

"Shut up," I said, shutting off the radio.

When we got home, I pulled my car into a spot in front of my house and ran toward the door.

"Rushing to get to that attic, are we?" Amber teased.

I rolled my eyes as I opened the front door. The house felt like a hollow shell, even though it was fully stocked with every type of furniture piece my mother could find. We even had a second living room set on the top floor. Who in their right mind would want two living rooms?

Quickly, I put two bowls of macaroni and cheese into the microwave and placed my book bag on the kitchen counter.

"What's for dinner?" Amber asked, grabbing an apple.

"Macaroni and cheese. I don't have time to create intricate cuisine, madame," I teased, running upstairs. "When it's done, take it out."

2

THE DIARY

The attic trapdoor was practically plastered to the ceiling. A string used to hang from it, but it broke off a couple of years ago and no one bothered to replace it.

Concentrating on the edges, I slowly cracked the paint lined around the sides of the door. I pulled the door down carefully, making sure it didn't smack against the wall. Once the door was steady, I focused on myself.

I could feel every molecule in my body as I began to float upward. When I was younger, sometimes I would sit in an Indian position and lift myself in midair. Amber used to laugh every time I levitated and would then beg me to float her around the room as well. Actually, not much had changed.

The attic was covered in sheets of dust. I was surprised I was able to see anything. Cool air whisked throughout the sullen room, which lacked windows. The place seemed empty, as if no human presence had ever stepped foot in it, even though there were withered cardboard boxes lining the room.

Looking down at my jeans and new sneakers, I realized I should have changed into something I never wanted to see again before cleaning the attic.

Taking a quick scan of the attic once again, I realized I should have told my mother I was allergic to attics, especially this one.

I began removing blankets of dust from the largest box on the left. The dust fell to the ground as if it had formed into a large, grimy rug.

"I wonder what's in here?" I asked myself, as I opened the box. The flaps practically crumbled in my hands as a swarm of spiders escaped from their cardboard home. Quickly, I lifted the spiders into midair and placed them inside another cardboard box.

I reluctantly sifted through the box, seeing if there was anything in it worth salvaging. The only things in the box were some stuffed manila folders, an old textbook, what looked like a yearbook, and a leather-bound book. Pulling out the textbook, I brushed cobwebs off the cover, which read *Theoretical Medical Techniques*. Interesting. Was this one of my father's books? No, he kept all his books in his office. Perhaps, these were his college textbooks. That would explain the yearbook.

Layers of cobwebs covered the yearbook. Spiders must have made that book their ancestral domain. I wouldn't have been surprised if I found a little spider graveyard underneath the webs.

The book was practically tearing at the seams. It looked too old and withered to be my father's yearbook.

I opened the book, trying not to rip the pages. The yearbook came from Locke High School. There was one public and three private high schools in the area, and none were named after John Locke. The first page showed a picture of over a hundred students standing in front of their school, which resembled a restored medieval castle. A banner that hung over the enormous entranceway read "Class of 1973." This yearbook definitely wasn't my father's, because he was born in 1974.

I flipped to the back of the yearbook, wondering if anyone wrote any comments in it. Luckily, I found a few that covered a couple of blank pages in the back. Though, the writing had faded over the years.

One person practically wrote a book, their comments covering a full page. The writing was curvy and slanted, but I was still able to make it out.

> These years we've spent together have meant everything to me. Every time I see you, I wonder if your presence is just a fantasy. Love has never been a word I've been comfortable with, but with you, that word completes me. You've stayed by my side throughout the part of my life that matters. I can't remember life without you. It seems like only yesterday that we met. Do you remember? I can never forget it. You practically ran out of algebra class. Your hair was so unkempt,

your tie was loose, and your slacks were torn on your left knee. I was walking down the hall with Beth and Mary when you dropped your books and they slid toward my feet. The first thing I noticed was your large, emerald eyes. You looked like a racoon that just ran out into the middle of traffic. I couldn't help but smile. Your helpless eyes melted my soul. I told you my name as I helped you gather your things. All you could do was mumble something about a compass and desks. I never understood your rambling. Honestly, half the time I'm too caught up in those pensive yet troubled eyes. It took me a few seconds before I noticed the large gash on your knee. I assumed you cut yourself because of your klutzy manner, so I took you to the nurse's office. That was the day I fell deeply and hopelessly in love with you. My sister agreed to help us with the wedding after gradua-tion. Marriage. That word sends lovely shivers down my spine. I can hardly wait. I love you so much, my darling. Love, Rose.

Rose? The only person I knew with the name Rose was my grandmother. That could only mean one thing: this was my grandfather's yearbook.

According to my mother, my grandfather died in 1986. My mother used to tell me how my grandfather wanted to be a famous doctor. He came from a poor family that hardly had enough money to put food on the table. My great-grandfather's clinic was bought out by Parkway Hospital. It figured; small businesses never survived in a world ruled by monopolies. No wonder the board game was so popular.

My mother idolized the man, even though she hardly remembered him. She used to tell me these fairy tales where my grandfather was a stoic knight who saved his daughter from the dreaded dragon in a dungeon. She knew her father would come because he was the only one who could break the binding spell that trapped my mother in the evil dragon's clutches.

It was one of my favorite fairy tales. Sometimes, after my mother told me the story, she'd look out my window for a minute, as if the tale existed somewhere outside the room. Whenever she talked about my grandfather, she had this nostalgic look in her eyes, as if she remembered every little detail about him. After a few seconds, she'd shake her head and say the only thing she could remember about her father was that he was quite clumsy.

He'd constantly let items slip out of his grasp. No wonder my grandmother constantly referred to him as "slippery fingers." I wondered why my mother had my grandfather's yearbook and textbooks in a disheveled cardboard box. The man meant so much to her; you'd think she'd keep them intact.

Placing the yearbook back into the box, my eyes fell upon the leather-bound book. Picking up the book, I brushed off the layers of dust that clung to the cover. I was tempted to bring the book downstairs and wash it, but I knew that would smear the ink; that is, if the ink hadn't already faded.

I didn't understand why my grandfather's books were in such bad shape. After forty-four years, you'd think they would only be a little dusty from sitting in the cardboard box in my parents' attic. Finally, when I got almost all the dust off the book, I carefully pulled at the black leather strap holding the book shut, but it was sewn to the binding.

I concentrated on the strap, feeling the leather slowly pull a part. However, I tugged too hard, and the strap ripped in half as if it were a mere piece of paper.

Opening the book to the first page, I noticed the ink was undamaged. In fact, the writing in the book looked better than the notes in my notebook. Not one word was smudged. It looked as if a hand had never even touched the page. Obviously, this person was quite neat.

I began to read the first page. The handwriting was familiar, but I couldn't put my finger on whose handwriting it reminded me of. The first page dated back to February 14, 1970.

> I never know how to start these journal entries. Let me start by saying that this journal is a gift from my beloved Rose. This is our first Valentine's Day together. I wish I could have bought her something a little more expensive than a couple of withering roses, but money has been tight since my father lost his clinic. I wish I could help. I offered to get a job at the pharmacy as a stock boy, but my parents wouldn't hear of it. My Da has a lot of pride and refuses to take charity, especially from his children. The way things are going, he might need that job for himself. I've been eating at Rose's house quite often so there will be more food for my parents and little sister, Sophie. I hope to get a scholarship to a great medical school so I can take care of my family. Perhaps I can slip some money into Da's wallet when I come over. Rose offered to help my family in any way she could, but I told

her my parents like to handle their own problems by themselves. We moved from Ireland almost ten years ago, and Da still doesn't trust the people in this country. He brought our family here so he could give his children the benefits he didn't have as a kid. I think that's another reason he doesn't want me to work; he wants me to only focus on school and that's all. He even disapproves of me being with Rose. If I ever get less than an A+ on my report card, he always blames it on me spending too much time with Rose. He's always telling me, "Maxwell, pretty girls are always trouble." But he doesn't know Rose like I do. She's genuinely kindhearted and cares deeply for others. She always tells me she hopes she can become a nurse one day. She's so perfect. I don't know why she puts up with me. She could have any guy she wants, and yet she stays with me. From time to time, I'll ask her why she stays with me after everything I've done. She always has the same response, "Oh, Max, I love you too much to leave you. If another guy spilt something on me almost every day and broke almost every glass figurine in my room, I wouldn't give him the time of day. But for you, I'll stay by your side forever." I love her so much. I wish I could be the smooth, charming fellow that she deserves. I wish, just for one day, I wouldn't screw everything up. I wish one day that everything could be perfect. Sincerely, Max.

It was obvious that this was my grandfather's journal, but how could my mother leave my grandfather's journal in a cardboard box in the attic? Did she even realize that a large part of her father lay in a deteriorating box practically encompassed by dust and cobwebs? I stacked my grandfather's journal, textbook, and yearbook near the attic opening and began to sift through the rest of the cardboard boxes. As I pulled open various cardboard flaps, finding the spider mothership, that journal still lingered in my mind. My eyes would inadvertently look toward the journal every now and again.

Why would my mother have this journal without reading it and trying to find out who Max McEwin really was? She always wished grandpa lived long enough for her to get to know him; this was her opportunity.

"Cooper, your mac and cheese is forming into ice!" Amber called from the kitchen.

"Coming," I yelled back, as I closed the last of the cardboard boxes.

I picked up grandpa's books and descended from the attic opening. His books felt right in my grasp, as if I was meant to hold them, especially his journal.

"Hey, what are those?" Amber asked, reaching for the yearbook.

"Believe it or not, they're Grandpa McEwin's books," I said, placing them on the kitchen counter. "Mom had them this entire time and never thought to take them out and read them."

Amber gently placed the yearbook on the table and stepped back as if it would explode any second.

"Grandpa McEwin? Whoa. This is unbelievable."

When Amber was five years old, our grandmother had a nervous breakdown when she saw a picture of Grandpa McEwin taken in the seventies, which she kept in a safe in the back of her closet, in my sister's hand.

Amber and I were hunting for "monsters" in our grandmother's house when we came across the safe. I didn't want to open it, but Amber kept pestering me to see what was inside.

"Nana has a secret closet, Cooper," Amber said in her high-pitched voice. "The monsters could be hiding in there. We'd be helping her by opening it."

Even at five years old, my sister had exemplary manipulation skills.

"It's wrong, Amber. Nana would be furious if we opened her safe. Now, I proved there were no monsters in the house, so let's go downstairs."

Amber's large, emerald eyes began to fill up with tears as I crawled out from under the hanging linen dresses.

"But I won't sleep if the monsters find Nana," Amber whimpered, wiping her tears on the back of her tiny, pale hand.

"There are no monsters, I promise."

"But Nana will die." Amber began crying so loud that I had to cover her mouth.

"Okay, okay. I'll open it, but you must promise you won't take anything. Pinky swear?"

Amber nodded as our pinkies interlocked.

I stared at the steel door as it reluctantly opened, revealing its secrets.

"Cooper the wizard." Amber smiled, showing the gap her front baby teeth had once occupied.

She didn't learn the proper name for my ability until she was ten years old. Amber always assumed I was some type of magician or wizard who could make people and objects fly around.

I expected to find checkbooks, dollar bills bound together by a bank seal, bonds, rare coins, jewelry, or anything else of monetary value. Instead, what we found in that safe were letters, pictures, and a couple of pieces of paper bound together by a withering, red rubber band.

"Pictures!" Amber squealed, and she started taking the photographs out of the safe.

As we sifted through the pictures, we found none of our grandmother, her parents, or hardly any of our mother. Practically all the photos were of Grandpa McEwin.

There was only one picture of our mother when she was just born as our grandfather held her in his arms.

"I stole grandpa's hair," Amber said, pointing to our grandfather's short, curly red locks.

Amber resembled our grandfather so much that our grandmother was always taken aback whenever she saw my sister. If she had been born a boy, she would have looked as if she were our grandfather reincarnated.

"You kids upstairs? I made cookies," our grandmother called from downstairs.

Quickly, I gathered the pictures, shoved them into the safe, and fumbled to lock it.

Amber and I ran downstairs to find our grandmother holding a plate of cookies. When I was three years old, I believed my grandmother was made of chocolate chip cookies because she was constantly baking them, even if no one was there to eat them. To this day, the smell of chocolate chip cookies lingered on my grandmother's clothes.

"Nana, I stole grandpa's hair," Amber said, presenting our grandmother with the picture.

Her smile faded as she stared at the picture, dropping the plate of cookies. For the first time, my grandmother's house seemed hollow.

"Where'd you get that?" our grandmother demanded, shakily reaching for the picture. "It was in a locked safe. You two couldn't have opened it. How'd you get this picture?"

Our grandmother lightly brushed her fingertips along the edges of the photograph as tears formed in her teal eyes.

"Grandpa wouldn't want the monsters to hurt you," Amber said, picking up a cookie from the floor.

I picked up the broken pieces of the cookie dish as Amber collected the cookies. Our grandmother seemed to stand in the same spot forever. It was as if time stood still around her as she was trapped within her memories.

"You—your grandpa? M-max? Max gave you this?" our grandmother asked. "Monsters. The monsters. He's coming. Max said he wouldn't come. How could he come? After all these years?"

I had to practically lift Grandma McEwin and sit her down on the couch. When our mother arrived twenty minutes after I called her, Grandma McEwin was in shock. She was taken to the hospital, where she had to stay for a week.

I told my mother what my grandmother had said to Amber and me, but she dismissed it as ramblings from a woman who had a nervous breakdown. However, I could tell there was something my mother wasn't telling me.

Now that I had found this journal, I definitely believed my mother was keeping secrets from Amber and me about our grandfather. What was so mysterious about my grandfather? He was an aspiring doctor who died at a young age. However, every time I asked my mother how Grandpa McEwin died, she always changed the subject.

"Did you read this book?" Amber asked, picking up the journal where I had ripped the strap.

"Yes. But I just read the first journal entry."

"You know, that's an invasion of privacy," Amber said, smirking.

I rolled my eyes and pulled the book out of her hands.

"So, why didn't you continue?" Amber asked, her eyes not leaving the journal. "You know as well as I do that there's something about grandpa we don't know."

I was itching to read the next entry, but I just wasn't sure if it was right. It felt right holding Grandpa McEwin's books in my hands, but shouldn't I show my mother the journal before I started reading them?

Amber whisked the journal away from me and began reading the first entry to herself.

Before I could grab the book back, Amber exclaimed, "Well, you read the first entry already, so what harm is there in reading the second?"

"You just said it was an invasion of privacy," I countered.

"Yes, but who started this?" she rebutted, as she began to read the diary to herself. "Wow. I didn't know great grandpa owned a clinic," Amber said, flipping through the journal. "I wonder what else is in here that Mom never bothered to mention to us."

"Mom might not have known. I mean, the books were packed in dusty cardboard boxes. Maybe she never knew about the journal." When Amber turned to the middle of the journal, I noticed there were a few strips of paper stuck to the binding.

"It looks like someone ripped these pages out," Amber said, running her fingers along the jagged edges.

She flipped back to the second entry and began to read it aloud.

> May 7, 1970. It's Rose's birthday today, and all I could buy her was some costume jewelry. Even though it's her birthday, she's baked me my favorite cookies—chocolate chip. I haven't been able to write until now. The schoolwork keeps piling on, and I have to sneak off to my job. I got a job at the pharmacy as a stock boy. May is one of our busiest months due to the excessive pollen.
>
> Every day after school, I tell my parents I'm studying at the library, when I'm really going to the pharmacy. I put some of my money in Da's wallet and placed the rest in my college-fund box I keep hidden in the back of my closet. I figure that by the time I'm eighteen, I'll have enough money to go to a decent college, even if I don't get a scholarship. Freshman year is almost over.
>
> Rose and I are going to celebrate by going to her favorite restaurant, McHale's. She loves Irish food. "It reminds me of you," she always explains. I, on the other hand, like Italian food better, but I'd never tell her that. Today, Rose and I were kissing when I knocked over her coffee table, which had her birthday cake on it. Rose tried to get the stain out of the rug, but it was no use. I ruined her perfectly clean beige carpet. I wish for once I wouldn't spill anything or knock anything over. My Da told me that it is just our way and can't be helped. He was lucky enough to get my mum. She found him endearing. My sister Sophie is so lucky. She takes after our mum in every way. She even has Mum's smile. Mum has a slight cold, but I'm sure it'll clear up soon. I must go to bed now. The last thing I need is for my Da to come into school because I slept in class. Sincerely, Max.

"Did Aunt Sophie ever go to college? Didn't she own an art gallery for a long time?" Amber asked, placing the journal on the counter.

"I think so. Our cousins put her in a nursing home after Uncle Alan died."

Our Aunt Sophie had Alzheimer's disease. After her husband, Alan Morris, died, she seemed to get worse by the second. Our cousins reluctantly put her in a nursing home in the city, Burke Rehabilitation Center.

"Poor Aunt Sophie," Amber said, picking up the journal and turning to the next entry. "This one wasn't written until two years later."

"Two years? Why?"

Before Amber could answer me, the phone rang. "Hello?"

"My parents just left," Sally said.

I almost forgot I promised to meet Sally tonight. If I said I was busy, she'd definitely break up with me.

"Who is it?" Amber whispered.

"Sally," I stated, turning my attention back to the phone.

"You are coming over, aren't you, Cooper?"

I could almost see her pouty lips, her illustrious blue eyes wide with anticipation, and her flaxen hair softly draped over her bronze shoulders.

"S—sure. I'll be there in a couple of minutes," I said, feeling as if my heart was about to burst through my chest.

"I'll see you then," Sally said, her seductive undertones still lingering on the line even after she hung up.

"Sally wants you tonight, doesn't she?" Amber asked, grinning.

I looked at my sister quizzically, wondering how she knew what we were talking about. I guess my pale skin and the way I fumbled to hang up the phone gave it away.

Amber giggled and pointed to my feet, which were levitating over the linoleum kitchen floor.

"I—well, I—shut up," I said, lowering myself to the ground.

"You know, it's a good thing she wasn't here. I think you defying gravity would have been a dead giveaway," Amber taunted.

"You should just tell her. Then you wouldn't have to keep avoiding her every time she wanted to screw you."

My sister was never one for subtlety.

"I can't tell her. I don't know how she would react," I said, looking at my watch. It was 6:00 p.m. Time really flies when you're uncovering a secret journal and fighting your way through spiders.

"Yeah, but you can't keep avoiding her. What are you going to do when you go over there tonight?" Amber asked, closing Grandpa McEwin's journal.

"You can't just say, 'Well, Sally, I love you and everything, but I just can't have sex with you. Why, you ask? Well, it's a secret, so I can't tell you. But I swear, it's a really good reason.' She'll definitely break up with you if you say that. I would break up with a guy in two seconds if he did that to me."

"Well, whoever said I was going to say that? I'll think of something," I said, placing our bowls in the sink. "Could you clean up? As you know, I have a date."

"Uh-huh. But will it be your last?" Amber called, as I grabbed my keys and headed out the door.

3

INNER TURMOIL

When I pulled up in front of Sally's house, I noticed the lights were off in every room except her bedroom.

"Oh God," I mumbled to myself, as I took a deep breath and got out of the car.

Maybe Amber was right. Maybe I should just tell Sally I had telekinesis, so if I lost control again, I wouldn't have to worry about being exposed. If I kept running away from her, both mentally and physically, she'd eventually leave me. I mean, she'd told me everything about herself, including her irrational fear of needles. However, if I told her, I risked others finding out. I loved Sally, but I had never entrusted her with a secret like this. I couldn't fully anticipate how she would react, what she might do.

Before I could ring the doorbell, Sally swung the door open and leaned against the frame. Her vibrant, sapphire eyes juxtaposed the midnight-black dress that clung to her glistening tan skin. Strands of flaxen hair escaped from her bun, framing her oval face.

"I see you dressed," she teased, running her fingers through my hair.

Perhaps ripped, loose jeans and once-new sneakers now caked with dirt and bits of cobwebs wasn't the way to go. I should have taken a shower before I came over, at least I should have washed my face. My light-green eyes must have look reddened and glassy.

"Um, yeah. I was cleaning out my attic when you called," I said, trying to brush off some of the dust on my shirt. "I didn't want to be late, so I headed right over."

Sally pursed her lips, which slowly formed into a seductive smile.

"Come in," she said, as my heart practically jumped into my throat.

The minute I stepped into her house, I was hit with a jasmine fragrance. I tried not to cough, but I couldn't help it. My anxiety escalated to new heights when Sally began to walk upstairs, lightly holding my hand in hers.

It felt as if her stairs went on forever. With every step, the jasmine scent strangled my lungs. I had to stop walking because I could hardly breathe. Sally must have bathed her house in perfume by the way the smell covered every crevice of it. There was no escape from it.

"Are you okay?" Sally asked. "Water," I managed to choke out. Sally raced to the kitchen, leaving me on the stairs, craving clean air that I could breathe. She returned with a large glass of water that she practically spilled all over the floor.

"Here you go," she said, holding the glass to my lips. "What happened? Is it the jasmine? I was afraid I sprayed too much. I'm so sorry, Cooper."

I gulped down the water, trying to drown out the smell from the perfume that seemed to make its way into every part of my body. If I had to have brain surgery right this very second, I swear, when the neurosurgeon began to operate, the potent smell of jasmine would leak out through every lobe.

"Air," I choked out, placing the empty glass on the stairs.

We rushed outside and stood on her stoop. I'd never appreciated oxygen as much as I did at that moment. I practically ate the air.

"I'll try to air out the house. Wait here," Sally said, running back inside.

How could that strong jasmine fragrance not bother her? After about five minutes, Sally sat next to me on her stoop. "I placed fans all over the house and opened all the windows, so the air should clear in a couple of minutes," Sally said, easing her head onto my shoulder. "In the meantime, we could look at the sunset. Isn't it romantic? I love dusk."

I nodded, closing my eyes and taking in the sweet, crisp air. The pink hue dripped into the orange tint outlining the vibrant golden sun. Everything and everyone seemed still, almost as if this moment was reserved for Sally and me. I wished Sally could have been satisfied with this stage in our relationship, but she wanted more, and honestly, so did I.

"I didn't spray the basement with perfume. Let's go down there," Sally said, leading me back into the house and quickly down the basement stairs toward her furnished cellar.

The distant memory of husky jasmine still lingered in the air, but it was beginning to dissipate. We sat on Sally's pink love seat couch facing her widescreen television.

"I wanted tonight to be special," Sally said, leaning in to kiss me.

As our lips met, I leaned backward, trying to get into a more comfortable position. I felt my elbow dig into something between the couch cushions. The faint glow of the television illuminated the dark room as I pulled the remote out of the couch.

"—and Samuel Murdoch, a junior at Erikson High School, was reported missing only a few hours after Debra Romer, a nurse at Parkway Hospital, was mugged near Erikson High School," I heard the TV news anchor say.

Breaking our kiss, I sat up and saw that the local news station was on.

"Samuel Murdoch? He's in my gym class. He and Michelle began dating a month ago," Sally said, interlocking her hand in mine. "Wait a minute. A person can't be reported missing until twenty-four hours after they haven't come home, right?"

"Well, that's usually true. But when your dad is the chief of police, I guess the rules bend a little." Sally shut off the television and placed the remote on the coffee table.

"It'll be in tomorrow morning's edition. Plus, I'd rather read the news than watch it," Sally said, brushing her fingers through my hair. "Now, where were we?"

The straps of her dress slid off her shoulders as we began to kiss. It felt like acid was splashing around in my throat as I tried to control my heart rate.

I felt Sally fumbling to find my zipper as she pressed her lips harder on mine. I wanted to rip off her dress and run my lips over every crevice of her body. I was more than tempted, but I had to resist. If Sally was going to find out my secret, she wasn't going to find out by realizing she defied gravity while lying on top of me.

I broke our kiss and gently held Sally's hands in mine.

"Sally, um, there's something—" I began, but then I heard the faint sound of Sally's front doorbell.

Sally grunted and reluctantly lifted herself off of me.

"I'll be right back, so hold that thought," she said, giving me a quick peck on the cheek.

I nodded as Sally ran upstairs to open the front door.

What had I been thinking? Had I seriously been about to reveal my secret to Sally? She'd think I was a freak, I just knew it. Then again, maybe I wasn't giving her enough credit. She accepted all of my other idiosyncrasies; perhaps this would be no different. Sure, there'd have to be an adjustment, but maybe she'd still love me. If she did, she wouldn't tell anyone. It wouldn't be my secret; it would be ours. Though, she'd probably be furious with me for lying to her all these years.

"We were supposed to have a date tonight, and now he's missing," a faint, familiar voice cried.

"Michelle, they'll find him. I just know it," I heard Sally reply. I was walking up the basement stairs when the door opened, and Sally peeked her head through the crack.

"Michelle's really upset. She needs me right now. I'm sorry Cooper."

"It's okay," I said, coming up the stairs. Although only a few minutes had passed, the jasmine fragrance seemed to have dissipated. I was incredibly relieved when I saw Michelle sitting on Sally's living room couch with her face cupped in her hands. Michelle looked up when she heard me walking toward the door. Her cheeks were streaked with mascara. A pang of guilt hit me as I opened Sally's door.

"I'm so sorry, Michelle," I said, not waiting for a response.

"I'll call you," Sally said as she closed the door behind me. Poor Michelle. I'd never felt sorry for her until that very moment. I was surprised to see her crying. From the way her cold, manipulative stare had practically cut through me the first time we met, I'd always assumed she'd never show her vulnerable side. Hell, I didn't even believe Michelle *had* a vulnerable side.

When I reached my house, I saw Amber sitting on the porch reading Grandpa McEwin's journal. Amber was never one to wait. She was probably the most impatient person I'd ever know.

"I see you couldn't wait—" I began, stopping when I saw Amber's eyes were puffy and her cheeks were smeared with trails of tears.

Sitting in the wicker chair next to her, I wrapped my arm around her shoulders. "What happened?" I asked, easing Amber's head onto my shoulder. "Was it Grandpa McEwin's journal?"

Amber's head snapped up at the mention of our grandfather's journal.

"Don't read them, Cooper. Something terrible happened. Grandpa McEwin's life is just so sad," Amber said, new tear trails forming over the old ones.

How could I just stop reading his journal? He was my grandfather, too. I had as much right as Amber did to read them. Maybe this is why the journal was hidden in the attic.

"I need to read them, Amber. If I don't, I'll always wonder. I can't just leave them in the attic and pretend they don't exist, like Mom must have done."

Amber nodded and reluctantly handed me the journal.

"Just don't say I didn't warn you," Amber said, going inside. I opened the journal, feeling Amber's tears on the cover. The third entry was dated May 30, 1972.

Today is the first anniversary of Mum's death. Da isn't taking it too well. He's become somewhat of an alcoholic since Mum died last year. The chemotherapy was too much for her. Rose sat by my side at that hospital every day, holding my hand. And what did I do? I broke up with her. After Mum died, I broke Rose's heart by telling her that I didn't, nor would I ever, love her. She didn't believe me. She knew me too well and knew I would have never said I loved her if I didn't mean it. She was my first love, and now I've lost her.

When I see her in the hall, I have to look away before our eyes meet. I want to tell her that I truly love her and want her back, but I can't. She's happy now with her new boyfriend, Joseph Illian. At least he has enough money to take care of her. If they get married, he'll be able to support her, even if she doesn't become a nurse. His father is the owner of a chain of pharmacies, including the one I work in. He'll inherit his father's money, live with Rose in a luxurious house with little children running in the yard, and they'll live happily ever after. I wish Rose all the luck in the world. She's with a man who is worthy of her love, unlike me. At least he won't spill things on her, knock over everything, and always hide half of himself from her. Right now, I need to focus on taking care of Da and Sophie. Sophie has taken Mum's death harder than anyone. It seems as if every time I see her, she's crying. She's about to become a teenager and she has no mum

> to explain anything to her. Her mum is dead, her Da has become distant. I have to take care of her or no one else will. I'll start with celebrating her birthday today instead of mourning our mum. Sophie will not cry every birthday. I won't let her go through that pain, at least not alone. I can't quit my job at the pharmacy because I have to support my family. They need me now more than ever, and I refuse to let them down. Even if I have to spend the rest of my life getting their lives back in order, I'll do it. I have to make sacrifices for them, including Rose. Sincerely, Max.

I could see why Amber was crying. At least I knew he and grandma got back together. After all my grandfather went through, he must have realized he couldn't just give up on his love for my grandmother.

"Home so soon, Cooper?" my mother asked from inside front door. She was peering out through the screen door as I fumbled to hide the journal from her, but to no avail. It slipped off my lap and onto the floor.

"What is this?" my mother asked, coming out onto the porch and picking up the journal.

She stared quizzically at the journal and opened it to the first entry. Before I could say anything, my mother's eyes grew wide with recognition. She dropped the book on the floor and stepped back.

"W-where did you find this? I've been looking for this for so many years."

"When I was cleaning out the attic. I found it in one of the cardboard boxes. I didn't have a chance to clear the boxes out of the attic, by the way," I said.

My mother slowly sat down in the wicker chair. She seemed to have either aged or regressed thirty years.

Her eyes were wide like a newborn's, searching for someone to protect her. And yet, every wrinkle on her face seemed to stand out.

"I thought you knew about Grandpa McEwin's journal because, well, it was in our attic. I mean, I know I'm the only one who can go up there, but I just assumed you or Dad put them up there," I said, placing my arm around my mother's shoulders.

Too many people in my life needed to be comforted that day. Next thing you knew, my father would walk out on the porch, frowning and needing a shoulder to cry on.

"I didn't even know it was up there," my mother said, rubbing her eyes where tears had begun to form.

If my mother hadn't placed the journal in the attic, then who did? It couldn't just place itself in a cardboard box and then hide itself in the attic. Then again, stranger things had happened. I would know. However, even if it appeared to put itself in a box and float up to the attic, someone would have had to control it with their will. To my knowledge, I was the only one with telekinesis in this household, so there had to be some logical explanation.

"Has anyone been in the attic except me?" I asked. "No, Cooper, just the movers. At least, I don't think anyone else was in the attic," my mother said, reaching for the dropped journal. "By the way, the strap is split, so I'm assuming you've read a couple of pages." My mother opened the journal to the first page, trying to hold it steady with her shaking hands.

"Mom, did you know that grandma and grandpa knew each other when they were fourteen years old?" I asked, wondering how much my mother really knew about my grandfather.

"No. I had no idea," she said, staring at the first entry as if it were written in Aramaic. "Your grandmother hardly told me anything about your grandfather. She loved him so much. When he died, a part of her also died that day. Any time I'd ask her even the simplest question about my father, she'd begin to cry. I'm not even sure how he died. In fact, when your grandmother had that episode when you were eight years old, she divulged more information about my father than she ever had before during my life. That's when she told me about his journal."

What was my grandmother hiding? My mother hardly knew anything about her father. Perhaps my grandmother placed the journal in that cardboard box before it was put in the attic. It could have been her own surreptitious way of explaining to my mother who her father really was and what really happened to him.

"Mom, why don't you take the journal? It's rightfully yours, and you should read it."

My mother stared tentatively at the journal, letting her fingertip caress the binding as if she were taking in everything she could of my grandfather's memory.

"We'll read it together, Cooper. I want you to know your grandfather just as much as I want to know my father," she said, handing the journal back to me. "Read me the entries, Cooper. I want to hear you read your grandfather's words."

I wish I had an authentic Irish accent; perhaps then it would have seemed as if my mother's father were reading her his own words. After I finished re-reading the first three entries for her, I turned to the fourth, dated September 11, 1972.

> Da is sick again. I keep pleading with him to see a doctor, but he refuses. He's lost all faith in doctors. He believes all they're after is your money. Da refuses to even walk past Parkway Hospital. He's become so bitter since Mum passed. I have to work double shifts just to keep our heads above water. We'd be living on welfare now if I hadn't taken that job at the pharmacy.
>
> Hopefully, I'll get promoted to manager soon. I'm tempted to put some of my paycheck in my college fund, but I won't. I know that soon I'll have to spend that money on bills, and medical school will be a distant dream. Da's enough to handle without trying to keep Sophie in line.
>
> She just started eighth grade, and I'm afraid she has already fallen in with a bad crowd. I swear, I smelt a faint scent of marijuana mixed with an overpowering aroma of Chanel No.5 perfume in Sophie's room. I told Da, but all he did was grunt and take another swig of beer. No matter how hard I try, my family is falling apart before my eyes. If Mum were here, she'd never let any of this happen. Mum was the glue that held this family together. With her gone, we're all headed for disaster.
>
> I heard Rose broke up with her boyfriend yesterday. For every dark cloud, there's a silver lining. When I heard, I wanted to hold her in my arms and tell her everything was going to be all right. But I knew better. The last person Rose would want to embrace is me. I tore us a part with my own stupidity. If Mum were still alive, she'd smack me over my head for being so ignorant. She'd tell me, "She was so caring. And look what you went and did. Well, don't just stand there. You know love is boundless, and you must fight any boundaries

placed in front of you to reach that love." Mum always had words of wisdom for me, even when she needed some herself. I will not let my Mum down, wherever she may be. I will fix my family and find my love. I will repair all damages so Mum won't look down and feel guilty for leaving us so soon. I love you, Mum. Sincerely, Max.

"That was beautiful," my mother said, wiping her running mascara with her fingers. "I have to get a box of tissues before we read on."

I couldn't believe that was my grandfather's life. He was not only self-reliant at seventeen years old, but he was the provider for his family. He was willing to risk everything to help his family.

What would I do if my mother died? Amber had a rebellious streak, which would probably go into overdrive if our mother died. My mother drew out the caring side in my father. Without her, I think he would turn to his work instead of the bottle.

I thought my life would have been quite similar to my grandfather's if my mother died, except I didn't think I would have had to break up with Sally. I was sure she'd break up with me after seeing gravity defy itself around me every second from me being so miserable. Perhaps she'd break up with me sooner because I kept hiding half of myself from her. She'd never know the true me unless she knew my secret. She might think I'm a freak, but at least I'd be an honest freak.

"Okay, now that I have tissues in hand, I think we can continue," my mother said, placing the tissues on the wicker table next to her.

"Sure, let's continue," I said, opening to the fifth entry. "Hey, how come you came home early?" my mother asked, parting my hair with her fingers. "Did something happen between you and Sally?" "No. Sally's best friend, Michelle, came over and was very upset because her boyfriend is missing," I said, closing the journal. "That's odd. Bernadette Peters, one of my colleagues at the agency, called me up earlier and asked me if I'd seen her daughter. She thinks her daughter is missing. She didn't come home and the school's closed, so she's sure her daughter isn't there. She's about your age, too. I think her name is Cynthia. I'm sure she'll show up though. Cynthia probably went to one of her friends' houses and didn't bother to call her mother, like Amber has done to me quite a bit."

Two kids that went to Erikson High School were missing. Perhaps it was just a coincidence. Both of them were probably at a friend's house. Maybe they were together. I didn't know Cynthia, but Samuel Murdoch dated my sister in the beginning of the year. I overheard him in the locker room telling some other guys that he was going to have sex with her, so I just "happened" to make him slip and sprain his ankle. I felt kind of bad that he got hurt, but it was probably well-deserved karma.

"They'll show up soon. You're probably right.

Now, where were we?" I asked, opening the journal to the fifth entry again.

My mother lightly placed her hand on mine and closed the journal.

"Actually, on second thought, I think that's enough for today, Cooper. I don't want to take in too much in only one day."

"Okay. Well, I'll just put these in a safe—" I began.

My mother picked up the journal and held it to her chest. A content smile spread across her lips as she took in the musky dust smell of the attic that still lingered on the journal's cover.

"Actually, I think it'll be safer with you than anywhere else," I said.

My mother had found a part of her father she thought was missing forever. I just hoped she would find happiness when reading the journal and not despair, like Amber did.

"I should check on Amber," I said, leaving my mother on the porch, holding the journal that was rightfully hers.

Amber had never reacted to any reading material, or even a movie, with tears. Even when she saw *Bambi* at five years old, she just frowned and asked me why animals had to die, but she didn't cry once. I wish I could have lied to her and told her that animals didn't have to die, but she needed to know the truth.

"Animals, and people, die so new animals and people can come into the world," I told her. I didn't know if that was the answer she was searching for, but that was the only one I could supply her with when I was eight years old.

4

HIDDEN SECRETS

"Is that you, Cooper?" Amber asked from inside her room, snapping me out of my daze.

"Yeah. Can I come in?"

"I guess," Amber said, opening her door. Amber always smacked me upside my head whenever I walked into her room because I couldn't help but laugh at the way her hair perfectly matched her wallpaper.

"Shut up and sit down," Amber said, giving me a good shove into her white rocking chair.

"Okay, in all seriousness, are you okay? That journal seemed to really bother you."

"Yeah, I'm fine," Amber said, checking her newly applied mascara in her vanity mirror. "It's just that Grandpa McEwin's life was so tragic. And, well, he had secrets.

Secrets that you'll have to find out on your own, though I wish you wouldn't."

"What secrets?" I asked, my curiosity piqued. "Well, you're reading it anyway, right? You'll find out on your own. I'm warning you though, Grandpa McEwin is a complicated guy."

Amber couldn't keep a secret for longer than two seconds, so why was she keeping this one? My grandfather's life was different than I'd once assumed, but I doubted there were any "secrets" my grandfather had that had to be kept hidden.

"Well, Mom and I are up to the fifth entry, so we'll find out Grandpa McEwin's secret soon."

Amber's emerald eyes seemed to turn a shade darker and grow twice as large.

"Cooper, you told Mom? Why would you tell her?" "It's Mom's father, Amber. It doesn't matter what skeletons are in Grandpa McEwin's closet. Mom has a right to know who her father was. Grandma McEwin never told her anything about our grandfather. Now that she has this information, she'll know her father. I think he would want that," I said, standing up to leave.

"Okay, whatever, Cooper. But I'm just warning you, Mom isn't going to be ready for what Grandpa McEwin put himself through." Amber was notorious for being overdramatic, so it was hard to take these types of statements seriously. However, was it possible that Amber wasn't overreacting? Was there something in our grandfather's past that was so disturbing and shocking that our mother shouldn't find out? "Cooper. I know you can hear me."

The school was a hollow shell waiting to be filled, but no one would ever come. I stood on the crumbling stairs, knowing that with each step, I was reaching my destination. I knew I had to go there. I knew that as I reached the top, the end of my world would soon be near, but it didn't matter; I had to go.

I gripped the railing, seeing the past I thought I left behind. Toys hovered over me, just as they hovered over my floor ages ago. The stairs were caked with dust, but the way had never seemed so clear to me.

It was as if time had rewound itself, and yet the present was preserved in a portrait that lay within my grasp. Nothing could stop me. With each subtle creak of every step, I knew I was getting closer to the truth, whatever that may be.

"I know you can hear me. You just don't want to."

The invigorating, chocolate chip cookie fragrance swirled through my senses. Jasmine lingered on the walls, slowly dripping in gusts of smoke toward an abyss that found its way through the cracks in the stairs.

"Why are you ignoring me? You'll never escape. No matter how hard you try, you will always stand on those stairs. You can't move. You'll never move unless you take the next step." The railing was sturdy, and yet it felt like sand in my grasp. Particles of dust sparkled in the foggy mist, flowing down and clinging to the stairs. My shoes were covered in sheets of gray grime, slowly seeping into my flesh. I had to move. It was now or never, and nothing could change my mind.

"Why try? You'll never be able to move. Stop trying. You're not ready."

"Who are you?" I screamed, shattering my vocal cords.

I choked on my own listless words, which seemed to linger in the forgotten dusty space.

"You know who I am. You'll never escape," the voice hissed.

"Why? Why can't I escape? Why can't I move on?

Why can't I reach that next step?" I tried to say, but my voice was merely a distorted whisper.

The voice formed into a laugh, seeming to twist every particle of dust, turning them against me. The sheet of dust pierced every sliver of flesh that gripped my bones.

I tried to scream, but it was no use. The laughter rose with each passing second. I tried to concentrate on my feet, believing I could lift myself over the stairs, but I couldn't.

"Why? Why can't you escape? Why can't you move on? Why can't you reach that next step?" the voice mocked. "You can't because you choose not to. You can't because secretly you don't want to. You can't because…you won't let go."

"Let go of what?" I demanded.

A sharp pang pierced through my chest. I heaved over, feeling myself fade.

"Let go of WHAT?" I screamed, but my voice didn't even carry.

"Cooper, wake up," Amber said, poking my back with a flat wooden pole.

I rubbed my eyes, seeing only blurry forms of what I assumed were pieces of furniture.

"Get down from there," Amber said, giving me another good jab with the stick.

I was just about to ask what she was talking about when I realized my body was pressed up against the ceiling.

"What the—?" I began to say, when I fell onto my bed, feeling the jolt of mattress springs press into me.

"Bad dream?" Amber asked, moving a pile of clothes off my chair.

"Kind of," I said, rubbing my back. My whole body felt as if it was still crawling with dust. "How is it possible that you're up before me? You haven't been awake before me since you were a baby."

"Well, it's ten, and I'm usually awake by nine. It must have been some dream you had to make Mr. Rise-and-Shine wake up after seven," Amber joked, kicking the pile of clothes into the closet.

"Yeah, it really was. So, any chance there's anything left for breakfast?" I asked, as we headed to the kitchen.

Apparently, we were having air, because there was nothing prepared. Usually, on Saturday mornings, my mother was in the kitchen cooking every breakfast meal she could think of. One morning, she actually made us blood pudding. Amber and I opted to skip breakfast that morning.

"Mom went to work today. She said a buyer wanted to look at the other warehouse in town. She mumbled something about the trouble she had selling another warehouse almost a year ago. At least that's what Mom told me when she was running out the door," Amber said, preparing a pot of coffee.

"Right. How about Dad? Oh, wait, let me guess, he barricaded himself in his office," I said, grabbing two mugs out of the cabinet. If it were Easter, Thanksgiving, or even Christmas, without fail, my father would be locked in his office, working. He even scheduled an appointment with one of his patients on my tenth birthday. My mother was furious with him, but that didn't prompt him to cancel the appointment, of course. He said the patient had a problem with rejection and he didn't want to add to it.

"He's not in his home office though. He has an appointment with some guy. I can't remember his name though. It was some type of emergency," Amber said, pouring the coffee. "You would think with his flexible hours, he wouldn't purposely make them inflexible. I mean, he owns his own practice. Do we have to constantly remind him?"

My father loved his work, which I could relate to. Whenever I had a test or assignment, the rest of the world shut down for me. I could only focus on school. Devotion sometimes took a toll on your personal life.

Amber resented our father for missing every dance recital she was in when she was younger. He'd disappointed us both quite a few times. I had to admit, sometimes I wished he would pay less attention to his patients and more to his family.

Sometimes, I wondered why my mother put up with him. I guess love made you blind, even when something's been in front of you for years. My father truly loved my mother and would never hurt her on purpose.

"Hey, did Mom leave the journal in her and Dad's room?" I asked Amber, as I finished up my cup of coffee.

"Um, I think so. But Cooper—" "Yeah?"

"Um, never mind. It's probably on her dresser," Amber said, putting my cup in the sink.

"Thanks."

My parents' room was forbidden to Amber and me when we were younger. We'd always take a peek inside when my parents weren't looking. Now, it was just a regular room covered with blue wallpaper and white wicker furniture.

Where would my mother put that journal? I knew she wouldn't leave it in plain sight for my father to see. However, it really wouldn't matter because he would probably be too preoccupied with his latest patient's case to worry about a mysterious book my mother brought into their bedroom.

Considering everyone in our family hid everything in the back of the closet, I looked there first. Eureka! It was hidden underneath a ton of shoes.

Sitting on the shag rug in my parents' walk-in closet, I opened the journal to the fifth entry.

January 1, 1973. I begin this new year with a fresh start. After hours of pleading and proving I would never hurt her ever again, Rose took me back. She understood I was upset when I broke up with her and nothing made sense to me anymore, but there's so much more I'm not telling her. Oh, I wish I could tell her everything, but I can't. At least, I can't for the time being. There are some things that are better left unsaid. My Da used to tell me that, before he was addicted to alcohol. These days, without a beer in hand, he looks incomplete. I tried to convince him to go to one of those AA meetings, but he refuses. "I do not have a problem" is the first sign of denial, which my Da has successfully accomplished. His personality completely flips when he's intoxicated. His responsible, strong disposition is replaced by a callous, irresponsible, weak being who is more like a lump on the couch than the da I used to respect and admire. I wish I could talk to Mum. She would know what to do. She would also know what to do about my rebellious sister. She's flunking out of the eighth grade. I keep trying to help her with her studies, but she refuses to listen. Ignoring my presence has become Sophie's favorite pastime these days. I don't know what to do. Brute strength wouldn't work, and harsh words would only provoke her further. She walks into the house with a joint in hand. I'm not her da, so any reprimand by me seems arbitrary to her. Rose told me she'd have a heart-to-heart talk with Sophie, but I fear Sophie has lost the part of herself that would listen. The only good news I have, besides having Rose back, is I made manager at the pharmacy. I'll be making twice as much as I make now. Rose thinks it's fantastic. I wish I could keep a few dollars for myself, but I have to pay the bills. I've circled plenty of want ads for Da, but he just uses them as a coaster for his beer. Sometimes, I want to run away from my family, but I couldn't do that to them. They depend on me financially. Their apathy drains any emotional dependence that could seep through. Sophie is out partying tonight, which I forbid her to do, but again, it is pointless to try to parent her.

Perhaps Rose can change things around for my sister. However, I cannot help but feel guilty for putting Rose in this position. Maybe Rose was better off when we weren't together. She wasn't involved in my dysfunctional family and didn't feel the need to take my responsibilities on her shoulders. Oh, Rose! I love you so and want you to never leave my side, and yet I wish you'd run away from me so you wouldn't have to deal with my life. I'm caught in quicksand, but that doesn't mean she should sink with me. Sincerely, Max.

"Cooper, could you come here for a second?" my sister yelled from downstairs. "Coming," I called back, placing the journal back underneath the shoes.

My grandfather's life seemed to become more tragic by the second. I didn't blame him for wanting to run away. If I were in that situation, I'd want to do the same thing. Of course, like my grandfather, I wouldn't. Even if his family didn't appreciate it, he took care of them and made sure they didn't crumble into the ground.

"I was just—" I began to say, when I saw Amber putting on her jacket. "Going somewhere?"

"Yeah, I'm going over to Darcy's. She just texted me. She's upset about Samuel and wants to talk."

"Why? Were they close?" I asked, believing that Michelle and Samuel were exclusive.

"Kind of. She's dating his friend Greg. She texted Greg a few times, but he hasn't texted back."

In a world where cell phones were practicably another appendage, it seemed a bit strange for someone to not text someone back, but not everyone was addicted to their cell phone. I misplaced mine most of the time.

"Okay, but don't be home too late," I said, walking Amber outside.

"How can I when I have Mr. Mom on my back?" Amber joked, cracking a smile.

I went upstairs again and found my grandfather's journal underneath various types of heels. My mother should really think about getting a shoe rack.

The sixth journal entry was dated March 25, 1973.

I haven't written in this journal for such a long time, I almost forgot how to start. I guess anyway you start a journal is fine. It's your journal and you're the only one who's going to read it, so it really doesn't matter how you begin or end it. My Da has joined my mum. He passed on January 29th, and I turned eighteen on January 30th, and since we do not have any other family members that I know of in the States, I was awarded custody of Sophie. My Da left me everything in his will. He even left a letter for me, in case he died when Sophie and I were still young. I found him lying on the couch, with his ubiquitous beer on the coffee table. The doctors at Parkway Hospital said he died of alcohol poisoning. I have failed. I failed to keep my Da alive and Sophie on the right path. I failed my mum, and I failed myself. If she were still alive, she'd probably smack me over the head for not doing a better job. Sophie made it into the ninth grade by the skin of her teeth. She had to make up a couple of classes in summer school, but she made it. My mum would cry if she could see my sister. She smokes marijuana almost every day, trying to numb the pain of losing our parents. I miss our parents just as much as she does, but grief comes out in different ways. Sophie called me heartless at Da's funeral because I didn't cry. I had already lost my Da when my mum died, so there was no need to cry twice. I was slowly losing Sophie, too. I wish I knew what to do. I am doing the best I can, but my best is not good enough. I wish I forced my Da to go to AA, but the program is ineffective if you don't believe in it. I shouldn't have snuck money into his wallet; that's how he paid for his addiction. Da deadened the pain with alcohol, and Sophie is trying to deaden her suffering with marijuana. Once she builds up a tolerance, who knows what she will take to alleviate the pain? Maybe I couldn't help Da, but maybe I still have a chance to save Sophie. All Sophie and I have is each other, and that will never change. Now that I am her legal guardian, I have to work harder to make sure she listens to me. Rose has never left my side through all this. She held my hand when the doctor told us my Da had passed. She cried on my shoulder as my Da's casket was lowered into the ground, and she stood by my side when Sophie came home so high, she could hardly stand. My love will never leave my side, even if I continue to make things fall and have hardly enough time to spend sitting next to her on the couch. Soon—and perhaps because I am crazy—I'm going to ask her to marry me. When I raise enough money to buy a suitable engagement ring, I'll get down on one knee and ask her to be my wife. Hopefully, she'll say yes. I still have to straighten Sophie out and wait for my college acceptance or rejection letters. There's a wonderful college in the area that specializes in pre-med. I'll probably go there, that is, if I'm offered a full scholarship. I've applied for many, so I should have enough money to pay for books and other expenses. I'm going to make it, and so will Sophie. She has to. Sincerely, Max.

"Wow," I muttered as I closed the journal.

Despite all the misery he went through, he still wanted to fulfill his dreams with my grandmother by his side. He had more courage than I could ever muster, then again, although he carried burdens, he did not carry a secret.

Just as I was about to continue reading, my cell phone rang. "Hello?"

"Cooper, can you come over?" Sally asked. Her voice sounded strained, as if she'd been talking for hours. "Sure, I'll be there in a few minutes," I said, grabbing my jacket.

5

LOSING CONTROL

When I reached Sally's house, I saw Michelle's blue BMW parked in the driveway.

Had Michelle spent the entire night? They were best friends, so I supposed it was more than likely, but why would Sally want me to come over if Michelle was there? Was it possible Michelle wanted me there? I brushed that thought off as I rang the doorbell.

"Hey," Sally said, as she opened the door.

Her glimmering, crystal eyes seemed dulled. The bun that was neatly pinned up last night was unraveling.

"How's Michelle? I saw her car outside, so I assume she's here."

"She's a little better. They still haven't found him yet," Sally said, fixing her unkempt, sleek black dress. "Come in."

When I walked into Sally's house, Michelle was asleep on the couch, lying underneath a thick quilt.

"As you can probably tell, I stayed up all night with Michelle. She just went to sleep a little while ago. She was so upset. I've never seen her that upset before," Sally said, rubbing her sleep deprived eyes.

As I walked her upstairs to her room, I noticed that the jasmine fragrance still lingered, but it wasn't as powerful. Chilled air came in gusts through her house due to the open windows she never shut and the fans she never turned off.

"I felt so bad that we had to cut our night short. Michelle didn't stop crying until a little while ago. She really needed to talk," Sally said, yawning.

"It's okay. I understand," I said, as she and I entered her room and sat down on her bed.

"I hope they find Samuel. Michelle will be crushed if anything happens to him," Sally said, as I slipped her shoes off her feet.

"I think she truly loves him, Cooper."

"I'm sure she does, but you need to get some sleep.

I'll look after Michelle while you get some rest," I said, brushing pieces of hair, which had escaped from Sally's messy bun, off her face.

Sally smiled as she lay down. "I wanted to make it up to you but—" she began, when her eyes fluttered closed, and she fell fast asleep.

As I tucked Sally in, her shoulder straps slipped off.

My fingertips skimmed her glistening, soft, tan skin as I pulled up her straps. I couldn't help but let my fingers lie on Sally's shoulder, watching her chest rise and fall. The edges of her black dress sculpted her breasts.

I was compelled to lie next to her. If we were together, we'd finally be whole, but I couldn't do it. I couldn't risk losing control again.

I was about to leave Sally, when I noticed her dresser, vanity table, and random stuffed animals were hovering five feet above the ground.

"Oh crap," I muttered under my breath, praying Sally didn't wake up.

Well, at least I didn't make Sally levitate. I closed my eyes, concentrating on the most mundane events in my life, like installing a jacuzzi in the upstairs bathroom or acing the French oral exam I took last week.

I felt the furniture slowly ease into its proper place; however, before I could feel any relief, out of the corner of my eye, I saw Michelle standing in Sally's doorway.

Any skin pigmentation I had escaped as I turned to face Michelle, her mouth agape.

"What the—?" she began, carefully walking into Sally's room. She stepped on Sally's beige carpet as if it were quicksand. Michelle stared at the dresser next to her, looking at it as if it were a monster that was about to attack.

"I—um. S-Sally's asleep," I said, feeling my voice crack with every syllable.

Oh God. My worst nightmare had come true.

Michelle must have seen the furniture levitating, so it was only a matter of seconds until she figured out the furniture was not just floating on its own, until she discovered my secret. Maybe I would get lucky, and she'd think she'd gone crazy and brush off the incident, but from the way she was staring around the room and touching the vanity table, which seemed unlikely.

"Cooper, what the hell did I just see?" Michelle asked, gesturing to the furniture that had been floating in midair just moments ago.

"W-what did you see?" I asked, nervously edging my way toward the bedroom door.

"Yes, what did I just see?" Michelle asked, refusing to let me go around her.

My heart was practically humming in my chest. I felt my control slipping again; everything felt a little too light. It was as if I would lose it any second, and the entire world would rip itself from the sun's gravitational pull.

"I-I don't know. What did you see?" I asked, trying to steady my voice.

"Cooper, I just saw Sally's furniture floating in midair and then slowly land. It was as if it jumped in the air, hung there for a second, and then slowly let gravity do its job," Michelle said, looking at me quizzically. "What did you see?"

"Me? What did I see?" I asked, obviously stalling for as long as I could. "I—um. I saw nothing. Nothing at all," I said, mentally hitting my head. Everyone knew "nothing" indicated you were being deceptive. Why couldn't I have just acknowledged I saw the furniture floating and chalk it up to one of those unsolved mysteries? No, that wouldn't have worked. Michelle was many things, but she was not naïve. "What do you mean you saw *nothing*?" Michelle demanded. I had no other choice than to deflect and refocus her attention on Samuel.

"You know Michelle, I think you've had a rough night. I mean, your boyfriend is missing, and you've hardly had enough sleep," I said, wrapping my arm around her shoulders and leading her out of Sally's bedroom. "I think all you need is a few more hours of sleep."

I felt guilty for bringing up her missing boyfriend, but I had to get her mind off what she had just seen. If she figured out I had telekinesis, the entire town would know in a matter of minutes. "Cooper, I know what I saw," Michelle insisted, stopping in the hallway and turning toward me. "I might be upset and tired, but I am not delusional."

Just my luck, Michelle couldn't be a skeptic who would rationalize away the entire situation. She couldn't think that she was hallucinating or that there had been a gust of wind strong enough to pick up the furniture. A skeptic would never acquiesce to the unbelievable truth, "Well, the boy obviously used his telekinetic powers to lift the furniture into the air and then placed it back down when he regained control." My fear was that this was exactly what Michelle would say to Sally, and then to reporters.

"Well, I didn't see anything," I said, walking downstairs.

"Well, I think you did," Michelle asserted, removing my arm from her shoulders. "I think you know something that you're not telling me."

If Michelle wanted to become a reporter when she was older, she had great potential. With her curious disposition and persistence, she'd be excellent. However, at that moment, I didn't care if Michelle had the potential to be the next Woodward and Bernstein. She was incredibly close to figuring out that the furniture's immediate defiance of gravity was my doing.

"Me? What could I possibly know?" I said, trying to sound as sincere as possible. "All I know is that my girlfriend is incredibly tired, and she needs her rest. Also, you need to go home and see if there's any new information on Samuel."

I practically threw Michelle's jacket and purse at her and shoved her out the door.

"All right, Cooper. I'll leave, but I'm going to figure out what's going on," Michelle warned me, placing her foot in the doorway just before I could close it. "I know you're involved somehow. And, when I figure out what's going on, you'll regret lying to me, Cooper O'Neil."

At that point, dramatic music should have been playing in the background. Michelle's threat struck a chord. I was surprised she didn't come out and ask if I was the one who made the furniture float in midair.

I could not help but wonder if, in a matter of minutes, everyone would know what happened in Sally's bedroom, and then I would be marked as a freak. However, Michelle didn't seem to know exactly what happened; nevertheless, it could be matter of time before she figured it out. Those nightmares I'd had since I was ten years old about scientists experimenting on me seemed like a possibility now more than ever.

When I went back up to Sally's room, she was still in a heavy slumber.

"Goodnight, Sally. I love you, and I hope you'll still love me when you find out the truth," I said, as I kissed her on her forehead.

6

FEARING DISCOVERY

An unfamiliar white Mercedes was parked in our driveway when I came home. I knew it wasn't my mother's because she still had that old van that I saved from being stolen.

"Cooper, there's someone here who wants to ask you a few questions," Amber called from the front door. When I came into the house, a woman in a plaid business suit was sitting on our couch and crying on my mother's shoulder.

My mother gestured for me to come into the living room. Hesitantly, I sat in the chair next to the couch and waited for my mother's next instructions.

"Bernadette, this is my son, Cooper. He's the one you wanted to speak with."

The woman's green eyes were overshadowed by the black, running mascara under her eyelids and on her flushed cheeks.

"Cooper," the woman said, reaching out to hold my hand. I'd never heard my name said with such definition. It was almost as if my name was what could make her stop crying. "Do you know my daughter, Cynthia Peters? You both go to the same high school."

She showed me a picture of a girl with straight, bleached blonde hair with a smile fixed for the camera, probably posted on Instagram a few moments later. Cynthia looked a little familiar, but I couldn't place her.

"She looks familiar, but I really don't know her. I'm sorry," I said, assuming Mrs. Peters had already reported her daughter missing.

"Maybe Amber knows her. I know she's a freshman, but Amber knows more of the kids in school than I do."

"No, I asked Amber. She didn't know," Mrs. Peters said, on the edge of tears. "She's mi—she hasn't come home."

I wish I could have told her more, but as I said, I didn't know the girl.

"Thank you, Cooper," Mrs. Peters said, carefully putting the picture back in her purse. "I should go home and wait by the phone. She might call."

Before Mrs. Peters left, a thought hit me.

"Did she leave her cell? Maybe you can call her contacts. Her friends might know something."

Mrs. Peters turned back to me, black tears streaming down her cheeks.

"I called all of her friends. None of them know anything," Mrs. Peters said, as she walked outside.

When my mother came back into the house, she muttered how it was such a shame.

"Isn't that weird?" Amber asked, plopping down on the couch.

"Her daughter doesn't look like the type that would run away."

"Amber, no one said that she ran away. And, even if she did, there are so many reasons why people run away," I said, sitting next to Amber on the couch. "Maybe she felt like an outcast, or there was a rumor going around that she did something that will ruin every chance she ever had at a normal life. She might be running from herself because she can't even stand herself sometimes. She might want to close her eyes and hope everything will just be all right, but there's no guarantee, is there?"

I was about to continue when I felt a hand on my shoulder. I looked up and saw my mother looking down at me with concern drawn all over her face.

"I have a feeling we're not talking about Cynthia anymore," Amber said, crossing her arms over her chest and sighing.

"Sweetie, did something happen that you want to talk about?" my mother asked.

"No. Nothing happened. Nothing at all. Why?" I asked, feeling my mom's palm pressing into my shoulder. Once again, I stupidly said the key word that indicated I was hiding something.

"Well, Mom's using all of her strength to keep you from flying up to the ceiling," Amber stated, pointing to the sliver of air separating me from the couch.

I concentrated on my body, allowing gravity to take over. I slowly descended onto the couch, and my mother pulled back her hand.

"Cooper, you can tell us. Whatever it is, we'll get through it together," my mother said, parting my hair.

My mother always thought every problem Amber, or I had could be solved in a matter of minutes, as long as we discussed it. When we were younger, that usually worked. However, now that we were in high school, our more complex problems couldn't be as easily fixed with a few words of wisdom.

However, it was difficult to brush away that something was bothering me, especially when my telekinetic outbursts were a dead giveaway.

If this issue only affected me, maybe I would try to deflect, but this dilemma probably concerned the whole family. After people figured out I was telekinetic, they'd wonder if my family had the same ability. Scientists would probably not only test me, but my family, too. That, or they would be under scrutiny for keeping my abilities a secret. Either way, normalcy would be a distant dream.

Why did they have to be dragged into my telekinetic screwup? They were normal. Amber was the typical teenager, with angst for miles. My mother and father were both hardworking individuals who'd raised at least one normal child.

At first, they were probably very frightened when they realized their twelve-month-old son could lift his bed by just staring at it, but they didn't have me tested and probed by scientists studying paranormal phenomenon.

Even though I didn't want my mother and sister to find out what happened, it was their right to know. If they were going to be tested for paranormal abilities, they should at least know why. "Well, yeah, there actually is something bothering me," I said, standing up to face my mother and Amber.

They sat next to each other, waiting for me to continue. "Okay, so I went to Sally's house this morning and Michelle was there. Michelle's boyfriend, Samuel Murdoch, is also missing. She was really upset, so Sally sat up all night with her. When I got there, Sally was so tired that I walked her up to her room and put her to bed. Well, to make a long story short—"

"I think you passed that point," Amber teased. "—when I was in Sally's room. . .well. . . I kind of lost control of my powers and half of Sally's furniture was floating in the air."

"Oh God, did Sally wake up and see her furniture?" Amber asked.

"Shh, let your brother finish," my mother told Amber, but I could tell she was wondering the same thing.

"Um, not exactly. Michelle saw," I said.

Amber and my mother's jaws simultaneously dropped.

"Everything?" Amber asked.

"Unfortunately, yeah. I don't think she knows I'm telekinetic, but she definitely thinks I'm hiding something about what happened in Sally's room."

Amber couldn't contain her laughter. She might have found the whole ordeal hilarious, but my mother wasn't as naïve. She knew there were horrible consequences to irresponsible actions.

"Cooper, are you sure she doesn't know you're telekinetic?" my mother asked.

I could see in her eyes that she wanted me to assure her there was nothing to worry about, but I couldn't give her that guarantee. "I don't know. I guess I'll find out on Monday."

———— ·+++++· ————

Their horror painted the walls black. I could feel their stares cutting through my flesh.

"I told you. You'll never escape."

Their bodies were plastered to the walls. They wouldn't dare go near me. I could see their mouths drawn into thin, pale lines. Some had fiendish, frightened grins.

"They know the truth now. They'll never leave you alone. They'll constantly pursue you until they have put a stop to people like us."

A spotlight shined overhead, showering light on my dark, eerie world. The faces became blurred, as if they were all the same person. In a crowd, there are no faces. They're just one big entity, set on destroying what destroys the normalcy that is supposed to exist.

"You're different. They won't stand for it."

I wanted to assure them I was no threat to them, but I couldn't. The minute I opened my mouth, a roaring howl escaped from it, which sent shivers through the dark halls.

"They'll never let you escape. Don't you see? You never trusted them. You have no allies."

They were starving to eradicate me; I saw it in their chilling eyes. They wanted to pounce, and yet they were too scared to. I could see that I was nothing but filth to them.

The marked being, the outcast, the one who was left to fend for himself and wait for the wolves to kill—that was me, and they knew it.

"They'll never understand. How can they? You're surprised your parents understood. They thought there was something wrong with you. They wanted to give you over to a scientist to test, but they feared you'd become a lab rat."

My feet refused to budge, as if mocking my racing heart. The people refused to move, but I could feel their eyes drawing closer. Their stares continued to slash through me. I could feel the sultry blood cascading down my back.

I tried to scream, but what came out was an inhuman wail that shattered the silence. Yet the tension defied my cries and grew more intense.

"Shut up! What do you know? You're not like me! You're not like me!" I wanted to yell, but all that came out were animal shrieks.

Laughter resonated through the halls, making the others press their fingers into their ears until blood started running down their hands.

"You're so naïve. You don't even know who I am," the voice mocked.

"Then who? Who are you? Who?!" I roared.

7

COINCIDENCES

"Sweetie, wake up," my mother said, shaking me awake. I looked around my room, trying to fight the pain caused by the sudden embrace of light.

"Your alarm's been ringing like crazy. You have school, don't you remember?"

I couldn't even remember who or where I was, let alone if I had school or not.

"Oh, yeah. I remember now," I said, the whole ordeal with Michelle coming back to me. Sunday had come and gone. I'd spent most of Sunday worrying about what I would find when I went to school. D-Day had arrived. "Maybe Michelle was suddenly struck with amnesia and forgot the whole nightmare."

My mother wrapped her arm around my shoulders and parted my hair. "We can only hope, Cooper," she said, pulling the covers down. "But, if she gossips like you told me she does, then you'll just have to deny it. I know, I know, I'm not going to win the 'world's greatest mother' award with that advice, but it's the best I can offer you."

My mother always hoped she had all the answers, but I knew that was impossible. I didn't know why she wanted Amber and me to think of her as Athena, the goddess of wisdom. We knew it was highly unlikely our mother had the right answers to all of our questions. What counted was that she never brushed our questions and problems under the rug; she was a problem solver. But our problems were not easily resolved, especially this one.

I think my mother felt the burden of raising two kids while her husband was more preoccupied with work than his family. Even when our father was on vacation, his mind was still at work.

After fifteen minutes of agonizing apprehension, Amber and I arrived at Erikson High School, which might have been bustling with rumors by then.

"It'll be okay, Cooper," Amber tried to assure me. "They're probably not going to believe a word Michelle says. Darcy told me that hardly anyone cares about half the things Michelle says about you." "This is different though," I said, bracing myself to enter the high school's halls. "Michelle saw my powers.

She saw that furniture levitating. She may have already connected the dots, and then helped others connect them as well." My sister gave my hand a tight squeeze and walked through the entrance, practically dragging me behind her.

When I entered the hallway, I expected a flood of eyes to be on me. Michelle had over a day to tell anybody about the paranormal incident at Sally's house, and that was a day more than she normally needed.

All I thought about were all those eyes staring at me in a matter of seconds. They had enough ammunition to make me do anything they wanted. But wait, why wouldn't Michelle want that ammunition? If she figured out I was controlling the furniture, why wouldn't she use that knowledge against me? She could use that information to make me do anything; I would be at her mercy. Both realities were horrific; however, the worst part of it all would be facing Sally. What would she think? Even if Michelle did not tell everyone that I made the furniture levitate, she would definitely tell Sally since they told each other everything. Would Sally believe her? Michelle might be a gossip, but as far as I knew, she never lied to Sally. If Sally did believe Michelle, would she accept me? I have feared the answer to that question for what felt like a lifetime.

Minutes turned into hours while I waited for the first person to look at me with a quizzical stare, but people didn't seem to be paying attention to me. In fact, all I heard were side conversations about those who had recently been reported missing.

I'd thought only Cynthia and Samuel were missing, but it turned out that two other students and a faculty member went missing, too. The two students were in the sophomore class, and the faculty member was a science teacher.

When I walked into my physics classroom and saw that we had a substitute, I knew who the missing teacher must have been. The name Samuel Divad, who I assumed was our substitute, was written on the whiteboard.

Michelle was sitting in her usual seat behind mine. Reluctantly, I sat in front of her and waited for her to tap me on my shoulder.

Surprisingly, Michelle seemed to be more fixated on the person in front of the room than on me. As I sat in my seat, I saw that Samuel Murdoch's father was standing next to the substitute. "Hello. For those of you who don't know me, my name is David Murdoch and I'm the chief of police," he said. He'd visited our classes in the elementary school and talked to us about crime prevention, and yet anytime he came to a school event, he seemed compelled to reintroduce himself. "I'm sure you've all heard about the recent disappearances. We'd like to ask you all a few questions concerning these disappearances."

Detectives had separate interviews with the students, trying to find some sort of information on the students and Mr. Nelson's whereabouts. By the number of detectives assigned to this case, you would think a massive crime spree had hit the town of Parkway. I thought the only reason David Murdoch was doing this was because he wanted to find his son as soon as he could. I didn't blame him, but he was abusing his power as chief of police. On the other hand, if I wanted to find someone I loved and had the power to do it, I'd probably use that power to my advantage, too.

Classes were hardly in session. The only thing we learned that day was how to stand in a line correctly, as that was all anyone did. Anyone who had any connection to the students and Mr. Nelson was interviewed, which was practically everyone in school.

"Hey, isn't this line just a joyous occasion?" Amber joked, standing behind me.

"Yeah. It makes me want to stand in the longest line at Six Flags," I replied sarcastically, rolling my eyes.

"If Murdoch says, 'this is police procedure' one more time, I'm going to make sure *he's* missing," Amber exclaimed, looking around to make sure no one heard what she'd said.

"Amber, his son is missing. At least he's looking for the other missing—" Before I could finish my sentence, my name was called.

"Hello, Mr. O'Neil. Won't you please sit down?" Murdoch asked, gesturing toward the chair in the guidance counselor's office he was temporarily using as an interrogation room.

"So, I hear you know a couple of the people who are missing," Murdoch said, sitting across from me in the dimly lit room.

"Well, yes. Mr. Nelson, who I assume is the teacher that's missing, is my physics teacher. Cynthia Peters' mother works with mine. Samuel Murdoch is my girlfriend's best friend's boyfriend. However, I don't know the other two students."

Murdoch leaned in and rubbed his chin, as if trying to judge if I'd told him everything I knew.

"Who is your girlfriend's best friend?" Murdoch asked, waiting in anticipation.

I was a little surprised Samuel hadn't told his father about Michelle. Perhaps, I shouldn't have even mentioned that I knew who his son was. However, it would probably come out that Michelle was Samuel Murdoch's girlfriend sooner or later.

"Her first name is Michelle," I stated. "Michelle what, Mr. O'Neil?" Murdoch asked, leaning forward a little further.

His bulky hands were clenched into fists, making them look like fleshy sledgehammers.

"Gibson. Why is it important?" I asked blatantly.

Murdoch looked right into my eyes, almost as if he was trying to see if I hid any secrets in my pupils.

"We are being diligent, Mr. O'Neil. We need to determine what is going on before more people disappear. Anything you know, or that this Michelle knows, could help us." He took an extended pause before asking his next question. As he continued to stare at me, I began gripping the chair, praying I would not lose control. "You look a bit nervous, Mr. O'Neil. Why?"

Before I could respond, a detective interrupted, stating that he wanted Murdoch to take a look at some evidence they found. I took this opportunity to get up to leave.

"I see that you are busy, so I will just show myself out," I said, inching toward the door.

"Mr. O'Neil, we'll be in touch," Murdoch asserted. Others would interpret what he said as procedural, but I could only view it as a threat. I had too many skeletons in the closet for the chief of police to be snooping through them. Even though I did not know anything about the missing people, I suspected that any investigation might somehow lead to my exposure.

As I walked toward my car, I felt someone grab my arm from behind.

"What did you tell Murdoch?" Michelle asked, spinning me around to face her. Her eyes were bloodshot and darkened. She looked like she hadn't slept in years.

"Nothing." I gave myself another mental slap. I really needed to remove that word from my lexicon. "Look, Michelle, I don't know what's going on with this investigation. I didn't say anything because I don't know anything. I only told Murdoch your full name, that's it," I said, walking toward my car.

Just as I opened the driver's side door, Michelle slammed it shut.

"Cooper, you know Samuel's father is looking for someone to pin this all on. He may suspect I had something to do with Samuel's disappearance," Michelle asserted.

"Don't be absurd," I scoffed. "It's not like you were the last one to see Samuel." From her widening eyes, I could tell I'd just made a big mistake. "Were you?"

Michelle turned around, crossing her arms over her chest.

"Maybe, but I can't be certain," she stated before spinning back to face me. "Look, Cooper, I don't know what is going on. This town's going crazy. First Samuel disappearances, and then others go missing. Not to mention that Sally's bedroom furniture somehow jumped in the air." She moved in a little closer and pointed her index finger at me as she continued. "I don't know how, but I know you are somehow behind that. I don't know if there are any connections between the disappearances and what happened in Sally's bedroom, but it's not a mere coincidence. I'll figure it out. You be sure of that, Cooper."

With her last warning, Michelle spun around and walked away. After about ten minutes of sitting in my car with the engine off, I heard a loud crash. I left the car door open and ran toward the school. When I arrived, students, faculty, and police officers were standing around two cars that had apparently collided with each other. Pushing through the crowd, I finally reached the front so I could see the state of the wreckage. When I saw a turned over, blue BMW's front end smashed into a parked car, I couldn't help but gasp. "Back, everyone back," Murdoch demanded, as other cops barricaded the crowd in with their presence. "We're trying to get her out, but you all need to back up."

Before a cop shoved me into the crowd, I saw Michelle's unconscious body upside down in the seat. Her thick, brown hair stuck to the blood running down from her scalp.

"Oh God," I muttered under my breath, realizing that gasoline was dripping from the car.

Any second, that thing was going to blow up. But the police were having no luck breaking through the doors. They were going to have to use the Jaws of Life to get her out.

"Who's in the car?" Sally asked, taking hold of my hand. "That looks like—"

I nodded, watching Sally's distorted countenance as the realization that her best friend was trapped in a car and there was a low possibility she was going to make it out alive sunk in.

Tears poured down Sally's cheeks. Her eyes became Niagara Falls as she pressed her head into my shoulder.

"It'll be okay. I promise. Michelle will make it," I said, as I stroked Sally's smooth, flaxen hair.

That was one promise to Sally that I was going to keep. I concentrated on the driver's side door of the car, slowly unhinging in. I could feel the rust weakening as I stared at the door. Suddenly, the door fell to the ground and the police rushed into the car. They ripped through the seat belt, picked up Michelle, and laid her down far away from the car. The police moved the crowd farther away from the car, probably seeing that the car was time bomb.

"Is she okay? What's going on? I can't see! Let me through!" Sally screamed.

I wanted to hold Sally back, but when Sally wanted to do something, no one could stop her. The police tried to keep her at a safe distance from Michelle, but Sally was so hysterical that not even trained cops could keep her at bay.

Looking back at the car, I wondered how it could have flipped over. Perhaps if she'd veered off the road and tumbled down a hill, the car could have turned over, but she'd been driving on flat concrete. Instead of parking in the large parking lot behind the school, she'd parked in the smaller one in front of Erikson High School.

"What happened?" Amber asked from behind me. "Is that Michelle?"

"Yeah. Her BMW flipped over and crashed into one of the parked cars. No one was inside the other car, but Michelle is pretty banged up."

"How'd they get her out?"

I craned my head back to look at the unhinged driver's door and then cast my eyes downward.

"They got a little *outside* help," I said, moving through the crowd.

"You *what?*" Amber asked in disbelief. Then she whispered, "You could have risked everything. You said Michelle's already onto you. What if she saw? What if the police officers saw?"

Ignoring Amber, who was surprisingly the rational one for once, I fought my way out of the crowd, toward my car.

"I had to do it. It was life or death. Plus, no one saw anything, especially Michelle, since she was unconscious. No one saw anything. I'm positive," I stated, feeling the need to repeat that no one saw anything, trying to reassure both Amber and me.

Amber nodded, following me to my car.

Just as I got to my car, I heard an explosion that almost made me jump out of my skin. Amber and I ran toward the heat that was radiating through the once-chilled air.

My skin felt like it was crawling off my bones as I looked at the charred, melting metal that was once Michelle's BMW.

"Is everyone all right?" Murdoch shouted, passing through the crowd.

A few people were injured from the intensity of the blast, but there were no casualties. Michelle and Sally were on the other side of the parking lot, so they weren't affected by the explosion.

"Is anyone going to call an ambulance? Michelle is dying and no one seems to care!" Sally screamed at the police officers, who were stunned by the strength of the explosion.

Murdoch pushed his way toward the burning car and began to talk to another police officer.

"Let's get a team to investigate that car. The explosion had too much force," Murdoch said to the other officer.

For once, I thought Murdoch was onto something. The force of that explosion felt more like several bombs detonating than a car exploding. There was something going on; I could feel it. That car was in such an odd position, and that explosion *did* have too much force.

"I should take Sally home. Wait for me by the car," I told Amber, pushing through the crowd toward Sally, who was practically hovering over Michelle.

Just then, the ambulance arrived. Sally refused to let go of Michelle's hand, even while she was being strapped to a gurney.

"Sally, I should—" I began, but then she spun around to face me. I had never seen her eyes so fierce and defiant, almost as if she were set to kill anyone who forced her to leave Michelle's side. I knew that if Sally was the one on the gurney, anyone would be thrown against a wall, with a literal blink of my eye, if they tried to pull me away.

"Call me if—*when*—she is better," I told her. Sally nodded and got into the ambulance.

CHAPTER

8

INHERITANCE

When Amber and I got home, our mother was there, waiting for us by the front door.

"Oh God, I didn't know what happened," my mother said, embracing both Amber and me.

I could hardly breathe with my face pressed into my mother's shoulder.

"The news said there was a car explosion, but it was so vague. I'm just so glad you're both okay."

"Mom, you're messing up my hair," Amber muttered, her face pushed into our mother's chest.

Reluctantly, our mother released us. Trails of new tears spilled over the old ones. I didn't know why our mother would think we were in a car crash. If my car were about to plummet into something, I'd stop it. That was probably one of the few good things about my powers: I could prevent accidents, at least ones I saw coming.

"We're all right, Mom. It was Michelle, Sally's friend...she was in an accident."

Somehow the word *accident* didn't sound appropriate. I couldn't help remembering how odd it was that the car was turned over and how the car explosion was more like a detonation. The feeling that something wasn't right was itching at the back of my throat.

"Is she okay?"

"I don't know. I hope so," I said, walking inside the house.

I didn't even look at any other part of the house; all I wanted to do was go to my room and lie on my bed for about four hundred years or so.

When I walked into my room, the first thing I noticed was my grandfather's journal lying on my pillow. I picked it up, feeling the weight of his thoughts.

Lying down on my bed, I opened the journal to the seventh entry. It was dated July 4, 1973.

Rose and I are finally married. At first, her parents forbid us from getting married so young, but after we eloped, they accepted our marriage. I have no idea how, but I got accepted into Columbia University with a full scholarship. It's going to be hard to get from my house to Columbia, but it must be done. Rose is going to a local university near the high school, mostly for Sophie's sake. Sophie is going to start tenth grade in the Fall. I sat her down and told her that if Mum were alive, she'd want her to live as if she was still alive, not try to deaden the present. I can still remember my exact words: "Mum wants us to succeed. She always dreamed that I would become a doctor and that you'd become a lawyer. She and Da wanted us to pave the way for others. Mum wouldn't want you throwing all of your knowledge and common sense away. Please, I already lost both of my parents, I don't want to lose my sister, too. I don't want you to live the rest of your life as if you're already dead, like Da did." It took months, but the days became easier. Sophie began to make more of an effort in school; she also promised she wouldn't try any drugs other than marijuana, but she has even begun to give that up as well. I'm not sure what else my sister had tried; I suspect she did not stop at marijuana. I just wanted my sister back. Slowly, I could see her blossoming into the Sophie I once knew. Between doing our own homework, Rose and I also check Sophie's and tell her that she must ask us for help. Rose is proud of Sophie, as if she were her own sister. My family isn't exactly the typical American family, but it's the closest I'm ever going to get to one. My life is as close to perfect as I'm ever going to get. I have a beautiful wife who loves me, a sister

> who's finally living as if she has something to live for, and I'm going to be a volunteer at Parkway Hospital, while going to a top university where I'm majoring in pre-med. Even though things still seem to drop, break, and spill everywhere I go still, I wouldn't change this life for anything. Sincerely, Max.

At least his tragic life seemed to take a turn for the better. He was fulfilling his dreams, with my grandmother by his side. I wished my life were as happy now as my grandfather's was in this journal entry.

I wondered if my mother knew her father had volunteered at Parkway Hospital. Maybe my grandfather was admitted there when he died. My grandmother never told my mother how her father died, but because he died so young, I assumed he didn't die after years of struggling with a debilitating disease.

I flipped to the eighth journal entry, putting aside the English and calculus homework I probably should have started instead. The entry dated back to December 24, 1973.

> This is the first Christmas Eve I'm spending with my wife. That word sounds so right. We haven't spent as much time together as we wish we could, but we're happy despite our other engagements. Rose is at the top of her class. She's taking nursing classes and already bandaged my hand perfectly after I burned it trying to make dinner. I keep telling her that she'll be the best nurse anyone's ever seen, but she's too modest. She keeps reminding me she's only a beginner, but I know she'll be the best yet. Sophie is doing quite well in her studies. I hope Sophie succeeds like Mum and Da hoped she would. I'm doing quite well also. My advisor told me that my volunteer work at Parkway Hospital can count as an internship. I've been working closely with my fellow volunteers: Brian Vara, John Slepton, and William North.
>
> They too hope to become doctors one day. William wants to be a neurosurgeon and follow in the footsteps of one of the top neurosurgeons in the hospital, Dr. David Leumas. In fact, I'm reading one of his textbooks in one of my classes, Theoretical Medical Techniques. Although the text is interesting, I am more interested in becoming a surgeon, like Dr. Malcolm Felone. He's one of the top surgeons at

Parkway Hospital, and he also graduated from Columbia. Brian and John don't know exactly what they want to specialize in yet, but then again, we have until medical school to figure that out. Dr. Felone said that when I become a resident, he'd like me to work under him. I told him it'd be an honor. Today, I promised not to talk about my work or school. Rose and Sophie agreed not to talk about school, too, but they're not obsessed as I am, or at least that's what Sophie keeps telling me. "We see it as just school.

You see it as your life." I've kept my promise, and I haven't spoken about work or school, so far. I hope Rose and Sophie like the gifts I've gotten them. I bought Sophie a Rolling Stones cassette. She seems to be obsessed with this band these days. I bought Rose a silver necklace, and I brought her engagement ring into the jeweler's so he could inscribe our names on the inside. "Rose & Max Fitzpatrick." It's bliss to my ears. Mrs. Rose Fitzpatrick. That name just sounds right. Sincerely, Max.

Max Fitzpatrick? My grandfather's last name was McEwin. Did he change his last name? I knew my grandfather was a first-generation Irish immigrant, and I knew some immigrants changed their surnames to more Americanized names but changing an Irish surname to another Irish surname defeated the purpose.

What would be the point of changing his surname then? Plus, his surname was still Fitzpatrick after he became an American citizen, so that didn't add up. Amber was right; my grandfather had quite a few secrets buried. Maybe this journal would help me uncover them. Before I could turn to the next entry, the house phone rang.

"Cooper, it's Sally!" Amber called from downstairs. "Got it!" I said as I went to pick up the phone. "Sally? Is everything okay with Michelle?"

"She's in critical but stable condition, whatever the hell that's supposed to mean," Sally said, her tone strained. "She has a concussion, a couple of broken ribs, a broken collarbone, and some tissues are torn in both her arms."

"Geez, I'm so sorry, Sally. Want me to come by?"

Sally paused for a second, probably wondering if it would be appropriate for me to sit in a room full of friends and family who Michelle actually liked.

"Maybe you could come tomorrow with me. I'm only going to stay an hour longer, and then I'm going to walk home," Sally said, sighing. "Plus, Michelle isn't awake yet. A couple of police officers are talking to her parents, as if they're going to investigate on an accident, which is what they said it was. I hate them being here."

"I know, I'd hate it, too."

They should investigate the car, though. There was something about the accident that made me think it was far from a simple accident. Luckily, the police officers did not suspect foul play, but if they did, then they might investigate the car door that had ripped off. Could they trace that back to me? Would anyone suspect that a cleanly ripped off car door was the result of telekinesis? I also had to consider whether or not forensics could get anything from the car door; after the explosion, the car was fried. However, if there was a slim possibility they could figure out that the car door had been ripped off, I had to make sure that it didn't get back to me. I shook off the thought; I could be worrying about nothing. Afterall, as I mentioned, I had a tendency to be paranoid.

"Well, I should get back. If Michelle wakes up, I want to be there. I love you, Cooper."

"I understand. If you want to talk later, whatever time, I'll be here to listen. I love you, too," I said, before hanging up.

I wish I could have held her in my arms and let her cry until she felt as if she were drained. I wanted to give her my strength until I had no more to give, and even then, I would find more to give her. However, Sally didn't want to lean on me just then. She put all of her strength into wanting Michelle to be all right.

And I needed to put all of my strength into figuring out why my grandfather's last name changed from Fitzpatrick to McEwin. "Mom, I need to talk to you," I said, walking into the kitchen. My mother was cooking for four, yet again, when she knew only three would be there to eat it.

"What about, Cooper?"

I turned to the entry where my grandfather revealed his true last name.

"Is McEwin grandma's maiden name?"

My mother stared at the journal as if the answer would be written somewhere between the lines.

"No. Your grandmother's maiden name is Sconza," she said, turning off the stove. "I've never heard the name Fitzpatrick in our family."

I was hoping the journal would provide answers to my grandfather's mysterious life, but it seemed to produce more questions than answers.

"Didn't you read the journal? Isn't that why you put it on my bed?"

"No, I didn't have a chance to read it. I thought you should read it first. I don't know if I am quite ready to find out the truth about him yet. There are a lot of ghosts in those pages," my mother stated, looking at me with her pensive eyes. "You, on the other hand, are far enough away that these secrets won't bother you. You never knew your grandfather, so learning about his secrets is more like reading a mystery novel. For me, it brings up a loss—the loss of a father and, with him, losing a piece of my mom."

Amber warned me that my grandfather had secrets, but I'd thought she was exaggerating.

"Mom, I'm sorry. I didn't know reading the journal would make you feel this," I admitted, feeling a pang of guilt, knowing what I was going to say next. "However, I have to keep going. There must be a reason why he changed his name," I told my mother, not giving her a chance to respond.

Opening the journal to the ninth entry, I noticed the writing was smudged, unlike the other pages. The entry was dated May 31, 1974.

> Something terrible happened at the hospital today. There was a shortage of doctors due to an influenza epidemic. Dr. Leumas and Dr. Felone were working practically triple shifts. The nurses who were there weren't as alert as they should have been. At 2:00 a.m., an emergency appendectomy was supposed to be performed. When a nurse, Simon Brane, was pushing the patient to the emergency room, he lost control of the gurney. It was going to crash into a window that was being repaired. The patient would have fallen out of a from the top floor of the five-story building if someone hadn't had stopped the gurney. I was on the other side of the hospital and couldn't reach it. Others chased it, but they couldn't grab it. Every doctor, nurse, patient, and intern on that floor seemed to be watching that gurney fly down the hall. I couldn't let that patient die, I just couldn't. So, I did what any other person in my position would have done; I stopped the gurney. I was risking everything. People would find out, but I didn't

care. As an aspiring doctor, I wasn't going to let a patient die if I could do something. Just before the gurney could reach the window, the wheels screeched against the linoleum floor, gaining friction. When the gurney came to a full halt without anyone touching it, every person stood agape. Everyone seemed to rationalize the situation in one way or another. Some said it was a miracle; others said the gurney's wheels hooked onto a nick in the floor. But I knew the truth. For once in my life, the curse my father passed onto me became a blessing. Another blessing happened today, too: Rose is pregnant. She's already one month along. I practically jumped through the roof with joy. A baby. A being made from Rose and me. Hopefully, it would be a child who could escape the curse that has been passed down through the Fitzpatrick line. Sincerely, Max.

I dropped the journal, feeling my fingers grow numb. A curse? My grandfather stopped a gurney without touching it? How was that possible?

For hours, I tried to rationalize the situation, just like the people at the hospital had done so many years ago.

However, I couldn't think of any rational explanation. There was nothing to think about. My grandfather had a curse that allowed him to stop a gurney without touching it. That could only mean one thing: my grandfather was telekinetic.

"You knew!" I screamed at Amber, barging into her bedroom. "You knew about Grandpa McEwin—Fitzpatrick—whatever the hell his name is!"

Amber dropped her lip gloss she'd been applying right into her blush. She stood abashed, unable to meet my eyes.

"I can explain," Amber said, gesturing for me to sit in the chair across from her vanity table. "Look, I stopped reading after that gurney incident. It took me a minute to recognize what it was, but all it took was memories of you to figure out that grandpa also had telekinesis."

"Why didn't you tell me?" I asked, the volume of my voice lowering quite a few decibels.

Amber sighed, picking up her now powdered lip gloss and cleaning it with a tissue.

"You needed to read it for yourself. Plus, would you have believed me if I'd told you, 'Cooper, by the way, grandpa was telekinetic too?'"

"Well, you still should have said something," I grunted, getting up from the chair and slinking onto the floor. "I had a right to know."

Amber slumped over the vanity table, fixing her perfectly kempt auburn locks.

"Cooper, our grandfather was telekinetic. He couldn't help it. From reading the journal, I realized I saw a lot of him in you and vice versa."

I closed my eyes, trying to imagine my grandfather moving objects to his whim and cursing every day that he couldn't fit in. He was a weed in a bushel of roses.

When items fell around my grandfather, when he couldn't hold onto anything without breaking it, he wasn't clumsy. I couldn't believe I hadn't seen it before; it all made sense now. It was foreshadowed. Maybe I should have focused on my English homework before reading his journal. He must have lost control of his powers every so often, just like me.

"That means I must have gotten it from him. He's telekinetic, therefore, so is his grandchild," I said, resting my head on my knees.

"It's unfair," Amber sulked.

I lifted my head to see that Amber had gotten up from the vanity table to lie face down on her bed.

"Yeah, it's unfair that I have this curse passed down to me, as if it's a family heirloom," I said, lying down on Amber's soft, plush carpet.

Her welcoming rug invited me to lie there forever, which I wish I could do. Stretching, I reluctantly lifted myself up and headed for the door.

"What are you talking about?" Amber asked, jumping up from her bed. "You have *powers*. You have abilities most people would *kill* for. It's not unfair that you got them. It's unfair that I *didn't*."

I'd always known Amber found my abilities entertaining, but I'd never suspected she was envious of me for having them. Did she seriously think these powers were a blessing? She had no idea about the agony I went through each and every day, hoping no one would discover my secret. Amber didn't know what it was like to strive for normalcy. How was it that everyone who *was* normal wished they were anything but?

As the adage went, people always wanted what they couldn't have. I wanted to be normal, while Amber wanted powers that were more of a burden than a godsend. I wished I could hand over my powers to her for just one day, so she would know what it was like to put on a façade. Amber would need to wear a disguise of normalcy, hoping the masquerade could continue, but there was always a high possibility that someone would rip off the mask and the charade would end.

"You think it's *unfair* that you don't have powers," I reiterated, trying to let Amber's naivety seep in.

"That's right. You have all the perks of being a McEwin—Fitzpatrick—whatever descendant, while I get the short end of the stick," Amber moped.

"Are you kidding me? You think these powers are a blessing from our grandfather's lineage?" I asked in disbelief. "Having telekinesis is a burden, if anything. I hope every day that no one will find out; I have to control my abilities at every turn; if I told anyone, I'd probably become the next article in the tabloids; I could be a science project at any second; I pray every day that I don't screw up when using my powers, otherwise someone could get hurt; and, I can't even get close to Sally, otherwise she will discover the truth about me, and who knows how she will react or what she will do with that knowledge. So, you think I'm the lucky one?

"You're the one who's lucky, Amber. You're normal. You don't ever have to pretend you're someone else. When people look at you, you don't have to fear they'll discover your darkest secret. No, Amber. It's *fair* that you didn't get our grandfather's awful ability. You're the fortunate one, not me. *I* got the short end of the stick, not you!"

Before Amber could respond, I stormed out and headed toward my room. I wasn't sure if Amber followed me or not, but I slammed the door anyway.

"I'm such an idiot," I told myself, as I collapsed onto my cool, disheveled sheets.

Amber didn't need to know that having powers was horrible. In fact, my abilities came in handy sometimes.

Perhaps I should have given her a pros and cons list before I rambled on about how terrible having powers has been these last seventeen years.

Without my abilities, Michelle probably would have died. Even if she told the entire world my secret, I couldn't have let her die. If I could prevent it, I wouldn't let anyone die. I would risk exposure to save lives.

Scanning my room, I noticed my grandfather's journal was opened to the tenth entry. It was as if it was coaxing me to read on. "Please, discover more horrifying secrets that will make you regret being a descendant of this man," the journal mocked, as if it could speak.

My curiosity got the best of me, and before I knew it, my fingers were gripping the pages, itching to read on. Before I could read the first sentence, someone softly tapped on my door. Reluctantly, I placed the journal on my pillow and opened my door.

My mother stood in the open doorway, hands on hips and eyes looking at me underneath furrowed eyebrows.

"I could hardly hear Mr. Murdoch on the phone with all the racket you were making," my mother said, tiptoeing around the piles of clothes I kept meaning to put away. "Now, why in the world were you yelling at your sister?"

I wondered if my mother knew about her father's telekinetic ability. She hadn't read the journal, so how could she? My mother hardly knew enough about my grandfather to make a family tree. However, maybe he revealed his secret to her and my grandma. It was unlikely, but I just had to know for sure.

"Did you know about grandpa?" I asked, ignoring her question.

"Know what? Now, Cooper, don't change the subject. Why were you—?"

"Did you know about his powers?"

"Powers?" my mother asked, sinking onto my bed. "What in the world are you talking about? What powers? He didn't have any powers."

Reluctantly, I handed her the journal and told her to read the ninth entry. I shouldn't have expected my mother to know anything about her father's telekinetic ability. If she hardly remembered the guy, she probably had no idea I'm just like him, in the paranormal sense.

When my mother finished the entry, she had a distant look in her eyes, as if everything around her was foreign. She opened her mouth to speak, but her vocal cords betrayed her. Every minuscule wrinkle around her lips and eyes seemed to magnify. Despite wearing blush, her cheeks were pale.

"I don't believe it," she stated, placing the journal gently on the sheets. "It must be a mistake." My mother shook her head, as if the words would leave her memory if she just shook hard enough.

"I couldn't believe it either, but it's right there. He didn't blatantly say he had telekinesis, but that's the only logical explanation," I said, placing my arm around my mother's shoulders. "It all makes sense. My grandfather's genes were passed onto me. Maybe they skipped a generation, I don't know. All I know is that he was definitely telekinetic. I'm sorry you had to find out this way, Mom." My mother brushed my arm off her shoulders and scanned my messy room.

"You know, I don't know why you just throw your clothes on the floor like this," she said, hastily picking up every piece of clothing she could get her hands on. "You know, you're a lot like your father in that sense.

Without me, this house would be a pigsty. God forbid you all clean up after yourselves. You're just like your father, you know that? Nothing like me in that sense. A mess of a room."

I stared at my mother as she swiftly moved around my room, hiding herself behind a large pile of my clothes.

Whenever my mother was upset, she cleaned and complained. When Aunt Sophie was put into a nursing home, my mother cleaned the entire house, both inside and out. My mother would tear up the floorboards and clean each one individually, if I didn't stop her.

"Mom," I said, ripping the huge pile of clothes from her grasp and throwing it onto my bed. "Why is this even different than me? What'd you do when you found out I had telekinesis?"

I didn't realize until I placed the clothes on my bed that my mother had been using the pile as a shield to hide the trail of tears spilling onto her pale cheeks.

"Oh, Cooper," my mother said, softly placing her palm on my cheek.

She sat me down on my bed and knelt in front of me.

"When your father and I saw what you could do, we thought of sending you to a specialist who could deal with your unique abilities," my mother said, cupping my hands in hers. "However, we decided you deserved a normal life. My father deserved a normal life, too. I just don't know. It's so hard to think that my own father had powers and I never knew about it. Like I told you, that journal just brings up ghosts—ghosts I didn't even know existed."

"I know. That's exactly what I thought. He gave me his curse, and I have to live with it."

My mother vigorously shook her head and reached up to part my hair. "No, sweetie. He gave you a *gift*. It might seem like a curse sometimes, but it's not. It's part of you. It makes you who you are," she said, pointing at my chest.

I gave her a meek smile and offered her one of my white T-shirts to wipe her eyes with.

"No, no. I'll get a tissue, but thanks," my mother laughed.

She wrapped her arms around me, holding on as if she would never let go.

I knew I was seventeen years old, but sometimes you just needed a mother's hug. Even when I reached fifty years old, my mother's bear hugs would still make me feel better.

"At least you're not the only one who thinks my powers are a gift. Amber thinks *not* having them is a curse," I said, smirking. "Maybe she should have inherited these abilities. She'd probably appreciate them more."

My mother gave a weak laugh, standing up.

"I do not think you received your powers by chance, Cooper. You shouldn't be ashamed of being special, sweetie."

She gave me a kiss on the cheek and left me to contemplate her advice.

My mother's accepting and understanding attitude never ceased to amaze me. I wished those words alone would convince me, but I had too many doubts to be persuaded so quickly.

I was about to complete what my mom started—putting my clothes away—when I once again noticed my grandfather's journal. His life was becoming a maze I couldn't figure out. One second, he was a normal guy with a pretty tragic life. The next second, he was a telekinetic student who changed his surname for some surreptitious reason.

Why did he wait until after his freshman year of college to change his surname? And, at what point exactly did he do so? Maybe knowing the answers to those questions would help me understand why he did so.

I rubbed my temples, feeling a migraine coming on. I knew the only way I would unlock my grandfather's personal Pandora's box was if I read the rest of his journal.

I turned to the tenth entry, noticing that once again the words were smudged. Perhaps he'd written it with a different pen. It dated back to September 30, 1974.

> My sophomore year is just as invigorating as I hoped it would be. I am taking my favorite courses, such as neurology and anatomical medical advances. I've also been encouraged to continue my internship at Parkway Hospital. I know my Da hated Parkway Hospital, but I think he would have been proud of me despite that. Before he slipped into an alcoholic oblivion, he told me he was proud of the goals I set for myself. I think that's why he was always so hard on me when it came to school. I didn't graduate valedictorian, but I was

third in my class. I hope he and Mum are proud of Sophie and me, wherever they may be. Speaking of Sophie, she's starting out well in eleventh grade. She received an A on her first chemistry test. Not too long ago, I asked Sophie if she'd like to pursue a career in science. However, she told me she'd like to study art and showed me a few of her paintings she'd hidden in the back of her closet. "Why would you hide such masterpieces, Sophie?" I asked her. She told me she didn't think they were that good. She was wrong. Her brushstrokes and eye for detail were amazing. When I was looking over one of her pictures, depicting the Parkway Pond at dusk, I felt as if I were standing on the grass, the breeze licking at my neck, with Rose's hands finding their way into my pockets for warmth. I told Sophie that she should submit the paintings in a contest, but she kept saying they weren't good enough to enter. I never thought I'd see the day when Sophie was modest. I finally convinced her to enter them in the art fair at the high school. Reluctantly, she set to painting yet another picture that she'd probably say was quite short of first place. Sophie has finally found her place in this world.

Rose is in bliss, but she's too hard on herself. She's five months along and believes that she's fat. I keep telling her that she is so beautiful. She thinks I'm just saying that because she's my wife, but I truly mean it. There's a glow around her that makes me want to sweep her off her feet. Rose placed my hand on her stomach the other day, and I felt the baby kick! It was as if my child knew that his/her father was waiting for him/her on the outside. I can't wait until the baby comes. Money will be tight, but I'm sure we'll make ends meet. I still have a night shift at the pharmacy, so a little money comes in. Da's life insurance also helps us pay the bills. I also still have a lot of money saved from when I was the day manager at the pharmacy, so we are able to get by. It also helps that both Rose and I have full scholarships. So far, I think we're in pretty good shape. Rose told me she wants to get a part-time job so she can contribute, but I told her there was no need. I told her that after the baby is born, and only if she wants to, she can get a job. I hope that when the baby is born, she/he won't have my abilities. They've gotten me in enough trouble. I wouldn't want my son/daughter to go through the same agony. I've already risked exposure quite a few times. When I first met Rose, a compass cut me in class. It must have been fate! The pain was so horrendous that it caused me to lose control of my powers. I ran out into the hall after the desks started moving, and I bumped into my love.

Recently, I saved a life by almost revealing my secret. I had to. If that patient had fallen out the window without me trying to save him, I'd have never forgiven myself. So far, no one has discovered the truth. However, everyone at the hospital is pretty distracted. There is something odd going around the hospital lately. A couple of patients and a nurse on the fifth floor have disappeared. The police have been notified, but an investigation isn't being conducted yet. I think they'll show up soon, but it's odd how they just disappeared like that. There were no notes left behind, so it wasn't a kidnapping, thank God.

Frustrated, I flipped through the first ten entries, hoping I might find a clue about the mysterious name change. As I turned the pages, rereading how my grandfather's mother died and how his father followed in her footsteps soon after, I found a little missing piece to the puzzle that hadn't fazed me at the time, but now, it was practically burning a hole in my retinas: my great-grandpa McEwin/Fitzpatrick left my grandfather a letter when he died.

It might lead to nothing whatsoever, but it was the only thing I had to go on, for the time being. The thought crossed my mind to speak to Aunt Sophie about my grandfather, but she had Alzheimer's. If I couldn't get any information from the letter or the journal entries, I would ask Aunt Sophie, but I doubted she even remembered she had a brother.

I began to turn to the eleventh entry when I realized I still had homework. Placing the journal on my desk, I took out my calculus and English textbooks and began to do my work, while my grandfather's mysterious life tiptoed through my consciousness.

CHAPTER

9

DISCOVERY

"You're just like him, in every way. He gave you this curse, and now you have to live with it. You hate him. You don't understand him, and for that, you also hate him."

I clasped my throat, feeling the air slowly work its way out of my lungs. My body defied gravity's grasp by clinging to the translucent, gray zenith of the clouds. The thin trail of oxygen I tried to keep inside danced its way out of my mouth.

"He did this to you. If you'd never found his journal, you wouldn't have blamed anyone. Now you blame him."

My feet dangled over millions of tiny ants running around the wide scape of smeared land. I could almost feel the soft touch of the grass tickling my toes, the firm dirt underneath my heels, forming to the arc of my feet, and the cool dew licking at the balls of my feet as I slowly descended to the ground.

"You're from a line of freaks now. Perhaps he changed his last name so he could find salvation in a new name. There's no mystery behind him changing his name. He did it to hide from his own curse. A name follows a curse from hell and back. He never escaped it, and neither will you."

My arms grew numb as I struggled to fight for air. I wanted to scream, "I want to live! Don't take that away from me!" But all I could get out was a *pathetic gasp that invited a toxic, pungent scent into my body. I wanted to cough to release the horrible musk, but I couldn't.*

The gray traces entered my body, ripping through the oxygen I managed to conserve. My entrails seethed with gray matter, causing my limbs to stiffen in pure agony.

"You are your mother's child. Her father wished for her not to receive the malicious gift, so she passed it onto you. He gave you the worst present possible: restraint. You have to hide a part of yourself, so you're never a full person and you know it. Even before you read those entries, you always knew it, didn't you?"

I gritted my teeth, trying not to bite off my tongue. The stifling gray air moved its way through my innards, making sure that not one part of my body escaped its callousness.

Streams of gray trickled down my cheeks, singeing my flesh. I opened my mouth to roar, but the only sound I could hear was the waves of seething gray odor pouring into my body, eradicating every part of pure flesh, bone, and intestines I might have left.

"The part of you that you repress will eat at you until it destroys you. You've always known that, and yet you continue to think everything will be fine. You try to convince yourself that you can fit into a world where you know you shouldn't exist. You're a creation meant only for failure, like your grandfather. Do you honestly think he made it? His dreams could never become a reality. He was destined to die early on because he didn't belong. It's inevitable, and you know it!"

I screamed in my mind for the voice to stop. Its malevolent cadence vibrated through my mind, serving only as a mild distraction from the torrential, gray stench excruciatingly tearing through my body.

"You're wrong!" I roared in my mind. "I will not fail! I have control over my own life! He didn't fail and neither will I!"

The rupturing musk's mission to destroy me was interrupted by the ripple of mocking laughter from the voice.

"You are him! You are damned! Your demise is soon to come! Only you can change the wheel of fate, but you'll never know how!" the voice taunted.

"Show yourself!" I thought, wishing I could yell. "Only a coward hides!"

The only response I received was yet another taunting laugh.

"I'm not damned! I'm not damned!" I wished I could hear myself yell as the gray-painted musk ate away at my body.

The only sound I could hear at that moment was the distant, spiteful laughter slowly forming into a piercing ring, which drowned out the musk that was munching its way to my soul.

I shot up, hitting my forehead on the ceiling.

Wincing, I rubbed the throbbing patch of skin that would soon turn into a welt.

Still thinking I was stuck in my dream, I checked my body to see if the acrid gray smell had made its way through my flesh.

"Cooper, I'm sorry—" Amber began, barging through my door. Noticing her eye contact had to aim a little higher than my bed, she smirked. "Okay, now who's the one taking their time to get ready, hmm?"

Rolling my eyes, I concentrated on my body, slowly lowering myself onto the cool sheets. I picked up my ringing alarm clock and shut it off.

"It's 7:00 a.m., so why are you up before me, again?" I asked, reluctantly rising from my bed. "This is becoming an odd habit."

"Yeah, me waking up before you is odd, but you waking up practically glued to the ceiling is completely normal," Amber joked.

I walked toward my closet. Shuffling through clothes, I could feel the pain in my bones leftover from the dream's gray musk that peeled me apart.

"I wanted to say...I'm sorry," Amber mumbled, fiddling with her curls.

"I'm sorry, I didn't catch that," I teased, taking out a pair of blue jeans and a T-shirt.

"I said, I'm sorry," Amber said through gritted teeth.

"It's all right. Although I can't empathize with you,

I know it must be hard to not have something you want," I said. "Trust me, if I could give them to you, I would."

"I'll hold you to that," Amber joked, and then made her way to her room.

After I got dressed, brushed my teeth, and ran a comb through my hair, I grabbed my book bag and went downstairs. It was 7:15 a.m., and Amber was nowhere to be seen.

I laughed to myself, grabbing a bowl of cereal. The day Amber was ready before me, I'd fly her around the town.

"Good morning, sweetie," my mother said from behind the largest coffee mug I'd ever seen.

I could tell from my mother's deepening worry lines that she needed about three of those cups, at least. "Did you have a good night's sleep?" she asked, offering me a cup of coffee.

I took a long sip of the brew, feeling the caffeine work its magic as my bones relaxed and a smile made its way across my face.

"I guess. And you?"

"Fine," she said, but I could tell by her uncertain tone that she was lying.

Perhaps my mother should know about the letter her grandfather left her father. It was a huge clue to the mystery that was my grandfather. However, since she did not know about her father's abilities and his name change, she might not know about the letter.

"Mom?"

"Yes, sweetie?" my mother said, finishing off the rest of her cup of coffee and making a second.

"How far did you get in Grandpa McEwin's journal?"

"About the first entry. Why?" she asked.

"No reason. I was just wondering," I said in a nonchalant tone.

I decided against telling my mother about the letter and how I wanted to retrieve it. There was only one person who would know what the letter was, and my mother would disapprove of me asking her: Grandma McEwin.

By 7:40 a.m., Amber was downstairs, followed by an overwhelming scent of rose perfume. I coughed, remembering Sally's overpowering jasmine perfume making its way into my lungs.

"Good morning," Amber hummed, placing her book bag on the kitchen counter and grabbing a Diet Coke out of the refrigerator.

"Finish that on the way to school. We have to go," I said, placing my bowl and mug in the sink while slipping my book bag onto my shoulders.

Amber grunted, placing the open can of soda back in the refrigerator. Just as we were heading for the door, our father walked into the kitchen.

"Good morning, everyone," he hummed, giving my mother a peck on the cheek.

"Morning, Dad," Amber and I said simultaneously. "Cooper, can I see you in my office after you come home from school today?" my father asked, just as Amber and I were about to walk out of the house.

"Sure, Dad," I said awkwardly, then I headed out the door without questioning why he wanted to see me.

"Why didn't you ask him why he wants to see you?" Amber asked in the car.

"I'll find out later, and I want to get to school on time, which I knew would never happen if you bombarded him with questions." Amber sighed, turning on the radio, finding yet another mind-numbing rap song. A momentary glance at the radio from me changed the station to static. Amber tried to fiddle with the stations, but I kept my mind set on that station. After a long struggle, Amber gave up on trying to change the station. I gave her a sly grin and shut off the radio. "That's what happens when you play rap in my car," I teased her.

When we reached the school, it seemed as if everyone was talking about yesterday's car explosion.

"There was a detonator in that girl's car that set off the whole thing," I heard a guy from my physics class, Anthony Desmond, say to a crowd, who were engrossed in his tale.

"She set the whole thing up. It was an attempted suicide that went horribly wrong," said another kid, in a different crowd.

"It was the principal's car she hit, I swear," another kid pledged.

Rolling my eyes, I made my way toward the front door, hoping the bell would ring soon.

"I guess people are fighting for the gossip-queen title while Michelle's away," I whispered to Amber, who I assumed was behind me.

Noticing that Amber must have left my side a while ago, I searched for Sally in the sea of gossiping students. I made my way through most of the kids, hearing tales of how Michelle got into the accident, but Sally was nowhere in sight. I thought of calling out for her but assumed she'd never hear me.

The bell rang just as I made my way to the entrance once again. Reluctantly, everyone put aside their tales and entered the school.

As I was walking toward my first period class, I realized I wouldn't be able to stop by my grandmother's house to ask her about the letter because my father wanted to see me in his office. Out of all the days he wanted to see me, why'd he have to choose that day? Sighing, I walked into my first period class, hoping I could think of something to get out of seeing my father.

Each minute seemed like an hour. The day dragged along as if it would never end. I thought of pinching myself just to make sure I wasn't having a dream in slow- motion, then again, lately my dreams had become nightmares that were trying to choke me with gray vapor. When my lunch period finally arrived, I bought a bowl of soup, which resembled and tasted like lava, and sat down where Sally and I usually met. I expected Sally to come into the lunchroom any second, carrying her usual brown paper bag filled with her mother's latest nutrition fiasco she was just dying to try on her unsuspecting daughter, but the lunch period came and went, and Sally was nowhere in sight.

I thought of calling her at home on my cell but figured Sally must have gone to the hospital to spend time with Michelle. Sally was the type of person who would stay by someone she cared about no matter what. That's why she'd tolerated me for so long.

Her loyalty astounded me. It also shocked Michelle, which was why she disliked me so much. I swear, one day Michelle was going to resort to brainwashing Sally to get her to break up with me. Michelle would probably throw a party on that day.

I still hadn't thought up a good excuse not to see my father in his office when school was finally over. Amber and I both knew that if our father put time aside in the day for one of us, he must have something important he wanted to tell us. Hopefully, it wouldn't take too long.

When I got home, Amber was dying to listen to the conversation our father and I would be having.

"He won't mind if I'm there," Amber whined. "I'm his kid, too, you know."

"Amber, I don't know. If you want to listen, fine, but it's not my idea. You'll have to ask Dad," I sighed, rummaging through my book bag for any homework I had to do that night.

With the lack of a proper AP Physics teacher, the bulk of my usual homework was missing.

"You know as well as I do that if Dad sets up a 'formal meeting' with you, I'm not allowed," Amber sulked. "Maybe I can put a glass to the door to hear or something."

"Amber, I don't care," I grunted. "Do whatever you want. I'd rather you take the meeting anyway."

Before Amber could respond, I walked into my father's office and shut the door behind me. Looking around his office, I almost thought I was transported into a psychiatrist's office in Belleview. The black file cabinets seemed to go on for miles; the brown leather couch looked as if it were the length of the Sahara Desert; and my father's large oak desk set him apart from those in his office by making him look like he was the biggest, most powerful being in the room. If my father wasn't trying to intimidate anyone, he failed miserably.

"Hello, Cooper. Good day at school?" my father asked, gesturing toward the couch.

"It was okay. There's nothing to complain about, if that's what you mean," I said, sitting down, practically sliding off the newly polished leather couch.

I snuck a look at my watch—3:30 p.m. I told myself I should go to my grandmother's by 5:00 p.m. Perhaps by that time, Amber would be so involved with texting her new boyfriend she wouldn't notice me leaving the house.

Amber always asked where I was going, even though she knew it was none of her business.

"That's good. Still keeping up those exemplary marks?" my father asked, picking at invisible lint on his sweater vest.

"Pretty much. Mom's always putting Amber and my report cards on the fridge, so if you want to see them…" my voice trailed off as I wondered when my father was going to get to the point.

Amber was right. My father didn't ask me into his office to have a simple chat. He had a method to his madness.

"Yes, I have. You kids are doing fine. Although, I wish Amber could pick up her GPA a little. If she put as much effort into her grades as she did into her boyfriends, she'd be set," my father joked.

"Yeah. I've told her that, in one way or another," I said, smiling to myself. "So, um, Dad. I'm assuming there's a reason why you asked to speak to me."

From years of experience, I've learned that when it came to my father, being straightforward was the best approach. He respected those who spoke their mind and asked clear-cut questions instead of beating around the bush.

Although, at that moment, he was contradicting himself by not getting to the point.

"Yes, of course," my father said, clasping his hands and placing them on his desk. "I was wondering what your plans were for the future. You have so many academic gifts, among other things, that I wanted to know what colleges you applied to and what you're going to pursue after college."

I should have expected that my father would sit down and talk to me about my future plans sooner rather than later.

"Well, I want to go into science, perhaps physics.

I've applied to a few reach universities, like the Massachusetts Institute of Technology, Harvard, and Stanford, but I also applied to a few target universities on the East Coast. Maybe I'll become a physicist. I'm not sure yet; I do know that I enjoy physics though, and it's what I am looking to major in."

"Well, that sounds like an excellent start, Cooper," my father said, getting up from behind his desk to sit next to me on the couch.

"However, I was hoping that by now you'd have more of a refined plan."

I was tempted to glance at my watch again, but I knew that would only make every second slower.

"Dad, I have an idea, which is better than most," I grunted. "I don't have a step-by-step plan because I might change my mind later on. Who knows what events might shift my focus? Maybe today I want to be a physicist, but who knows what tomorrow holds? Who knows how other things in my life might change what I want to be? Like I said, who knows?"

My father studied my calm expression, trying somehow to look beyond my countenance and into my true feelings. In my eyes, he could probably see how annoyed I was by his questions. He should see that I needed to do something and would rather have this conversation when I actually got into a university and was deciding exactly what I wanted to pursue.

If he did see all that, he didn't let on. Pressing his forefinger and thumb across his face, chin cupped in his palm, he tapped his cheek, as if that somehow would help him come up with a reasonable response. If there was anything my father considered himself to be, it was reasonable.

"I realize that life alters what you might become, but it's always good to have a structured plan in mind. That way, you have a sound, detailed idea of what you want to be, so you won't worry about it later. There's nothing wrong with planning ahead, son," my father suggested, trying to brush out the creases from his khaki pants.

I should have told my father that there are other factors in life to think about besides my career, but I decided against it, for the time being. He wouldn't understand. He'd always had a plan.

However, I was positive that having a son with telekinesis hadn't fallen anywhere in his plans. Maybe that was why he was pressing me for answers about my future. He wanted his odd son, who lived outside of his organized life, to have an arranged future.

"I'm sure I'll figure out something soon, Dad," I said, forcing a smile. "I'm applying to colleges with excellent science programs, and I'm sure I'll become a physicist. In fact, most of the colleges I've chosen specialize in physics in their science departments. So, if we're done—"

"Where are you going?" my father asked as I was about to get up to leave.

I should have told my father I was going to do my homework, or I was going to see Sally. Anything would have been better than what actually came out of my mouth.

"I just have to go somewhere. I'll be back later," I said through gritted teeth.

"Well, I think your future plans are more important than whatever you have to do. I mean, we are talking about the rest of your life," my father insisted.

"How would you know?" I asked. I knew I shouldn't have, but I couldn't help myself.

There was this insane little voice in my head telling me I needed to say this or it'd swim around in my head for the rest of my life, never quite reaching the surface.

"Excuse me?" my father asked innocently, but I could tell there was an underlying awareness in his voice, as if he knew what was coming.

"Well, you don't know enough about my life to know where I'm going or whether or not it's important," I declared, feeling a long, overdue speech coming on. "I could be planning for my future, or I could be trying to solve a mystery that's haunted this family for years. But you'll never know, will you? Amber and I have been as patient as we'll ever be; I even try to empathize with how dedicated you are to your work. Even when we were kids, we understood your career was more important to you than anything, even us. If you missed a birthday, it was because you were providing for our family by doing something you loved. We were both smart kids, so we understood; however, understanding doesn't make it hurt any less. You not being there for us affected our lives just as much as it shaped yours. You know, one day you're going to look back on your life and wish you took the time to get to know your kids better." I paused to take a much- needed breath.

"Cooper, now, I—" my father began, but my lungs were filled enough to continue my speech.

"I know you want a long-lasting career plan for me, but you're not thinking about all of the other aspects of my life. I might get married one day and have a few kids.

Perhaps my kids might have powers like me, and that's fine. My powers might have been a nuisance in your life- long plan, but that doesn't matter to me. I'm fine without planning out every detail of my life, unlike you. I'm not, nor will I ever be, you," I insisted. When I was done, I felt the color drain from my face with each second I waited for a response from my father.

His face flushed as he digested everything I'd just thrown at him. Regretfully, I'd revealed over a decade of repressed hostility toward my father, much I hadn't even realize I had until I'd spewed it out in that moment.

"First of all, you're right about almost everything you said. No, I never expected to have a son with telekinesis, but you were never a nuisance," my father assured me, adjusting his rimless glasses. "I recognize that I need to be more involved. That was what this conversation was about. With the recent disappearances on the news and from the conversations with your mom about what you told her about your grandpa, I realized I need to appreciate and find time for the people I love. Maybe I didn't go about it in the best way."

"Well, making after-school appointments may not be the best way to go about it. We are not your patients, Dad. Just talk to us. We're around," I assured him.

"So, making an appointment with Amber is probably not a good idea," he joked.

"I don't know. She may be intrigued by that.

Speaking of Amber, if you find her outside with a cup to the door, I think she's ready for her appointment," I said, glancing at my watch. "I, on the other hand, have another appointment."

As I was leaving, my dad asked, "Will you be home for dinner? Let's try to have the whole family there."

"Yeah, I'll definitely try."

By the time my father and I finished our conversation, it was already 4:30 p.m.

When I arrived at my grandmother's house, I reminded myself that she might not provide me with the answers I was looking for. My grandmother had never been a talkative person. If she didn't tell my mother a thing about her father, I shouldn't expect her to tell me anything about my great-grandfather's letter he'd left for my grandfather. She might not even know about it.

Hopefully, the mention of his name wouldn't give her a nervous breakdown again. Taking a deep, needed breath, I rang the doorbell. When my grandmother answered the door, the usual chocolate chip cookie scent escaped from her house to the streets, where everyone would probably think a bakery suddenly opened.

"Hello, Grandma," I greeted her, as she looked me over.

Even though my grandmother lived in the same town as my parents, Amber, and me, we hardly visited her. My mother invited her to our house for the occasional holiday, but besides that, we barely saw her.

"Cooper? You've grown so much since the last time I saw you, dear," my grandmother laughed, welcoming me into her house with a wide smile.

I sat on my grandmother's dull, beige couch, which was covered in thick plastic. She asked if I wanted a cup of tea and cookies, but I said, "No, thank you."

Taking a seat on the dusty piano bench, my grandmother made herself as comfortable as possible with her walker placed in front of her legs.

When I was about thirteen years old, my grandmother fell off a chair she'd been standing on, trying to reach a jar on the top shelf of the pantry. She injured her vertebrae, and it healed asymmetrically, so she needed a walker to get around.

"You haven't been here in quite some time, dear," my grandmother said, placing her cup of tea on the coffee table and fixing the pyramid of chocolate chip cookies she'd set in front of me, even though I'd told her I didn't want any.

"Yes, I know. I'm sorry, Grandma. I've been busy with school."

"Oh, yes. Your mother told me all about your interest in science last Christmas. I'm so proud of you, dear," my grandmother said in her usual sweet, compassionate tone.

I felt a pang of guilt when she mentioned she hadn't seen my mother since last Christmas.

When I was younger, I never understood why my mother wasn't close with her mother. The reason became obvious when I found my grandfather's journal. My grandmother must've had a few secrets of her own about my grandfather, otherwise she wouldn't change the subject with the mention of his name.

"Thank you, Grandma."

"You still keeping up those exemplary grades?"

Nodding, I reminded myself why I had come: I needed to ask her about the letter my great-grandfather left my grandfather. I could not be sidetracked by small talk. If anyone knew anything about my grandfather's secrets, it had to be my grandmother. At least, she was the first step toward the spiraling mystery that was my grandfather's life.

"Grandma, is there anything of Grandpa's you still have?" I asked, hoping she wouldn't turn three shades of white at the mention of his name and have to be admitted to the hospital again.

My grandmother's smile quickly formed into a frown.

"I have to take out the second batch of cookies I made," my grandmother stated, rising from the piano bench and walking to the kitchen as fast as she could.

Well, at least she hadn't gone into shock, which was progress.

The last thing I wanted to do was press my grandmother for answers, but I had to know the truth. I had a feeling she might know where that letter is. But, even if she didn't, I knew she knew more about my grandfather than she'd willing to let on.

Walking into my grandmother's flower-printed kitchen, I watched her busily tend to the mound of chocolate chip cookies she'd made for no apparent reason.

"Would you like one, dear?" my grandmother offered, placing the freshly baked cookies on a few clear plates.

"Um, no thank you, grandma," I said, wondering what she wound up doing with all the cookies she baked. She was too thin to have eaten them by herself. "Grandma, I know it's hard for you to talk about Grandpa, but I really need to know if there's anything of his that you have, besides those pictures of him and a couple of scraps of paper in the safe in the back of your closet."

The second I ended that sentence, I realized one of the letters or pieces of paper wrapped in the withering, red rubber band that Amber and I found in the back of my grandmother's closet so many years ago could be the letter my great-grandfather left my grandfather after he died.

At the mention of my grandfather's picture, my grandmother dropped the plate of cookies she was going to bring into the living room. Avoiding eye contact, she cast her eyes downward, picked up another plate of cookies, and walked out of the kitchen.

I picked up the pieces of broken glass and soiled cookies and threw them in the garbage, where I found mounds of other uneaten cookies. At least that was one mystery solved.

When I went back into the living room, my grandmother was nowhere to be found.

"Grandma?" I weakly called for her, but there was no reply.

I was about to call for her again when I heard the floorboards squeaking from upstairs. On the second floor, there were only three rooms, and I had a feeling my grandmother wasn't in the bathroom or my mother's old room, so I lightly knocked on her bedroom door.

"Grandma? Can I come in?"

After waiting about two minutes for a response, I tested the doorknob to see if she left the door open.

Surprisingly, she had.

Cautiously, I stepped into my grandmother's bedroom. I immediately noticed pictures of my grandfather spread out over her bedspread. Taking a few steps into my grandmother's room, which seemed to stand still in time, I tripped over her walker, which she left in the middle of her room.

"So much like your grandfather," my grandmother chuckled, who was sitting on her bed with her back facing me.

"Yeah, I guess," I said uncertainly, trying to untangle my legs from the walker. "He was pretty clumsy, wasn't he?"

"That he was, Cooper," my grandmother stated, gesturing for me to sit in the rocker beside the bed.

Sitting down in the rocker, I noticed I had a clear view of the safe. But, to my dismay, it was empty. Why would she take out the contents of the safe that might lead me to an answer about my grandfather's surname change?

"Why the sudden interest in your grandfather?" my grandmother asked, her face a silhouette in the dim light.

I should have known my grandmother wouldn't forfeit any information without a just cause. However, I'd assumed my grandmother would try to turn me away and that I would have to keep asking until she gave in. I never thought she'd take the calculated route and turn the Q and A session on me.

Should I tell her about the journal? Perhaps she was the one who put them in our attic. It was not like my grandfather could have done it, so she was the only other suspect.

Neither of us seemed sure about what the other one knew, and we were both certain of that. Well, at least I was.

"There's something of my grandfather's that I think you have," I stated, trying not to show my hand as long as she wasn't revealing hers.

My grandmother was about to reach into her blouse pocket, but then she hesitated before her hand could slip out of sight.

"What would that be, dear?" my grandmother countered. Her tone was more sharp than compassionate now.

She wasn't going to make her move until I made mine. My grandmother would stay on the defensive as long as possible, until I was on the offensive. I felt like I was playing a game of chess.

It was as if my grandmother had suddenly gone through a metamorphosis and changed into this calm, surreptitious person. If I was going to get answers, I had to tell her what I wanted and why, otherwise I'd never uncover my grandfather's secrets.

"I want the letter his father left him after he died," I stated, wondering if she'd give me what I wanted.

At first, I thought my grandmother was going to reach back into her blouse pocket and pull out the letters. However, instead, she turned toward me, revealing the glistening tears rolling down her pale cheeks.

Perhaps I shouldn't have acted as if the whole ordeal was some type of metaphorical chess match. I knew my grandmother could hardly stand hearing his name without falling apart. What made me think anything had changed just because I mentioned the pictures and letters in the back of my grandmother's closet?

I was about to say I should go home when my grandmother took a photo off the bed and handed it to me. It was the one Amber took out of the safe and handed to my grandmother when she was little. My mother was an infant, looking up at my smiling grandfather, who was holding her in his arms.

"That was the day your mother was born," my grandmother sighed, wiping away her tears with a tissue she kept tied to her wrist with a rubber band. "Your grandfather was so happy. You know, he used to always carry that picture in his wallet. He gave it to me the day he..."

My grandmother's eyes filled with distant memories she'd probably moved to the back of her mind the day her husband died.

"Grandma, I'm sorry about Grandpa. I know it must have been hard for you to let go. But he's still with us in a way," I said, wanting to kick myself for saying the most cliché response in the world.

My grandmother gave me a slight nod, reaching inside her blouse pocket and pulling out the withering letters and the few scraps of paper held together by the red rubber band.

Taking one last look at the papers in her hand, she reluctantly gave them to me. Part of me wanted to hand back the last papers she had left of my grandfather, but the logical, curious side of me won the battle and took the papers.

I told myself that after I figured out my grandfather's mysterious life, I was going to frame the papers for my grandmother.

The letter was what I came to my grandmother's house to retrieve, but I knew there was more I could get out of her. In some respect, it was cruel to pick at a scab my grandmother had tried to keep bandaged for decades, but my inquisitive nature got the best of me and I had to know more.

"Grandma, did you know about grandpa's journal?" I inquired, feeling like I was pushing the envelope just a bit too far.

My grandmother dropped the picture she'd been studying on the bed and looked at me with magnified, glossy, teal eyes.

"How do you know about it? I left it with your mother years ago," my grandmother stated, shifting the clutter of pictures spread across her bed. "When she moved into your house with your father, I put a cardboard box in the attic filled with your grandfather's things he wanted her to have. At the time, I couldn't bear to tell her what was in the box. I figured she'd open it and discover the journal and other things for herself."

"Well, I found them recently and came across some interesting entries," I stressed, helping my grandmother sort out the pictures. "And I was wondering, since you gave them to Mom, if you know why grandpa changed his last name?"

I waited in anticipation for the answer. Hopefully, my grandmother would provide more answers for me than my great-grandfather's letter could.

"Dear, now's not the best time to ask me. I'm tired and need to take my pills," my grandmother said, struggling to put the photos back into the safe.

Nodding, I helped her clear the photos off her bed and close the safe. I should have anticipated that she would avoid the issue.

Well, at least I left my grandmother's house with more answers than what I'd come in with. I knew my grandmother placed the journal in the attic, and I had a few more clues that would lead me to the truth about my grandfather.

10

THE STORM

When I got home, the sun had already set. Tucking the papers into my pocket, I went into my house.

"Sorry I didn't leave a note, but I went out for a little bit," I called to anyone who was listening.

Not hearing a response, I shrugged and went into the kitchen to make myself something to eat. When I entered the kitchen, Amber and my parents were sitting around the table, whispering to each other. The minute they saw me, their heads shot up.

"Hey, everyone," I said, almost in the form of a question.

Ignoring their staring eyes, I went to fridge to grab a piece of fruit. I could feel their eyes on me, watching my every move. This must have been what it would feel like to be a science experiment if my powers were ever discovered.

Placing the piece of fruit on the counter, I smiled awkwardly at my family.

"Something wrong?" I asked. "I said I would be home in time for dinner. Am I too late?"

They whispered among themselves, trying to find a response to my question. Finally, my mother became the spokesperson for the group.

"Cooper, um, come sit down," my mother said, gesturing toward the seat next to her.

"All right," I said, cautiously sitting down. My parents and sister gave each other a wary, knowing look and then turned toward me.

"Is there something you have to tell me?" I asked, starting to worry.

The last time my family sat me down at the kitchen table, they told me that my beloved hamster, Bailey, died. I had a feeling these were similar circumstances. Although I didn't have a pet, something had happened that was hard for them to tell me.

"Actually, yes, sweetie," my mother said, placing her cool hand on top of mine. "Sally's mother called while you were out—"

"Is it about Michelle? Did something happen?" I asked, not allowing my mother to finish her sentence.

"No, no. I'm not sure about Michelle's condition," my mother said, glancing at my father and giving my hand a light squeeze. "Sweetie, um, Sally left the hospital last night after visiting Michelle. Sally's mother called to ask if you'd seen her."

"She wasn't in school today," Amber mentioned, casting her eyes down at her freshly painted nails.

"Sweetie, Sally's been reported missing," my mother stated.

"Missing?" I blurted.

Suddenly, my mouth went dry, and the people at the table seemed foreign. Who were these beings telling me that my girlfriend was missing? Why would someone say that?

"Yes, son," my father said, awkwardly placing his hand on my shoulder.

"Missing?" I asked again.

It was as if the only word in my vocabulary at that moment was *missing*. How could Sally be missing? Sally couldn't be missing. She must be at home right now, trying to reach me.

It was at times like this when I wished I knew where I'd placed my cell phone. Instead, I raced to our home phone before anyone could stop me and vigorously dialed Sally's number. My mother tried to pull the phone out of my hand, but I gripped the thick plastic as if it were my life.

The phone rang five times before anyone answered. "Sally? Is that you?" Sally's mother asked in a frantic tone.

"Is…Sally…there?" I slowly asked, already knowing the answer. A whimper and a loud click were the last sounds I heard on the other line. Slowly, I hung up the phone.

"Missing?" I asked again, watching my mother nod sadly.

"I'm so sorry, sweetie," she said, placing her arm around my shoulders. "I'm sure she'll be found."

"Yeah, Cooper," Amber chimed in. "Sally's probably just lost or something. Someone's bound to see her and help her get home."

"Son, this is a small town. I guarantee she's somewhere around here. Or, she might have wandered toward the city and will be home soon. I'm sure she'll be found," my father tried to assure me.

"Can you stake your life on it?" I hissed, turning on my father.

It was as if someone set off a detonator inside of me. I couldn't control what I said. At that moment, I blamed anyone who came in contact with me for Sally's disappearance, and my family just happened to be in the line of fire.

The kitchen table began to shake as I shrugged my mother's arm off my shoulder. My father and Amber firmly placed their hands over the table, trying to stop it from moving.

"Now, Cooper, I know you're mad, but there's no reason to—"

"No reason to what?" I asked, not allowing my father to discuss *reason*.

There was no *reason* why Sally was missing. There was no *reason* why I shouldn't lash out. At that moment, there was no *reason* left in the world.

I cast my eyes downward, feeling the pantry and cabinet doors opening and closing. The chairs at the table began to energetically move around, as if they had a mind of their own. My father and sister jumped from their seats when they realized they could no longer hold down the table and let it fly up to the ceiling.

"Cooper, I know this is hard, but you have to calm down," my mother pleaded, trying to grab the silverware that was jumping out of the cabinet drawers.

"Calm down?" I echoed, flicking my wrist toward the dishwasher, which immediately came to life.

Why was she missing? She couldn't be missing. I loved her too much for her to just disappear. I felt as if I could reach her if I tried hard enough. If I just used all the power I had, maybe I could find her.

I didn't care my thought process was irrational. In a world that seemed to lack anything rational, what else did I have to turn to?

"Cooper, you have to stop this!" Amber shrieked over the rattling of the dishwasher. "She's going to be fine. You have to calm down!"

Amber jumped at the chorus of shattering glass. Plates levitated in the air just before they hit the linoleum floor.

"Cooper, that's enough!" my father roared, grabbing my arm. "I know you're upset, but that's no reason to cause destruction."

Wrenching my arm out of my father's grasp, I rose to the ceiling, feeling every molecule in my body charged as I controlled all the objects around me. Kitchen utensils swirled in the air, making a mini tornado underneath my legs.

"Cooper! Stop being such a baby!" Amber screamed, trying to pull objects out of my hold.

Snapping my head in Amber's direction, I flicked my wrist, forcing her to rise so I could meet her eyes. Her skin turned a deep red as she screamed, while all of our kitchen appliances whirled underneath us.

"Put your sister down!" my father commanded, trying to pull Amber to the floor.

Closing my eyes, I felt the entire house move in my grasp. Every atom, every particle was trapped in my telekinetic rage. Picturing the world outside my kitchen, I envisioned trees uprooting from the comforting grass, bodies of water rising from their prisons and floating freely in the air, and the ground unearthing itself from the world's grasp.

"Cooper, please! Please, stop it!" Amber cried.

My eyes snapped open, taking into view Amber's tearstained cheeks. My parents clasped her legs, trying to get her away from the peril that was their own son, but I couldn't stop. Reason had already escaped from my mind. Wrath was all I had left.

I ignored my pulsating temples, extending my powers past their limit.

I imagined Sally's shimmering, petrified eyes staring out at me from a torture chamber. Knowing full well I couldn't reach Sally, I focused on her, trying to release her from the prison that trapped her.

"Sally!" I roared, feeling my grasp slipping as her image faded from my mind's eye. And then my entire world went black.

CHAPTER

11

DON'T MAKE ASSUMPTIONS

"You lost her you fool! You know you'll never find her! Even if you do reach out for her, she's lost, and you know it. Those kids are missing, and so is she. They can't be found, and neither will she!"

Liquid washed over me, boiling my flesh. I screamed out in agony, feeling my skin burn away. I tried to move my arms, but they were buried underneath the earth's surface. I could feel clods of soil melding with my flesh, as I became one with the earth.

"You deserve to suffer! She was your love, and you let her go. You should have met her at the hospital and walked her home, but no. You just let her walk home by herself and allowed her to go missing!"

I could feel my teeth piercing my tongue. The warm, red blood trickled down my lips, making its way into the patches of burnt, fleshy tissue left on my deteriorating body.

My screams were quieted by the pooling blood inside my mouth. I opened my lips, gurgling for help, but no one was there to hear me. And, even if someone heard my pleas, they shouldn't come.

"You're right," I thought, giving into the voice's iniquitous words. "I should have been there to save her. It's my fault she's gone, and I feel helpless."

The usual mocking laughter reverberated against the hollow, dark walls.

"Yes, I know. But you can change it, you fool," the voice hissed.

"How? How can I change it?" I thought, wishing I could scream.

"Find her," the voice simply said, giving me one last wicked laugh before it left.

"How?!" I heard myself scream, seeing only darkness.

When I opened my eyes, I noticed three blurry heads looking down at me. At first, I thought I'd been abducted by aliens, like in some type of cheesy sci-fi movie from the sixties. Then, when the faces came into focus, I realized I was looking up at my parents and sister.

"Sweetie, it's okay," my mother said in a soothing tone.

"Are you guys floating?" I asked.

"Well, I was, and I thought you were going to pile drive me into the floor," Amber stated, handing me a compress.

"Huh?" I said, placing the cool, damp compress on my forehead.

"You passed out, son," my father said, helping me sit up.

The minute I sat up, little fluorescent balls began to explode in front of my eyes. A wave of darkness soon followed, trying to wipe out the vibrant sprays of fireworks exploding in my head.

Wincing, I took the compress off my forehead, waiting for the intense throbbing to lessen. But, as the seconds passed, the excruciating pressure in my mind refused to settle.

After a few minutes, when my sight finally returned, I groaned, surveying the broken pieces of glass and wood that covered the linoleum kitchen floor.

Did I really ruin my parents' kitchen? It seemed like a terrible horror movie parody, where I was Carrie, and my family were the frightened students running for their lives from the blood-soaked, wrathful, telekinetic teen.

Being in a sci-fi movie had become a self-fulfilling prophecy. All we needed was a mad scientist hell-bent on revenge and we would be all set.

"Sorry about the kitchen," I said, feeling like a greater apology was in order.

"It's okay, sweet," my mother assured me, folding over the cool compress and placing it back on my forehead. "I can replace the glasses, plates, table. You know, I was meaning to get new pieces for the kitchen anyway." My mother gave me a wide smile, but I could tell she was crushed. I'd broken almost everything in the kitchen.

"I'll clean up, Mom," I said, trying to stand up.

My father put my arm around his shoulders and helped me to my feet. The vibrant explosives went off in front of my eyes again. I waited a couple of minutes for them to pass, staring at the dark curtain that fell over my field of vision.

When I could finally see clearly, I tried to stand on my own, but I slipped back onto the floor.

"I'll buy you new kitchen pieces, Mom. I swear I will," I pledged, feeling pangs of guilt as I got a really good look at the shards of broken glass and wood covering the floor. "And I'll clean up this mess as fast as I can."

Focusing on the pieces of shattered glass on the floor, I tried to lift them off the ground and into the trash can, but I couldn't. My telekinetic prowess was replaced by a horrendous migraine.

Giving my head a good shake, I concentrated on a smaller pile of glass shards near the garbage can. The throbbing made its way to my sinuses as I focused on the broken glass.

I stared at the pieces of glass until I was practically blue in the face. The shards moved slightly before the fluorescent explosions blinded my sight.

Falling back onto the floor, I waited patiently for my vision to clear once again.

"Oh, sweetie, are you okay?" my mother asked, placing her hand on my aching forehead.

My parents helped me to my feet again and brought me into the living room. Surprisingly, the furniture was only tipped over in that room. I was thankful I didn't have to replace all of the furniture in the house.

"I couldn't move it," I murmured, in a state of disbelief. "I tried, but hardly anything happened."

"You're probably just drained, sweetie," my mother tried to assure me, inadvertently parting my hair. "You went through a tough ordeal today. Your powers will return, I'm sure of it."

"How can you be sure?" Amber asked, studying my pale, damp face.

I lay back, letting the pain wash over me.

With my temporarily malfunctioning powers, I somehow felt empty, as if a vital part of me had escaped. I never realized how hollow I'd feel without my abilities. It almost felt like I had a phantom limb; I could feel it there, but I couldn't do anything with it.

I kept expecting to be able to concentrate on an object and have it easily float to me, but I knew if I tried to use my powers again, I might pass out from the unbearable pain.

"Well, at least the playing field is level now," Amber jested, giving my arm a light nudge.

I rubbed my temples, trying to massage away the pulsating agony in my brain.

"Let's see how you feel about that when I get my powers back," I weakly laughed, wincing at the increasing pain.

I wished my throbbing migraine and momentary loss of powers could distract me from Sally's disappearance. Unfortunately, nothing could make me forget Sally wasn't at home, safe.

I yearned to wrap her in my arms and tell her I would never let anyone hurt her. Why hadn't I tried to call her when I was at school? Why hadn't I walked her home from the hospital the other night?

Over the next few hours, I lay in bed, trying to ease my headache with the compress placed back on my forehead like a cool, damp, regenerating covering, I kept thinking about what I could have done to prevent Sally's disappearance.

Although no one said she had been kidnapped, I could not help but suspect these disappearances were not coincidental. It was the only logical explanation.

If she'd been kidnapped, I had to find her. Even if my abilities never returned, I was determined to bring Sally back, whatever the cost.

"Do you really think you can find her?"

Despite the shards of glass embedding themselves deeper into my flesh, I stood my ground. I refused to allow myself to give in.

Stakes spitefully drove themselves through the fleshy tissue of my thighs and abdomen. I could feel fiendish energy driving the sharp pieces of wood deeper into my flesh. But I didn't flinch. I couldn't. I knew what I had to do.

"*Nothing will stop me from finding her. Neither you nor anyone else, can keep me from bringing her back home,*" *I said to the disembodied voice.*

I could feel the voice's sneer from fifty miles away. For once, the voice's laughter didn't ripple throughout the atmosphere.

"*What makes you think you're the one who's supposed to find her?*" *the voice countered.* "*Maybe you should leave this matter to the police.*"

"*No!*" *I roared, feeling the reverberation of my voice licking at the hollow walls.*

I wished I could hear the echo of my voice as it sliced through the thin sheet of space, but the feel of my vocal cords somehow lessened the atrocious pain the shards caused as they sawed through the first layer of my bones.

"*What do you mean, no?*" *the voice jeered.*

"*I'll find her without the police's help. I don't care if I'm destined to find her or not. I'm going to discover where she is and rescue her, no matter what anyone says,*" *I shouted, determination ringing in my voice.*

I could sense the voice's invisible lips form into a grin.

"*Then do it,*" *it merely stated.*

———— ·+·+++·+· ————

"I can do it. I know I can," I mumbled, waking up to the sound of my own strained voice.

Slowly sitting up, I realized the throbbing in my head had subsided a little. However, I still felt like my head had been used as a set of bongo drums.

As I got out of bed, I realized I hadn't heard my alarm ring. Wondering if I'd woken up too early, I looked over at my clock to see that it was 9:00 a.m.

I threw on the first clothes I found, grabbed my book bag, and ran downstairs.

I practically fell down the stairs in my rush to get out of the house.

"Going somewhere?" Amber laughed, as I was about to run outside.

She was lying on the couch, scrolling through her phone, acting as if nothing were amiss.

"We're late!" I shouted, trying to concentrate on Amber to get her off the couch, but she only slightly moved forward.

Dropping my book bag, I grabbed my head, feeling the pounding severely increase.

"Mom shut off your alarm," Amber said. "She wanted you to take it easy today. Plus, it's a superintendent's day, so we don't have school."

"Right, I forgot," I said, wincing at my increasing migraine.

"Look, about yesterday—"

"Forget it," Amber cut me off, helping me to the couch. "Plus, it was entertaining. It was like a really intense rollercoaster with collateral damage. By the way, that's all coming out of your allowance."

"Perfect," I said, as Amber eased my head back on the couch.

"It's not like I have anything to spend it on anyway."

"Cooper..." Amber began, leaving her thoughts lingering. "I...I don't really know what else to say other than sorry."

Before I could respond, Amber got up and went to the kitchen, returning with another cool compress our mother kept in the freezer.

"Here, this will help," Amber said, laying the compress on my forehead. "Cooper, there's something I want to ask you about yesterday, you know, when you went power-crazy in the kitchen."

"Shoot," I said, wincing at the memory, cringing at the thought of going into the kitchen to take a look at the destruction I caused. Now that my vision was not blurred, I would be able to clearly see the aftereffects of my telekinetic tantrum.

I knew if I was going to get angry, I had to use that anger strategically. I needed to put all of my energy into finding Sally. The only way I could rescue Sally was by using my intelligence, not my telekinesis—not that I was able to use it at the moment anyway. I knew I had to start my investigation at the hospital. And, I had to talk to the one person who I knew must have seen Sally last: Michelle. That is, if she was conscious yet.

"Well, when you were using your powers, something happened that I didn't know you could do," Amber said, twirling her freshly curled red locks. "I thought you could only use your powers through your eyes."

Sitting up, I took the cool compress off my head, trying to figure out what Amber was getting at.

"Yeah, that's right," I affirmed. "Why?"

"Well, when you were levitating, you flicked your wrist a couple of times," Amber said, showing me with her own wrist how mine had flicked the day before. "I was just wondering if you were able to do that before?"

"I did, didn't I?" I asked. Amber nodded. "I've always used my eyes to move things. I don't know why I was moving my wrists."

Groaning, I placed the compress on my forehead once again, feeling my migraine worsen. I had never lost control of my abilities like I had in the kitchen. Everything I'd done was so instinctual. For the life of me, I had no idea why I'd flicked my wrists or if doing so had any effect on how I exerted my abilities. However, there must have been a reason why I'd done it.

"Do you think you could do it again?" Amber asked, removing the compress from my head. "I know you are having difficulty moving things around by looking at them. Maybe this is how you can use your powers."

"Ugh, not now, Amber. I have an incredibly large migraine. I can hardly think straight," I moaned, pulling the compress out of Amber's grasp and placing it back on my forehead. "Plus, wrists or eyes, I still use my brain to move things around, and right now it feels like it's out of commission."

Amber pulled something out of her pocket.

"I found this on the kitchen floor, and I thought it might belong to you," she said, holding the withering papers held together by the red rubber band.

Taking the papers from her, I realized I'd forgotten all about trying to discover why my grandfather changed his name. As I turned the papers over in my hands, they didn't seem as important to me as they had the day before.

I had to find Sally. I had to put all of my energy into that, nothing else. After I rescued her, I'd have time to unlock my grandfather's secrets.

"What are they?" Amber asked, eyes focused on the papers.

"Letters," I merely stated, shoving them into my pocket.

"From who?"

Rolling my eyes, I took the letters back out of my pocket and handed them to Amber.

"Grandma gave them to me. They were in the safe we opened when we were younger. Here, read them if you like. I think one of those letters is to grandpa from great-grandpa McEwin, or Fitzpatrick, whoever they are," I said, helping Amber take off the red rubber band. "There might be something in there about why he changed his last name."

"These look familiar, why?" Amber asked.

Amber just looked at me for a moment. I could see a flood of questions forming in her eyes, but she chose to ask just one. "Want me to read them aloud?" she inquired, unfolding one of the letters.

"Fine," I grunted, sitting up.

"Hey, I think this one is from his diary. Remember, there were missing pages?"

I nodded, wondering why he had ripped them out.

"It's dated June 15, 1973," Amber said, beginning to read the diary entry.

I wish I could tell Rose about my powers. As I bent down on one knee, asking her to marry me, I felt a little pang of guilt. She had a right to know what she was marrying into. When we had children, they might have my abilities, and Rose will be so scared. One second, her little boy/girl will be playing ball on the ground. The next thing she knows, the ball will be spinning in midair while the little babe is laughing. My poor love. Perhaps, she shouldn't have said yes, but I wanted her to so much. When she said yes, I nearly lost control of my powers and let the ring levitate. Luckily, I kept my telekinesis under control and was able to place the ring on her finger. This really doesn't count as a diary entry because I plan to give it to my beloved so she knows what she's getting into. If I were to marry a person with powers, I'd like to know about it. Hopefully, she won't leave me when she finds out my terrible secret. Rose, I know I've lied to you for so many years. I should have let you see all of me, so you could love all of me, but I just couldn't. I wrongfully hid the part of myself that scared my mum when she married my da. My powers come from his line of the family. He always told me the power we hold is both a gift and a burden, but we have to accept it. After years of struggling, I finally accepted my powers. My Da showed me how to use them by practicing with his own. But I was never a match for him. He could lift up an entire town if he tried hard enough. I, on the other hand, can't even lift a person. The most I can do is make some objects levitate or change a person's movements. I've made people stop running, but no matter how hard I try, I can never levitate a person. Though, I see that as a good thing. The more power you have, the further away from normal you are. When you read this, my love, please think before you leave me. I'm so sorry I didn't share this part of myself with you. You've already had to endure a painful breakup and my parents' deaths. I didn't want to burden you even more by telling you that your fiancū is a monstrosity. I hope you'll still be with me, Rose. I love you so much, my darling. I will never keep anything from you again. Our lives will be joined and so will our secrets. I love you, Rose. I hope your compassion will lead you to see that I didn't tell you about my powers because I love you. Please, forgive me. Love, Max.

So, my grandmother knew about my grandfather's powers. Did that mean she knew about mine? She must have known that someone in our family would have telekinesis.

Perhaps she believed my mother had telekinesis. As far as I knew, my mother hadn't told my grandmother about my powers. However, she might have figured it out already and just hadn't mentioned it. Maybe I was just being paranoid, but then again, that was my specialty when it came to my abilities.

"Well, that was idiotic," Amber said, wrapping the red rubber band back around the diary entry.

"What are you talking about?" I asked, not understanding why Amber thought my grandfather was an idiot. "He was trying to protect her. He also loved her so much that the fear of losing her was too much."

"Well, granted, he was doing it out of the goodness of his heart," Amber stated. "But he shouldn't have hidden any part of himself if he truly loved her like he said he did. He had no right to decide how she would judge him. Who says she wouldn't have accepted him with his abilities? Obviously, she did, considering they did get married."

"Just read the next letter," I grunted, shoving the diary entry back into my pocket.

I refused to admit it, but part of what my sister said made sense. My grandfather should have let my grandmother decide how she felt about his powers before he decided for her. That was exactly what I'd done to Sally. Believing she'd leave me or tell her best friend about my abilities, I didn't tell her about my powers, and now I didn't know when I'd see her again. I shook my throbbing head, almost as if I were trying to erase the pessimistic thought of Sally being lost forever. I couldn't think like that. I would find Sally, no matter what.

"Okay, well, some of these letters aren't even letters," Amber said, studying the papers.

"What do you mean?" I inquired, pulling a paper out of Amber's grasp.

Looking over the piece of paper, I realized what I'd assumed were letters were really medical records.

Diagnostics, blood types, allergies. An entire medical history was typed onto these withering papers.

"Wait, this one is an actual letter," Amber said, as I put the medical papers aside.

"Is it from great grandpa?" I asked, unable to contain my curiosity.

"Well, if you give me a second…" Amber's voice trailed off as she read the letter. "Yes, it is. I'll read it aloud," she offered.

Before Amber began reading, I took a glance at the writing. Like my grandfather's first journal entries, the words were not smudged. I finally realized that my grandfather must have written in his diary using his telekinesis. However, in the later diary entries, the ink was smudged. I wondered why he'd no longer used his telekinesis to write those letters.

> To my darling children. If you are reading this, your mum and I have passed. No matter what happens in your lives, no matter who takes care of you, you both will always have each other. Your mum and I will always look after you from wherever we are. We'd never let anything happen to either of you. You two will never be alone. Sophie, when you look in the mirror and see those lovely auburn freckles spread across your face, you will be looking at your mother's face. Max, when you look down at your strong hands, you'll really be seeing my hands.
>
> When you both set your mind to something and follow through on your goals, this will be your mum's determination. Max, when you lift an object without touching it, you'll be using my powers. Sophie, when you look into a person's eyes and can see their soul, you'll be using your mum's intuition. Even in death, may we always stay fresh in your minds. As you grow up, you'll have questions that your mum and I won't be able to answer. Depend on each other. When you're scared, hold each other and know that you are holding us. When you have a problem, ask each other what to do and know that you're asking your mum and me. There might be times when you have no answers. It's a long, rough road ahead, and your mum and I will live

through you both to guide you. We love you more than the world will ever know. Love, Mum and Da.

That letter would have brought comfort to two scared children. It was a lovely sentiment. However, it didn't help me figure out why my grandfather changed his surname.

A couple of days ago, the letter would have been a huge disappointment to me, but at that moment, I cared more about finding Sally than discovering why my grandfather changed his last name.

After Amber finished the last sentence, I took the compress off my forehead, got up, and headed for the front door.

"Where are you going?" Amber asked, jumping up from the couch. "Mom will kill you if you're not here resting."

"Out," I stated, opening the front door and heading toward my car.

"Well, I'm coming," Amber insisted, following close behind.

"Amber, you can't come with me," I asserted as I headed toward my car.

"Come where?" Amber prodded. "What in that letter set you off? Where are you going?"

I sighed. "Amber, forget the letter. It led to nothing.

I can't focus on the mystery of grandpa's name change. There are greater mysteries to unravel."

"You mean Sally," Amber affirmed. "You are going to try to find her."

"Yes," I admitted, opening my driver's side door. Before I could get in, Amber placed her hand on the door.

"Look, Cooper, if you are going to play detective, fine, but you are not doing it alone," she asserted. "And, before you say anything about not wanting to put me in danger, take a lesson out of grandpa's literal book. Don't make assumptions about me. I don't need a 'big, strong male protector.' I can take care of myself. Got it?"

Looking into Amber's defiant glare, I knew that if I wanted to leave our street, I would have to take Amber along for the ride. I knew Amber had no idea what she was getting herself into, but then again, neither did I.

"Fine, but if there is any danger, you need to leave," I warned, feeling fresh and powerful pounding throughout my brain

12

UNRAVELING MYSTERIES

When we arrived at the hospital, I scanned the emergency room waiting area, which seemed rightfully pristine and packed. Across the room of potential patients filling in charts, waiting for their turn, I found the nurses' area.

Walking up to the desk, I smiled at the nurse, whose name tag was so large, you couldn't miss his name: Brian Vara. It took a second for the name to register, but then I recognized it. My grandfather mentioned the name Brian Vara in one of his journal entries. However, this Brian Vara couldn't be the same person my grandfather described in his journal. This guy looked like he was in his mid-twenties.

Perhaps, when I wasn't preoccupied with discovering where Sally was, I could ask this guy if he had a great-uncle or grandfather or someone who used to volunteer at Parkway Hospital. However, finding Sally was my first priority.

"Hi. I am here to see Michelle Gibson. She was brought in the other day," I asserted, hoping I would be able to see her.

"Why are you here to see Michelle?" Amber whispered, moving even closer to me.

"I have to ask her something about Sally," I whispered back, as the nurse typed something into the computer.

"She's in room 203," the nurse said, pointing down the hall and to the right. "However, the family requested that no visitors see her at this time."

It was as if he was hanging a piece of cheese in front of a rat, so it was just out of reach. Well, I was not going to be played for a mouse. I needed to find my girlfriend, and Michelle was the first step toward discovering where she was.

"Oh, okay," I said, grinning as a plan formed in my mind.

I turned my back on the nurse, making it seem as if I'd given up.

Trying to settle the throbbing in my mind, I concentrated on the file cabinet behind the nurses' desk. Subtly, I flicked my wrist in the direction of the cabinet.

The sound of drawers flying open and files bursting out brought a smile to my lips.

"Let's go," I whispered to Amber, as she stood agape, watching the nurse curse as he tried to reorganize the files.

"I thought your powers weren't working," Amber whispered back, grinning as we neared Michelle's room.

"Yeah, well, I fought through the pain," I said, both feeling and hearing the pounding in my head crank up a few notches.

Opening the door, I was surprised to see Michelle awake, hooked up to an EKG and an IV. A splash of purple and red bruising covered half of her forehead, and a vertical line of dried blood cut across her swollen, split bottom lip. I didn't realize how banged up she was after the accident.

Although Michelle and I were usually at odds, it was difficult to not feel sorry for her at that moment.

When Michelle saw Amber and me standing in the doorway, she quickly sat up.

"They let you in?" Michelle mumbled, "I told my parents I didn't want any visitors."

"Apparently," I said, stepping into the room and sitting in the chair across from Michelle's bed. "I was wondering if you've heard about Sally?"

Michelle's hardened eyes softened at the name of her best friend.

"My mom told me this morning. The police wanted to interview me, yet again, but my mom said I wasn't up to it," Michelle said. "However, I let them ask me a few questions. I'm assuming you're here to ask me about it, too," she stated, as if she were reading my mind.

"Well, yeah. I wanted to know if she said anything to you before she left the hospital?"

Michelle cleared her throat, then she began to cough. Amber quickly grabbed the pitcher on the nightstand beside Michelle's bed and poured her a glass of water. Michelle waved the water away as the coughing subsided.

"Of course, she said something to me," Michelle hissed, wincing at her pain, which probably made my headache seem like a mild pinch. "I came to just as Sally was about to leave. Great timing, huh? Anyway, Sally was about to leave when my sister ran to get her. We spoke about the accident. The police were saying they were going to conduct a full investigation into the car crash, but I don't think they have any leads. They were pretty cryptic about what they were going to do. I don't know, maybe I just lost control of the car."

There seemed to be a hint of doubt in her tone. However, I didn't know if she doubted the police's investigation, calling the car crash an accident, or both.

"Well, I suppose you're going to ask me the same questions the police asked? 'Did Sally associate with the others who have gone missing? Did she say anything to you about where she was headed that night?' Blah, blah, blah," Michelle said, trying to imitate the investigator's voice.

"Something like that. Anything would be helpful," I said, hoping Michelle gave me at least a sliver of something to go on in order to find Sally.

"I don't know if this means anything, but I overheard the police talking outside my room after they finished interviewing me. They think the people who have recently disappeared, including Sally, have been kidnapped," Michelle stated.

Michelle's and the police's suspicions matched mine. The number of disappearances were increasing too quickly. Although the police did not find any ransom notes, how likely was that this many disappearances, occurring within a few days, were not kidnappings? However, if people were being kidnapped, who was doing the kidnapping and what did they want? I mean, who could even say whether there was only one kidnapper? There were too many unknown variables. However, many kidnappers there were, they must want something, but what? Also, were the people who were kidnapped randomly selected or did they have something in common? So far, they all had ties to the high school, but there had to be a greater connection between these individuals, otherwise the kidnapper—kidnappers—would need to practically kidnap everyone in town.

"Oh, really?" I asked, feigning surprise.

"Yeah," Michelle asserted. "Look, Cooper, I want Sally back as much as you do. She's my best friend, and I'll do anything to get her back. I know you feel the same way."

Michelle was becoming quite the mind reader. That, or she was incredibly intuitive. I thought the latter was more likely.

"I'll find her," I assured her.

Before I could ask Michelle any more questions, Amber nudged my shoulder.

"I can hear the nurse coming," she whispered.

Reluctantly, I rose from the seat, but before I could sneak out, Michelle called me back.

"You better," Michelle demanded.

"As I said, I'll find her," I promised, as I slipped out of the room with my sister.

When I pulled up to my house, I noticed my mother's car was parked in the driveway.

I winced, anticipating a lecture. Amber and I glanced at each other, knowing our mother wasn't going to be too happy about us leaving the house when I had such an excruciating migraine.

"I told Mom you'd rest," Amber stated, opening the passenger door and walking toward the house. "She's going to bite my head off for letting you go out, and then she's going to go after you."

"Hey, you weren't too eager to stay home yourself, so don't rest this all on my shoulders," I reminded her as I opened the front door.

When Amber and I entered the kitchen, we immediately heard our mother drumming her finger on the counter before we noticed her angered countenance.

Black garbage bags, assumedly filled with shards of glass, broken utensils, and splintered wood, lined the back wall of the kitchen. Surprisingly, the kitchen table was positioned in its rightful place, adjacent to the stove. It was a miracle I hadn't split it in two.

"Where have you two been?" our mother demanded, gesturing for me to come to her.

Reluctantly, I walked over to her, allowing her to study my face.

"Well, your eyes aren't as glassy and your color's better, but you two still shouldn't have left the house without calling," my mother asserted, reflexively parting my hair. "I was watching the local news, and three students and two teachers from the high school have gone missing since we heard about…" my mother's voice trailed off.

She probably assumed I couldn't handle hearing *Sally* and *missing* in the same sentence. Hopefully, I'd figure out who kidnapped Sally, and those two words would never be used together ever again.

By finding Sally, I might find the others as well. At least I had one connection to work off of: Erikson High School. However, other than being associated with the school, what other connection tied these individuals together? Did they all know something about the school? Did the faculty members work in the same department, and the students take the classes they taught? Even if that were the case, why would they be kidnapped because of this connection? Maybe there was a secret about the school I didn't know but they did. Once again, I was left with more questions than answers.

"Cooper. Are you even listening?" my mother demanded, as I snapped to attention.

"Could you repeat that one more time?" I asked, ruffling my parted hair.

"I *said* that if you leave this house one more time while you're sick, I'm going to ground you until the turn of the century," my mother stated, poking my chest with her index finger.

"He wasn't sick. He was…telekinetically unbalanced," Amber joked. "Plus, I was with him."

Raising her eyebrow, my mother looked over at Amber.

"Yes, and you said you were going to look after him, at home," my mother stated, before addressing me again. "Well, Cooper, you've had a long day. Why don't you go rest," she said.

Nodding, I went up to my room, with Amber close behind.

"So, where are you going to go next?" Amber asked eagerly, following me into my room.

"Excuse me?"

"Well, you went to see Michelle to get some clues about Sally because she's her best friend," Amber reasoned. "So, what's your next step in this investigation, Detective Cooper?"

Rolling my eyes, I lay on my bed and pressed my palm to my forehead. At least my migraine had subsided enough for me to use my powers at the hospital. However, I still felt a little drained.

"I don't know, but this case definitely isn't closed just yet," I announced, pushing my grandfather's journal aside.

Amber picked up the journal, flipping through the pages.

"I thought you weren't going to continue to read it," I said

"I don't know. . .that letter just pulled me back in, you know?" Amber said, taking our grandfather's papers out of her pocket and putting them in his journal. "There are just too many mysteries here potential kidnappings, grandpa's last name. I thought this town was boring, but I was wrong," she said, a little too excitedly.

"Boring would be great. If only I could have a boring life. Now that's the dream" I stated, closing my eyes.

Suddenly, I felt a hand nudging my shoulder.

Opening my eyes, I saw Amber staring at me. "Cooper, wake up."

I could feel the rhythmic pangs—though they were more subtle—inside my head as I opened my eyes. I hadn't even realized I'd dozed off.

"Cooper, you need to read this," Amber insisted, placing the journal in my hand.

"Why?" I inquired.

"Just read it. This entry," Amber instructed, opening the journal to the twelfth entry, dated January 5, 1975.

Rose gave birth to a beautiful baby girl today at 3:35 a.m. She has her mother's smile and my hair.

Brian, John, and William told me she looks more like her mother, thank God. Even Dr. Felone and Dr. Leumas came to see my daughter. They said she stood out among the blondes and brunettes in the nursery. Sophie made her niece a portrait of her late grandparents, so she'd have some memory of them. Rose and I were so excited about the birth that we almost forgot the name we'd chosen for her. We both agreed to name the baby after my mum, Anne. My beautiful little Annie. If she'd been a he, we were going to name her Daniel, after my da. If the next child we have is a boy, then he will be Daniel. I still can't believe Rose and I created a human being. We made a life. Hopefully, our daughter will not have to go through the tragedy Sophie and I endured. Speaking of tragedy, four patients, two nurses—Simon Brane and Victor Fran—and Dr. Natalie Mernus have been kidnapped. The police have finally determined the recent disappearances are kidnappings, even though there are no signs of a ransom letter. Why are the hospital staff and patients disappearing? I know I shouldn't get involved, but I work here. I can't allow innocent people to be taken from a place where they should feel safe. The police are surveying the hospital to see if they can pick out any suspicious characters.

However, anyone can be a suspect. Maybe, they're one of the doctors, interns, nurses, or patients. I've only figured out that the kidnapper must be taking these people because they have something in common that this kidnapper wants. There's no way these kidnappings are random, but what do they have in common? I'll figure it out. I have to. Sincerely, Max.

After finishing the entry, I felt compelled to put the journal down. How was it possible that people were being kidnapped almost fifty years ago and now history was repeating itself? Parkway was not a crime-free town by any means, but I had never heard of any kidnappings occurring—at least, I hadn't until today. This had to be more than a coincidence; the kidnappings had to be connected. By whatever means possible, I had to find out what my grandfather knew and whether he ever discovered the identity of the kidnapper, or kidnappers.

"Cover for me," I told Amber, as I opened my window.

"Why? Where are you going now?" Amber asked, as I climbed onto the roof.

"Look, I have go check on something. All I'm asking is for you to cover for me until I get back," I pleaded. "I don't ask you for much."

"Why can't I go? Maybe I can help," Amber moped, crossing her arms over her chest.

"Who will cover for me if you come?" I asked, trying to balance myself on the inclined, slippery roof. "I promise the next time I need to go somewhere important, you can come with me, deal?"

13

THE KIDNAPPINGS

I knew my promise would have consequences, but I couldn't think about that at the moment. Solving this mystery and finding Sally were my only concerns.

Finally arriving at my destination, I walked into the library, making sure my library card was in my wallet in case I needed to take some reading home with me.

I asked a librarian if I could look at some microfiche from the local paper during the 1970s. I figured I would not be able to discover this information on my computer. If people disappeared in the 1970s, the local newspaper, the *Parkway Chronicle*, had to have covered it.

The librarian helped me find the records and told me the library closed at 6:00 p.m.

I must have scanned over a hundred articles before I found something on the kidnappings at Parkway Hospital. The paper was dated January 21, 1975.

"Police are investigating the kidnappings taking place at Parkway Hospital.

The once safe haven of this tiny hamlet has turned into one of the biggest crime spots. Six patients, three nurses, and one doctor have been reported missing, according to police spokesman and chief of police, Roger Murdoch. The police will not release the names of the kidnapped at this time.

So far, the department has no leads on the kidnapper's identity.

'I can't believe this is happening at this hospital,' David Leumas, a neurosurgeon at Parkway Hospital, said. 'I have never seen a crime of this magnitude here, and I never expected our hospital to be involved in something like this. These patients come here to recover and expect us to care for them. They shouldn't have to worry about being kidnapped.'

Murdoch told the hospital staff and patients that he and officers Henry Garrison and Daniel Biros will have around the clock surveillance in the hospital. Officers will be stationed inside the hospital on each floor.

Malcolm Felone, a surgeon at Parkway Hospital, said, 'There should be no safer place than this hospital.'

This newly established hospital has been crime- free until now."

I read the rest of the article, but it didn't provide me with any additional information I could use. However, one name in the article caught my eye: Roger Murdoch. Considering the time period and location, Roger Murdoch must have been David Murdoch's father. Perhaps, I could talk to Murdoch to see what he knew about the prior kidnappings, so I could find a motive. If I could find out how the police solved the Parkway Hospital case in the seventies, perhaps I could find a correlation and solve this case. And then, Sally would be safe.

The next three articles I read mentioned there was no ransom to be found, the police still didn't have any leads, and two more patients and another nurse were kidnapped.

Ripping my eyes away from the screen and looking down at my watch, I realized the library was going to close in ten minutes. Quickly, I searched for one more article before the librarians dragged me away from the microfiche.

The last article dated back to December 30, 1975.

"The Parkway Hospital kidnapper, or 'Infirmary Napper' as he's come to be known, has struck again. But, this time, he abducted an eleven-month-old girl.

The eleven-month-old infant is one of the youngest to have been kidnapped.

Two nurses, one doctor, and three patients, including the female infant, whose names aren't being released despite the demand for them from the frightened public, have been kidnapped.

So far, thirty people residing or working in Parkway Hospital have been abducted. According to the local police, which is the largest recorded number of people who have been kidnapped in the history of Parkway.

'This is outrageous!' William North, a premed student, said. 'My best friend's baby girl has been kidnapped and it seems as if the police aren't doing anything about it. Staking out the hospital hasn't stopped him.'

The police still have no leads. The hospital security has tripled since last Tuesday."

I immediately recognized the name North as belonging to one of the premed students who volunteered at the hospital with my grandpa. Unless he had other friends whose daughter was approximately the same age as my mom, the baby girl he was referring to *had* to be my mom. Before it could even register that my mother was a victim of abduction, the librarian who'd showed me to the microfiche tapped me on the shoulder and told me the library was closing.

Millions of questions roamed through my head as I walked home. What happened to my mother when she was kidnapped? Did someone find her, or was she returned?

Why would someone kidnap my mother out of all the other infants in the nursery? Did the police find her, or did my grandfather take matters into his own hands?

When I arrived at my house, I didn't even bother trying to sneak back in. I entered through the front door and went into the kitchen, where I found Amber and my mother eating dinner. I sat down at the counter in a daze.

Getting up from the kitchen table, my mother brushed wisps of damp hair away from my forehead and placed her cool palm on my cheek.

"Well, you look a little flushed, but you look better," my mother said. "At least, you do for someone who's grounded for the next two weeks."

I looked over at Amber, who mouthed, "I tried." Normally, I would have been annoyed with Amber for not covering for me more effectively; however, in that moment, all I could think about was that my mother had been kidnapped and I had no idea how she was sitting in front of me.

"You should have used your telekinesis to get back in. I wouldn't have known," my mother stated, fixing me a plate. "And I assume Amber was covering for you, considering she didn't follow you. So, Amber, you're grounded for two weeks like your brother."

"But that's not fair!" Amber whined. "I'm not his keeper."

I wanted to walk away, but I couldn't. My mother had been kidnapped, and there she was, sitting in front of me, alive! I realized people who had been kidnapped could lead normal lives if found, but I thought most of those people *knew* they'd been kidnapped. My mother had been too young to know she was an abduction victim.

"Did grandma ever tell you that you were kidnapped?" I blurted out.

Perhaps I should have waited until I had all of the facts. I should have talked to my grandmother first before I revealed to my mother that she had been abducted. There was no possible way she remembered what happened to her, and I doubted my grandmother told her. She was probably so relieved to have my mother back in her arms that she never thought to tell her daughter about the horrific period she went through, when her baby was ripped from her grasp and she had no control over whether her daughter would ever be returned. However, I couldn't help myself. If this information somehow led to me finding Sally, I had to know the truth.

"What are you talking about?" my mother laughed, loading the dishwasher. "Where would you get such a silly idea?"

"I snuck off to the library, thinking I could find some information on grandpa," I said, rubbing my throbbing temples. "I found an article that said an eleven- month-old girl was kidnapped from Parkway Hospital in 1975. In Grandpa McEwin's journal, he wrote about the kidnappings in the hospital and seemed to be determined to discover what was happening. It stands to reason that you were the eleven-month-old girl referred to in the newspaper, that you were…kidnapped."

My mother stopped loading the dishwasher and sat back down at the counter.

"Cooper, that is ridiculous. There's no way I was kidnapped when I was little. My mother would have told me," my mother said.

"I know, but from reading Grandpa's journal. . .I just don't think your parents told you the whole truth," I said, placing my hand on top of my mother's.

I couldn't believe I was having this conversation with my mother. I wanted this to be just another one of my nightmares. I wanted this whole ordeal to be a nightmare, so I could just wake up and discover the oddest part of my life was still having telekinesis.

"I'll have to read it for myself," my mother said, getting up to resume loading the dishwasher. "I'll go to the library tomorrow."

Leaving my mother to ponder her family's mysterious past, I went to my room, determined to read the rest of my grandfather's journal so I could tie up the loose ends of not only my grandfather's mysterious life as a witness to the Parkway Hospital kidnappings, but also to discover how I could find the Erikson High School kidnapper and rescue Sally.

Flipping through my grandfather's journal, I noticed there were only three entries after the twelfth one. The rest of the pages were blank.

The thirteenth entry was dated January 21, 1975.

> Ten people have been kidnapped from Parkway Hospital. I can't believe it. I was reading an article on the matter in the Parkway Chronicle, and I couldn't believe people were being taken in such a small town. I used to think the hospital was the safest place in town. That hospital is like my second home. My friends work there. My mentor, Dr. Felone, practically lives there, and my daughter began her life there. Innocent people could be dying, and the police have no idea what's going on. So far, I've figured out that the kidnapper wants something from the patients and staff rather than from the hospital itself, otherwise, why wouldn't he have left a ransom note? Also, these patients must have something in common that makes them targets, and that information could probably be found in the hospital. The kidnappings cannot be random, so whoever kidnapped the staff must know what the patients and staff have in common. So, that would mean whatever the kidnapper wants from these people has to be something each one of them has. First thing tomorrow morning, I'm going to check the medical files on these patients to see if they have anything in common that could be of any significance. Sincerely, Max.

My grandpa made a valid point in his deduction.

Whoever was kidnapping those patients and staff members from the hospital had to be abducting them because they all had some sort of information in common, which he suspected was in their medical records. Could the same person—or people—be kidnapping the students and teachers now, or was this a copycat?

Regardless of whether the kidnapper was the original or a copycat, why was this kidnapper taking staff members and students from Erikson High School? Unless the medical records truly were the key, and the kidnapper had access to the medical records the students and staff submitted to the school.

However, why wouldn't the kidnapper, original or copycat, continue to abduct patients and staff from Parkway Hospital? Why shift their attention to the high school?

Whatever the kidnapper was searching for had to be at the school instead of the hospital. Like my grandfather, I had to get my hands on the staff and students' medical records. After I obtained the school records, I could compare them to the medical records my grandmother gave to me.

14

INTERVIEW WITH THE CHIEF

"Cooper? Is that you?" Sally asked, squinting at the dawn's glare.

Wrapping my arms around Sally, I squeezed her so tight, I felt as if our skin would melt together. My life flowed into hers as my warmth seeped into her ice-cold flesh.

Caressing her arms, I wanted to fill every crevice of my senses with her jasmine fragrance, supple skin, and glimmering eyes. She cried into my shoulder as I pulled her into my coat.

"I wanted to tell you where I was," Sally sobbed, unable to control her breathing. "But I didn't know."

"I love you so much, Sally," I said, kissing her forehead. "I would tear the earth apart to find you. I would never let anyone hurt you."

Raising her chin with the tip of my finger, I noticed Sally's face was somewhat different, as if her coloring were smudged. Wiping a tear from Sally's cheek, I felt her flesh peel off in my hand.

"Cooper, what's wrong?" Sally asked, as I backed away.

It wasn't Sally. Sally was real. Whatever this thing was, it wasn't her.

"Please, Cooper. I love you," the thing said, as it teared layers of flesh off its cheeks with its fingernails. "I thought you said you'd never leave my side."

I wanted to scream at the being to bring Sally back, but before I could even open my mouth, the flesh melted away. Instead of bones and muscle, all that was left was a voice.

"It's you," I choked out, hoping it could feel the malice in my tone.

"Did you think it'd be that easy?" the voice mocked, its laughter stripping away pieces of my skin. "You just can't be her knight in shining armor without working for it."

I wanted to rip out my own heart so the voice wouldn't have the satisfaction of killing me, but I couldn't. My hands weren't my own anymore. Every part of me now belonged to the voice because I'd let my guard down. I'd thought I was letting Sally in, but the only thing I'd done was reveal my vulnerability.

"I...will...save...her." I struggled to breathe, feeling as if I was suffocating.

"If you want to save her, don't just say it," the voice demanded. "Words mean nothing now. Your actions will speak for you."

I gasped for sweet, fresh air as I shot up from my bed, waking to the sound of my alarm clock. Feeling my heart practically pounding out of my chest, I hit the off button on my alarm clock. Surprisingly, I found my cell phone right next to the alarm clock. It had been charging for days, so the battery might be swollen. I picked it up and stared at the screen, waiting for my vision to clear. It was 7:00 a.m.

Everything suddenly seemed to fall into place after my nightmare. I had school today, I had to find Sally, and I had to get the school records of the staff and the students who'd been kidnapped from the nurse's office.

When Amber and I arrived at Erikson High School, we noticed security had doubled, and David Murdoch was checking the students' and staffs' IDs.

"Can I see your ID, Mr. O'Neil?" Murdoch asked. "Sure," I said, taking my ID out of my wallet.

He studied the ID intently with his dark, beady eyes, as if he were making sure it was real. I knew he still wanted to interview me, and I had a sneaking suspicion that second interview would be scheduled soon. As much as he wanted to interview me, I knew I needed to ask him a few questions as well, specifically about Roger Murdoch and the Parkway Hospital kidnappings.

Perhaps, Roger Murdoch solved the case, but it was strange that the case was not more well-known.

"You can go in," Murdoch said, moving his bulky mass of a body away from the entrance.

When I went into my physics class, Mr. Divad was standing in front of the room, setting up the SMART board for the lesson.

Sitting in front of Michelle's empty seat, I waited for Mr. Divad to begin the lesson.

"All right, settle down," Mr. Divad said in a firm tone, adjusting the black frames of his thick glasses. "We're going to start on Newton's laws today. I think that's what Mr. Nelson was planning to go over. Mr. O'Neil?" Mr. Divad asked, still unsure of his new students' names.

"Yes?" I said, snapping to attention.

"What is Newton's third law?" Mr. Divad asked. "What's in motion, stays in motion, unless a tangible object stops it," I stated, feeling a little uncomfortable answering the question, knowing I had stopped objects using an intangible force.

"Thank you, Mr. O'Neil. That's—" Before Mr. Divad could finish his sentence, a security guard entered the room and told me the chief of police wanted to see me.

Trying to hide my grin with a yawn, I followed the security guard to the guidance counselor's office, which Murdoch had turned into his temporary station.

When I arrived, the office was somewhat brighter yet emptier than the last time I was interviewed.

"Mr. O'Neil. I'm glad we can continue our interview. Won't you take a seat?" Murdoch asked, gesturing to the chair.

I nodded, knowing this time, this would be a two-way interview.

His father had to know more about the Parkway Hospital case than the news indicated. All I needed to know was how the case ended. If I could learn how that case was solved—if it had been solved—then maybe I'd have more insight into the Erickson High School kidnappings.

"Before we continue, I need to ask you about your father," I said, leaning forward. "I know your father was the chief of police during the seventies, and—"

"And he was one of the best chiefs of police. My father had a practically spotless record," Murdoch growled. "However, that's not why you are here, Mr. O'Neil. We need to—"

"Wait, what do you mean by *practically* spotless?" I asked, cutting him off.

"That's confidential," Murdoch huffed, getting up from his chair.

"He didn't solve the 1975 case of the Parkway kidnappings, did he?" I asked.

Watching how Murdoch's beady eyes narrowed, I knew I was right. If anything, I wished I were wrong.

Even though the case was unsolved, I wasn't at a standstill. I could still find out if those who were kidnapped were returned. Once the kidnapper got whatever he wanted from these people from the hospital, I imagined he either returned them or killed them. Unfortunately, the latter seemed like the more logical answer.

However, since my mom was still alive, maybe he let everyone live. If that was the case, I still didn't understand why those kidnappings weren't public knowledge. Sure, it happened over forty years ago, but as far as I knew, it was one of the greatest crimes in Parkway, so why didn't more people know about it?

Murdoch slowly cracked his knuckles "How'd you know that?" he asked, leaning in.

"I need to know what happened, and something tells me your father told you about the case," I said, hoping I was right and that Murdoch would provide me with the information I needed.

"Again, that's confidential," Murdoch repeated, sitting back down in his chair.

I guess I was wrong. Perhaps I could convince him to tell me something if I gave him some information.

"Chief Murdoch, my grandfather was involved in that case. He might have known something that'll lead you to the kidnapped. I know it's been over forty years, but I'm sure someone's alive."

"There's no need for that," Murdoch said, leaning back. "Most of the kidnapped were returned. There were only two people who weren't, and one man died."

"Who were they?" I asked.

"Why do you need to know?" Murdoch countered suspiciously.

I wondered if Murdoch thought my line of questioning connected the two cases. Perhaps that was why he was humoring me.

All I needed from him were names; however, if he were uncooperative, I would just need to obtain his father's cold case files. I never thought I would stoop to stealing, but I was willing to do anything to figure out who kidnapped Sally, even if I had to break into the police station and retrieve the confidential files. Hopefully, Murdoch would provide me with the information I needed, so I wouldn't have to resort to breaking the law.

"My grandfather was involved in that case. He wanted to solve it as much as your father probably did. He risked his life to save…someone from the kidnapper. I guess you could say I'm trying to finish what he started," I stated, hoping to tap into Murdoch's compassion and family loyalty.

"After my father died, I took a look at that cold case. I also tried to find the kidnapper," Murdoch said, wiping the beads of sweat that were forming on his brow. "My father would have wanted that kidnapper convicted, but I didn't have much to go on. The people who were returned were completely fine, but they didn't have any recollection of what happened, nor did they know their kidnapper's identity. Max Fitzpatrick, the man who died, gave my father a few tips, but they didn't lead anywhere.

Then Fitzpatrick died, and the kidnapper got away with murder."

That confirmed it; my grandfather risked his life to catch the kidnapper. However, Murdoch called him Max *Fitzpatrick*. If my grandfather died a Fitzpatrick, then why was my grandmother and mother's surname McEwin? Also, did my grandfather save my mom, or did the police save her? If he did rescue her, then had my grandfather known the kidnapper's identity? Perhaps, my grandfather even rescued the other people who were kidnapped. If the reason why they were kidnapped was in their medical records, then it was imperative I take a look at those. I'd also need the names of the two men to see if they were in the medical records. I could determine if they had anything in common, and then cross-reference those commonalities with the others in the medical records. Maybe Murdoch would reveal their names; it couldn't hurt to ask.

"And the names of the two men who are still missing?" I asked blatantly.

"They were two doctors at the hospital. I think their names were Felone and Leumas. My father never found them or the kidnapper," Murdoch stated.

Murdoch had to be referring to Dr. Malcolm Felone and Dr. David Leumas. However, knowing this information just led to more questions. Why were they not returned? Did the kidnapper dispose of them before the others were rescued, or did the kidnapper find something he needed in those two that he didn't find in the others?

"There was nothing on the victims that would lead you to what the kidnapper was looking for?" I asked.

"As a matter of fact, every one of the people returned had puncture wounds on their scalps and forearms," Murdoch said. "Again, no one knew how it happened. Everyone went to the hospital, but everyone was fine. However, my father mentioned that all of their medical files were gone. To this day, they have not been recovered."

So much for trying to retrieve those records from Roger Murdoch's files. However, in the pile of papers my grandmother gave me, there were a couple of medical files, but thirty people had been kidnapped. There was no way that pile contained thirty medical records, so where could the others be?

Murdoch continued, "At first, my father thought the kidnapped were poisoned, including Max Fitzpatrick, but there wasn't a trace of detectable poison in their systems."

That was definitely a clue I could use. I certainly knew I was on the right track by checking the medical records. Whatever that kidnapper wanted was inside those hospital staff and patients. Perhaps this kidnapper was looking for the same thing in these kidnapped students and staff from Erikson High School.

"That's very interesting," I said, itching to retrieve the school's medical records. "Did your father find the same puncture wounds on Max Fitzpatrick?"

"Actually, there were twice as many on Max Fitzpatrick than there were on anyone else. He was very weak from the head trauma. My father couldn't understand what happened to him, or anyone else."

The fact that those people weren't poisoned didn't surprise me. I assumed the kidnapper was trying to extract something from those people. He wouldn't put something in his victims. That is, unless he was using the abductees for experiments. Perhaps, he injected them with some type of drug that wasn't detectable. Afterall, in the mid-1970s forensics was not as advanced as it was now.

Whatever these people had in common, maybe that led the kidnapper to believe those particular people were the perfect guinea pigs for his experimental drug. It was a longshot, but it *was* plausible.

"Did Max Fitzpatrick tell your father anything that would lead him to a suspect?" I asked, hoping the answer would be yes.

"Unfortunately, no," Murdoch said, rising from his seat. "Mr. O'Neil, now it's my turn to ask the questions.

What do you know about the disappearances?"

Reluctantly, I sat back, gingerly turning over my suspicions, determining what I should reveal.

"I think what you probably think—that these *disappearances* are kidnappings—but that's it. I only have my suspicions; I don't have any proof," I admitted, hoping Murdoch would be satisfied with this answer.

Murdoch's beady eyes widened as he considered my response. He took a long pause before asking his next question.

"What makes you think these are kidnappings?"

"The volume," I declared. "It's highly unlikely all of these people ran away together, as if they were all joining the same cult or something."

"I see," Murdoch muttered, taking another long pause. He narrowed his eyes and tilted his head as if contemplating something about me. Before I could say anything, he reached into his pocket and pulled out a card. He placed the card on the table and slid it toward me.

When I picked it up, I saw it was a business card, with a number written on the back.

"Call if you see anything," Murdoch stated before he stood up.

"You can go back to class now, Mr. O'Neil."

"Thanks," I said, getting up from my chair.

"Hey," Murdoch said before I left. "Make sure to call if you see *anything.* That's my home phone number on the back."

I nodded to him as I left the office. I wondered if his father had the same conversation with my grandfather over forty years ago. Well, the only way I was going to answer any of the questions I asked myself was to gather and review the evidence.

CHAPTER

15

THE MEDICAL FILES

When I was in English, I asked my teacher, Ms. Conway, if I could go to the nurse. After about five minutes of trying to convince her my head was still bothering me from the day before, she reluctantly gave me a pass to the nurse's office.

"I thought I'd recovered from yesterday, but my head is killing me," I tried to explain to the skeptical nurse.

I just needed a couple of minutes alone in that office to find the files of the staff and students who were missing. The file cabinet was right behind the nurse's desk. All I had to do was cause a distraction in order to sift through the files.

"Well, all right," the nurse said, putting a thermometer in my mouth. "Keep that in there for three minutes and sit over there."

I sat in between a kid gripping his stomach and another who had his hand over his eye. Maybe these two students could provide me with the perfect diversion.

There were only two nurses in the office. They could both become easily distracted if something went amiss. I hated using people for my means, but it was the only way I could get the files I needed.

Concentrating on the guy gripping his stomach, I tipped his chair forward, causing him to fall to the floor, where he began to writhe in pain.

Hearing his moaning, one of the nurses rushed to him and led him into the back.

The other nurse was still behind the desk, sifting through the files I was itching to get my hands on.

Focusing on the other guy sitting next to me, I also made him slip to the floor, making sure he did not hit his bad eye.

At the sound of this kid's groaning, this nurse, like the other, took him into the back.

I was finally alone. Quickly, I went to the filing cabinet and pulled out the files I needed on the people who were missing. I pulled my cell phone from my back pocket, grateful I'd been able to find it this morning.

Unlike his father, Murdoch released the names of the kidnapped, so I only took pictures of their files.

After I'd finally taken pictures of all the medical files I needed, I quickly shoved them back into the filing cabinet, closed it, left the thermometer on the seat I'd been sitting in, and left. They'd probably assume I felt better and went back to class. Hopefully, I'd been meticulous enough in putting the files back that they didn't suspect I'd riffled through the cabinet.

⋆ ⋆⋆⋆⋆⋆ ⋆

When school was finally over, I raced home to compare the medical files my grandfather had kept with the ones on my phone. The medical records my grandmother gave me looked a bit thin, and I again wondered if all thirty records were in the pile.

"Forget something?" I heard Amber call from the kitchen.

At the sound of her voice, I realized I raced home so fast that I forgot to wait for Amber. I stopped in my tracks and headed toward the kitchen to apologize.

"I'm sorry Amber. I got caught up in this intricate mystery," I admitted, pulling out my phone, preparing to review the pictures. "It won't happen aga—hey, wait a minute, how did you make it home earlier than me?"

"Easy, I can fly," Amber joked, smirking. She knew only members of this family might actually take that remark seriously. "No, Steve drove me. But, going back to this mystery, how has it become intricate?"

134

I looked at my phone, hesitating before I said anything. I knew it was useless to try to avoid Amber; however, I was conflicted because I didn't want anything to happen to her. Perhaps I was making the wrong choice, but I knew nothing could stop Amber when she was invested in something, so I decided to let her in on the secret.

"Fine, I'll show you, but this stays between us," I demanded, waiting for Amber to nod in acknowledgement. "Did you leave the papers grandma gave me in grandpa's journal?" Another nod.

Once we were in my room, I pulled the medical records out of our grandfather's journal. However, there were only a couple of files in that pile. Amber quizzically took a glance at the pieces of paper.

"These are too few," I said, remembering what Murdoch had said about the missing medical records. "Where could the others be?" I asked myself.

"The other what?" Amber asked, gingerly taking the medical files from me. "These look like medical records.

What do these have to do with anything?"

"I don't know," I said, furrowing my brows, trying to figure out my next steps. "I do know they hold the answer. I'm sure they are the key to why certain people are being kidnapped."

We both took a long, pensive beat. Then Amber spoke. "Maybe Grandpa McEwin's journal—or where you found the journal—could offer a clue. Didn't you find it in the attic?"

The attic! That's when I realized my grandfather must have taken the missing medical files. He was trying to discover the kidnapper's identity, and he probably died before he could return the files.

After sifting through cardboard boxes in the attic for a couple of minutes, I finally found the manila folders I'd seen when I first sorted through my grandfather's box.

After pulling out the two folders, I went back down to my room, where I placed the dusty manila folders next to the two medical files and my phone on the bed.

Gingerly picking the records up by their yellowing corners, I fanned them out on my bed. Now, all I had to do was find the correlation between all of the school records and then compare that connection to the association my grandfather found in the Parkway Hospital's medical records of the kidnapped.

"Before you study the records, why don't you see if Grandpa McEwin had anything to say about the medical records he took. It could provide you with some insight into what you're looking for," Amber suggested.

Grabbing my grandfather's journal, I said, "Amber, I may not say this often, but you are a genius."

She smirked. "I know." Amber nodded to the journal. "Now that you know, read it out loud."

My grandfather's fourteenth entry dated back to April 5, 1975.

> Anne is a three-month-old infant today. Sophie wants to throw her a party, but Rose told her we should wait until she's at least a year old. As a present, Sophie painted little Anne a picture of a cabin by a lake to hang over her crib. She's the cutest little baby I've ever seen. Her eyes are wide with curiosity as she watches her mum and me talking or playing with her. I took Anne with me to the hospital today because we couldn't find a babysitter. Everyone instantly fell in love with her.
>
> While Anne was with me today, I took a couple of medical records I needed. I planned to type up the medical records on my typewriter and return them the next day. I snuck behind the nurses' desk and started to sift through the file cabinet, but hardly anything was in there. So, I went to one of the offices where I knew the doctors kept the medical records. After about a half hour, I retrieved all of the records I needed and returned to the waiting room. I was about to put Anne in the daycare center at the hospital when I noticed that the pencils on the nurses' desk were moving on their own! For a second, I thought I might have lost control of my powers, yet again. That's when I heard Anne giggle for the first time. I looked down at the little babe in my arms, who was staring at the dancing pencils. I could feel the blood drain from my entire body and my jaw drop to the ground as I watched my precious, little daughter control the pencils with her mind. Quickly, I focused on the pencils and prevented them from entertaining my little babe. When the pencils were still,

Anne began to cry. Holding her eyes close to my chest so she couldn't use her powers on anything else, I signed out and raced home. My worst fears were realized. My little Anne, my loveable, adorable infant, had telekinesis. I looked down at my tiny little daughter, and I just couldn't believe it. She was only three months old. My Da said I didn't move anything with my mind until I was two years old. Not my daughter though. Here she was, three months old, and she was making pencils dance for her. What will be next? I can't explain to her that she has to be careful about using her powers in public; she is too young to understand. My little Anne, what am I going to do with you? I'll have to tell Rose and Sophie. Maybe they can come up with a better solution. They haven't come home yet, but when they do, I'm going to tell them right away. Right now, all I have to worry about is copying these files and getting them back to the hospital before anyone realizes they're missing. Sincerely, Max.

Dropping the journal on the floor, all I could do was stare at the white wall of my bedroom. My mother was telekinetic? My mother, who I assumed didn't completely understand what I was going through, had—at least, at one point—the powers I had? Why would she keep them a secret? Why didn't she tell my father or my sister? Why didn't she ever use them?

Pressing my palm to my forehead, I felt another migraine coming on, as I slunk down to my floor. I always assumed I was the only one with telekinesis in the family, and now I'd found out that not only did my grandfather and great-grandfather have telekinesis, but my mother had it, too! Although, I had to admit it made sense. The gift, and the burden, was passed down from one generation to the next. However, if that was the case, why didn't Amber have it? Maybe there was still time; maybe she would get her wish and develop telekinesis later in life.

I really should have researched the effects of telekinesis, but I didn't think there was a reliable source out there. It wasn't not like telekinesis was a common power. Many people claimed to be psychics or mediums, but I'd never heard of a person who claimed to have telekinesis, besides myself and the McEwin/Fitzpatrick line.

"Damn," Amber exclaimed. I jumped, almost forgetting she was there.

"Does this mean Mom has telekinesis, too?"

I looked at Amber, gulping air, not realizing I'd been holding my breath. "I'm not sure. She never mentioned anything about it. I don't know why she would keep it a secret. Then again, her side of the family keeps a lot of secrets."

I have to find Sally, I reminded myself, as I brushed dust off my jeans and stood in front of my bed.

"We'll figure that out later," I told Amber. "First, we need to figure out how these records connect to the kidnappings. We'll get to Mom later."

A sheet of medical records covered my ruffled white sheets, which I'd love to burrow under until everything passed; however, that just wasn't an option.

First, I stared at the medical records my grandfather typed up. Some of the patients had similar diseases, but that didn't explain why staff members were taken, too. Then, I looked at the vaccinations on each of the medical records. Most of the patients and staff had a smallpox vaccination, booster shots, a Salk vaccination, TBA tests, and tetanus shots. However, not all of them did.

I tried to find a faded pencil mark or any type of clue my grandfather may have drawn on the files to indicate what I should be looking for, but the papers were mark-free. Even if my grandfather had circled or underlined anything, the marks probably would have faded over the years the papers aged in the attic and in my grandmother's safe.

Taking a deep breath, I opened up my grandfather's journal once again, hoping the next entry provided more clues.

The fifteenth entry of the journal was dated December 30, 1975.

> She's gone. My little Anne is gone. How could she be gone? Even after the reporter spoke to me and we filled out the missing person report, I still didn't believe it. I didn't believe my daughter was snatched away from me until I read the article. I thought life was so perfect, but now everything is ruined. I left her in the daycare at Parkway Hospital, and when I came back, she was gone! I practically tore the hospital apart looking for her. She was nowhere to be found. It's obvious she has been kidnapped like the others. That's what I told Chief Murdoch. Rose can't stop crying. All I can do is hold her as she weeps. Our daughter has been ripped away and the wound will

always be fresh. I promised Rose I'd find her, even if I have to hunt down the kidnapper myself and kill him. Whoever took my daughter is going to regret it. When I first found out my daughter was missing, I couldn't control my powers. Every object I looked at tipped over or hung in the air. With the rage I have inside me, I feel as if I could move mountains with a single blink of my eye. I keep looking in Anne's empty room, hoping she'll be lying in her crib, staring up at the stars Sophie painted on her ceiling. But she's never there. My little Anne is gone. Even writing those words feels wrong. She can't be gone. She can't be missing. I'll hunt down the kidnapper even if it takes me the rest of my life to do so. I will not let this kidnapper tear my family apart. Rose will not lose her daughter. Our child will come back. Our child will be found. And the person who took her will pay dearly. I'll risk everything to hold Anne in my arms once again. I've taken the semester off to solve this mystery. I told Rose she should stay in school, but she refused. Sophie's the only one who's still in school. Every day, Rose just lies on the bed, gripping a large box of tissues. Sometimes, her tear ducts are depleted, and she shoves her face into her pillow and screams. A couple of days ago, Rose almost smothered herself with the pillow. I won't ask her if she was trying to end her life because I can't handle the truth. I will not lose Rose. I will find Anne. Rose and Anne will live, even if that means I have to die. I will see Anne in Rose's arms. I will hold my babe once again. She'll look into her parents' eyes and know she is safe. Anne will be home. I can feel it throughout every nerve of my body.

My daughter will not be another missing person on the back of a milk carton. She's my little girl, and it's my job to find her. I'll risk everything to find you, Anne.

Like my grandfather, I was willing to risk everything to find Sally, even if that meant losing my life, too.

I was dismayed my grandfather didn't reveal how he solved the case yet.

Flipping to the next journal entry, I noticed it was shorter than the others. It was only about half a page, and it was smudged almost beyond comprehension. I was barely able to make it out.

The sixteenth entry dated back to January 5, 1976.

> Anne's one year old today. I want to hold her in my arms, but she's not with me. The police are quite vague about what's going on, which means they have no idea where the kidnapper could be. I need to find him.
>
> Sophie thinks Anne might be dead, or at least that's what I overheard her telling Alan Morris, her new boyfriend, on the telephone. She's not dead! Anne has to be alive. I won't give up. I'll find her. I tell Rose that every day, but she doesn't believe me. She hasn't spoken since Anne disappeared. I miss my Rose. She's dying inside, just like my Da did when my mum died. Not again. I won't lose two of the three people I love more than anything. Even if I lose myself trying, I'm going to find Anne. That's a promise I'll die to keep.

"Damn," Amber muttered. "Well, obviously, he succeeded somehow, because Mom is alive."

I nodded, flipping to the last journal entry. I was hoping he wrote something—anything—about the medical records, but there was nothing finite I could work from.

Before I could read the last journal entry, Amber and I heard the front door open.

"Now's our chance," Amber exclaimed, turning toward my open door. "Mom! Is that you? We're up here!" she called, to which I heard footsteps nearing my bedroom.

"What are you doing?" I hissed. "I still haven't figured out the connection between these medical records."

"Look," Amber said, compiling the once-fanned medical records and organizing them into a neat pile before hiding them under the sheets. "Can you face Mom right now without telling her?" Before I could answer, Amber asserted, "Well, I can't. I need to know, Cooper. None of this makes sense."

"What doesn't make sense?" our mother asked, standing in my doorway.

"Hey, Mom," I said, placing my hand over the covered medical files.

"Hi, sweetie," she said. "So, do you kids need anything?"

As we glanced at one another, Amber nudged me. "You ask," she whispered to me.

"It was your idea," I countered.

Chuckling, our mother asked, "Ask what?"

After what felt like a five-minute staring contest, I finally gave in.

"Mom, you know how I have telekinesis," I said awkwardly.

"And, you know how Grandpa had telekinesis."

"Yes, Cooper. I've come to terms with that," she said, uneasily shifting her eyes.

I could tell my mother still felt uncomfortable about her father's powers, but I didn't think it was the powers themselves that she had an issue with; I thought it was the secrecy that bothered her. She had a parent who had abilities she never knew about it. She felt as if part of her life was a lie. At that moment, I felt the same way.

If my mother knew about her powers, I couldn't make sense of why she would lie to us about them.

"Well, you'd tell me if *someone else* had powers in our family besides me, right?" I asked, hoping that, if she was pressed, she would reveal the truth.

"I would, if anyone else in this family had abilities. Why are you asking?" my mother inquired, crossing her arms over her chest.

"Well, I was reading Grandpa's journal, and he wrote that someone else had powers besides him and his father," I said, careful not to reveal too much too soon.

"Who?" my mother asked, her eyes widening in anticipation.

Part of me was hoping she'd come clean and admit she had telekinesis, but I guessed I was just going to have to say it.

"Well, I think you should sit down first," I suggested, gesturing to the chair in my room.

After she sat down, I took a deep breath and brushed my fingers through my hair.

"Um, well, I really don't know how to tell you this," I said nervously, trying to avoid eye contact with my mother. "It's...well, it's you."

"Me? You think I have telekinesis?" my mother blurted out, laughing. It took her a minute to regain her composure. Amber and I looked at each other a few times, wondering if we should get her a glass of water or wait until she finished.

"Aunt Sophie used to always tell me that I had powers. And then, my mother would constantly tell me that my aunt was lying. I didn't know who to believe," my mother stated. "One day, Aunt Sophie told me she was going to train me. I had no idea what she was talking about, but I went along with it. Every day, after school, Aunt Sophie would take me to her room and demand that I move these pencils she'd laid on her desk. And every day I'd try to move them, but I couldn't. She made me promise to never tell my mother what we were up to because she'd disapprove.

"At first, I was excited about hearing I might have powers. I imagined moving the world as I walked on the sun. But, as the days passed, and my aunt grew impatient because nothing was happening. One day, my aunt put aside the pencils and told me she was going to try a different tactic.

She assured me she'd seen it done a million times and that it would definitely work. Trusting my aunt, I did exactly what she said. I stood perpendicular to her bed and placed my arms by my sides. As I waited for her next instructions, she took out a small box from her drawer. I stood perfectly still as she opened the box and pulled out the first knife.

Without warning, she started to throw the knives at my feet. 'Concentrate, Anne. Make the knives stop,' she commanded. I tried, but I was too terrified to focus.

"Disobeying my aunt, I jumped away from the knives and ran out of her room. I went to my mother, tears running down my cheeks, and told her I didn't want Aunt Sophie to test me anymore to see if I had special abilities. After my mother yelled at my aunt, she made my aunt promise she'd never try to test me for powers I obviously didn't have."

My mother cast her eyes downward and smiled to herself. Amber and I, on the other hand, looked at our mother in disbelief. How could my aunt do that to our mother? There were other, less dangerous ways to test for telekinesis. She could have made her meditate, or she could have watched her sleep, and then my mother might have levitated in a relaxed state. My aunt should have inspired my mother to use her powers rather than scare her to death.

"I'm so sorry. I really don't know what to say," Amber said.

"It's okay, sweetie. You brought back some memories I thought I'd lost," my mother said, smiling. "Maybe I knew my father had telekinesis all along.

Perhaps I just didn't want to think about it. It all makes sense now, though. Now I know why Aunt Sophie constantly tested me." As our mother started to leave, Amber inquired, "If you don't have telekinesis, then why did grandpa write that you made the pencils move in the hospital?"

My mother stood in the doorway, tapping her cheek with her index finger in contemplation.

"I'm not sure. That would also explain why Aunt Sophie expected me to have powers," she said, sitting back in the chair. "I guess if I did have powers that I showed when I was little, they disappeared."

So, my mother lost her powers; why couldn't I have been that fortunate? No, of course not, I had to keep my powers. Well, at least I didn't have knives thrown at me to test my abilities.

"I better get downstairs and start preparing dinner," our mother said, getting up from the chair again. Before she left my room, she turned to Amber and me. "Don't go too far down the rabbit hole with Grandpa's journal, okay? I don't know what other skeletons are buried in his closet and discovering them can sometimes hurt. Okay?" Both Amber and I nodded as my mom left my room. I closed the door behind her.

"That was some story," Amber exclaimed, pulling the medical records out from under the sheets.

"Well, we'll have time to psychoanalyze the whole ordeal later. At least one mystery is solved. Now, we need to figure out the connection between these records," I said, as I picked up our grandfather's journal. "And the last entry may hold the key."

The last entry was dated February 8, 1976.

> She's safe. My little daughter is home. He'll never take her again. I said I'd find her, and I did. I can sleep happily now. Unfortunately, I won't be sleeping at home tonight. I'm in a hospital bed at Parkway. Rose brought me my journal and one of my textbooks.
>
> Theoretical Medical Techniques. It's hard for me to speak. The chief of police asked me quite a few questions after I woke up. I can hardly concentrate. I can hardly move. I was only able to answer a few of his questions. I can barely keep my eyes open. Even now, I feel like sleeping for an eternity. Anne is safe. That's all that matters. I rescued my daughter. My little babe is with her mum. That's all I wanted—for my daughter and wife to be safe and happy. And now that they are, I can sleep peacefully. My fingers feel numb. Can't write well. Must find journal. AB. Doc. Kid.

I feverishly flipped through the remaining blank pages of the journal, but there was nothing else. That was it. I had no more clues from my grandfather.

Taking a deep breath, I stared at the medical records on my bed and began to study them once again.

Fifteen minutes later, Amber received a text from her boyfriend and left my room, but not before asking me to text her if I found anything. About thirty minutes passed as I stared at the medical records, trying to find the connection. Looking over the vaccinations once again, I was surprised that some of the people who were kidnapped didn't have the same immunizations.

After comparing the medical records for about the tenth time, I laid them down and shut my eyes. I could still see images of files in my mind, in a vibrant hue.

There had to be something I was missing. I was overlooking something. But, what? It didn't make sense.

Opening my eyes, I flipped open my grandfather's journal, hoping he'd given me a clue I'd missed.

For the next fifteen minutes, I practically dissected the last journal entry my grandfather wrote. Assuming the beginning wasn't going to lead me anywhere, I focused on the last few sentences, where my grandfather struggled to finish the entry. There had to be a reason why he kept writing despite the pain he was probably in.

"What does it mean? 'My fingers feel numb. Can't write well. Must find journal. AB. Doc. Kid,'" I said to myself.

Well, his fingers were probably numb from the pain, he couldn't write well due to the numbness in his hand, and he wanted to find his journal—or did he want someone else to find his journal? I flipped through the rest of the journal entries; however, I soon realized the connection between the medical records was nowhere to be found in these pages.

The last few words in the last journal entry had to be some type of clue. Otherwise, why would he use the rest of his depleting strength to write those last words?

"AB. Doc. Kid," I kept repeating.

My eyes shifted between the medical records and the last journal entry several times. The writing formed into small, black blurs as I kept looking from the medical records to the journal entry.

"I need a break," I said to myself, brushing my hand through my hair and exhaling a breath I didn't realize I was holding in. When I went downstairs, Amber was sitting at the kitchen table across from our parents. Surprisingly, our father made it to dinner.

Smiling, I sat at the kitchen table and laid my head on the cool wood.

"Homework getting to you?" my mother asked, placing her hand on my shoulder.

"Yeah, homework," I mumbled.

Maybe if I did my homework, I would be able to concentrate on the medical records later.

"Well, you can get back to your homework after dinner. I hope you're in the mood for lasagna," my mother said, offering me a piece. "I made it from scratch."

"Thanks," I muttered, moving the square piece of lasagna around on my plate.

Pushing my fork into the top layer, I noticed the tomato sauce oozing out in between the bottom layers. The thick, red sauce covered the translucent glass plate's surface.

"It looks like blood pouring out," Amber teased, pushing her plate of lasagna aside.

Studying the sauce flowing over the layers of pasta, I agreed with Amber. The way the red sauce spilled out of the layers of pasta, it looked as if the lasagna was bleeding.

The lasagna was bleeding. Blood! That's it!

I practically toppled over the kitchen table as I ran to my room.

I didn't even wait to see if anyone followed me before I closed the door behind me.

I started looking over the medical records to see if my hunch was right. I knew it was a longshot, but AB was a blood type. Before this realization, I had scanned over the blood types in the medical records, but I didn't take a *really* close look at them. Perhaps by the time I began to look at the blood types, my eyes had already betrayed me and I started to see the world through kaleidoscope glasses.

I double-checked the medical records from the hospital and the ones I photographed today just to make sure my eyes weren't playing tricks on me. Every person who was kidnapped had an AB blood type, even my mother.

That must have been why my grandfather wrote AB in his journal. He probably wrote it down for whoever he thought would read his journal.

My grandmother told me that my grandfather wanted my mother to have his journal, so he must have wanted her to know what happened to him. Also, he may have been warning her about the kidnapper.

Now that I'd discovered the connection between the students, staff, and patients, with a little help from my grandfather and sister, I had to figure out why their blood type was significant.

Why would someone kidnap the students and staff at Erikson High School with an AB blood type? What was so vital about having AB blood?

Again, I thought back to the Parkway Hospital kidnappings. The kidnapper abducted those with AB blood. According to my grandfather, the first kidnapping occurred around September of 1974. My mother was the last person reported missing, and that happened around December of 1975. My grandfather died trying to save my mother, and it could be assumed he confronted the kidnapper, so he knew the identity of the kidnapper. Nevertheless, he didn't have a chance to tell the police. Dr. Malcolm Felone and Dr. David Leumas were still missing, and they might be dead by now. However, why were those the only two who hadn't returned?

As far as I knew, no one had died yet; everyone was still just missing. Also, the location of the kidnappings moved to the high school, but the AB blood type connection still didn't explain why. What made this kidnapper target Erikson High School instead of the hospital? If this were a copycat kidnapper, wouldn't he try to recreate the kidnappings exactly? That would mean taking people from the hospital, not the high school.

I needed to speak to those closest to my grandfather; maybe they had additional insight into what happened to Grandpa McEwin and mom during those kidnappings. Tomorrow, I'd be making yet another trip to my grandmother's house. In the meantime, I'd try to trigger Aunt Sophie's memory by visiting her at Burke Rehabilitation Center.

16

DOC. KID.

"It's only 7:00 p.m. I'm sure Aunt Sophie would be happy to see a few familiar faces," I pleaded with my mother. "She's so alone. In Grandpa's journal, she was full of life. After reading the entries, I feel really bad for her."

My mother stopped loading the dishwasher and looked down at the journal I was holding.

For a second, I could have sworn she was going to dismiss my request and tell me to go back up to my room, but she seemed to want to visit her aunt almost as much as I did. Maybe remembering what Aunt Sophie did to her unearthed some questions she needed to ask her; however, I didn't know if Sophie would be able to answer my mother's questions, or mine.

"I think you're right, sweetie. She has no one to talk to. It's kind of late, though. I highly doubt we can see her tonight," my mother said, beginning to load the dishwasher once again.

"You can call and find out," I suggested, hoping my enthusiasm wouldn't make her suspicious of my ulterior motives.

Agreeing, my mother called the nursing home.

Unfortunately, visiting hours were only from 10:00 a.m. to 5:00 p.m.

"We can go tomorrow after school," my mother stated.

I was just too impatient to wait. I was hitting a dead end with the medical records. I needed any additional information Aunt Sophie and Grandma

McEwin could provide. There was only one thing to do: I had to see my grandmother tonight.

Before I could sneak out my window, with the journal in hand, Amber barged into my room. The breeze coming from the open window licked the back of my neck, trying to lure me outside.

"I thought I would find you up here, staring at the medical records," Amber exclaimed, walking toward the window. "Going somewhere?"

"Yes, I have somewhere important to go, but it's best if I go alone, Amber," I asserted.

"Important, hmm?" she questioned, smiling. "Remember what you said about going somewhere important?"

"Ugh! Amber, I don't have time for this," I moaned, climbing out the window.

"C'mon, Cooper!" she called after me, as I clung onto the gutters. "I've been helping you out. Let me come. I'll be fine. I told you, I can take care of myself."

Holding my grip on the gutters, I hung my head downward and groaned.

"All right, but this is the last time you tag along," I stated, knowing full well that Amber would *always* follow me.

"Scout's honor," Amber promised, giving me a mock salute.

<hr />

By the time we arrived at our grandmother's house, the lights were already out. She was asleep.

"So, this was what was so important?" Amber grumbled. "You wanted to go to Grandma's house?"

Walking up to our grandmother's door, I prepared to ring the bell as many times as necessary until she opened the door and answered my questions.

Sally was missing, and I had a feeling that time was running out. Besides my grandfather, and possibly two doctors, none of those kidnapped in the seventies had died. However, who knew if that would be case this time. Perhaps the kidnapper killed those he didn't need.

"Wait, what are you doing?" Amber asked, following me to the door. "You're not going to ring the bell, are you? She's asleep, Cooper. I don't understand why we can't wait until tomorrow."

Amber never had someone she loved ripped away from her. She didn't understand that tomorrow wasn't an option. Every day I wasted was another day Sally was in trouble.

I was getting too close to the truth to wait until tomorrow for answers I could get right now.

When Amber noticed the doorbell pushing inward without a hand touching it, she realized I couldn't wait.

"Well, I guess there's no time like the present," Amber stated, rolling her eyes.

After the fifth ring, lights flickered on in the house.

"Who is it?" my grandmother asked, her voice strained from sleep.

"It's Cooper and Amber," I stated, waiting for her to open the door.

"Cooper? Amber?" my grandmother repeated in disbelief, as she unlocked the door.

When she finally opened the door, I barged in and turned on the hall light.

"Hi, Grandma," Amber said awkwardly. "I'm sorry we're here so late, but Cooper wanted to see you."

As if my grandmother had expected me to come to her house that night, she pulled out a couple of pictures of our grandfather from her robe pocket.

"Come into the living room," she stated, gesturing for Amber and me to sit on her couch. "I see you brought the journal, Cooper. I knew you would finish it soon."

It was as if our grandmother had been waiting for this moment. Maybe she knew it was inevitable. She left the journal for my mother to read, and she knew I was already asking questions about our grandfather's past.

However, I still wasn't sure if she realized what unanswered questions our grandfather left behind. He seemed to be the only one who could solve a case that was repeating itself forty years later. Even though our grandmother might not be able to answer every question I had, I still thought asking would be better than letting the mystery die and potentially risking those innocent people's lives. "What did Grandpa McEwin tell you about the Parkway kidnapper?" I asked, hoping our grandmother would supply me with more answers than I had.

"You know, I feared this day would come ever since your grandfather died," our grandmother laughed. "I knew I'd never be prepared for it, and

I was right. In fact, I assumed your mother would be the one to ask me, not her children."

Did our grandmother know everything? Had she been hiding these secrets for over forty years? Well, now she was going to reveal her secrets to Amber and me. Why didn't she tell her daughter? My mother shouldn't have had to go through the painstaking effort of uncovering my grandfather's journal and reading it before she learned the full truth.

"Grandma, *do you* know about the Parkway hospital kidnappings?" Amber asked.

"Yes, dear, I do," my grandmother said, as a sheet of tears covered her teal eyes. "When your mother was taken from us, your grandfather was determined to find her. I thought I would never see her again, but your grandfather refused to give up. He stayed by my side in our bedroom every day, thinking. I thought that was the only way he could grieve. The only time he left our bedroom was to go down to the hospital. He said whoever took Anne was there. One day, after coming home from the hospital, he told me he was going to rescue Anne. I didn't think anything of it because he said that every day, but one day, he did. He rescued our daughter. He risked his own life to rescue our little Anne."

My grandmother excused herself to get a box of tissues.

"Grandpa McEwin was always a man of his word," Amber stated, a satisfied smile spread across her face.

When our grandmother returned, both Amber and I sat at attention, waiting for her to finish the story I'd been longing to hear.

"I got a call from the hospital a day after your grandfather left to find Anne," our grandmother continued. "They said Anne had a few puncture wounds on her head and forearm, but besides that, she was perfectly fine. Your grandfather, on the other hand, had twice as many puncture wounds and was quite weak. He couldn't even stand.

"I practically lived in the hospital. Every day and every night, I sat by your grandfather's side. Your grandfather only lived a week after he saved Anne. He lost his voice two days before he died. The doctors claimed his Broca's area—I think that's what they called it—was damaged beyond repair. It's the part of the brain that controls speech. The doctors said the part of the brain that controls the senses, the somatosensory area, had more puncture wounds than any other part of his brain. The needle went straight through, could you believe that? The doctors were baffled. Before Max lost his voice entirely, he told me he wanted to write something down. He used every bit of his strength writing that last journal entry of his.

After that, he just lay in bed and waited for death to come. He looked like he was paralyzed.

"But, before he wrote in his journal, he spoke to me.

He told me he lost his powers. He said they wanted power and they found it in him."

My jaw practically fell to the floor. I looked over at Amber, who looked five shades paler than usual. The kidnapper wanted his *powers*? How? Why?

"Did Grandpa tell you who the kidnapper was?" I asked anxiously, hoping our grandmother knew.

"He only had the chance to tell me it was a doctor. He was going to tell me who, but he could only talk for so long. He fought so hard to tell me, but I kept insisting he reserve his strength," our grandmother said, as trails of tears streamed down her cheeks.

Oddly enough, it all made sense. A doctor would have access to medical records. And, who other than a doctor would think to shove a needle through the brain and know how to do so? That's what *Doc. Kid.* probably meant. He was trying to write that a doctor was the kidnapper.

I was so close to the truth that it was killing me. The two most important questions left were: who was the doctor, and why did he want telekinesis? The latter question was easier to figure out than the former.

"Grandma, was there anything else he said?" I asked hopefully.

I just needed one more piece to the puzzle, and then I'd be able to solve this mystery.

"He kept repeating the word *foam*. And he whispered your mother's name every day until he could no longer speak. Even when he couldn't speak, he would mouth her name, and mine as well," our grandmother said, wiping her eyes with the last of the tissues from the once-full box. "He also told me this was the safest town to live in because the kidnapper would never come back. That *monster* wouldn't return because he got what he wanted."

Foam? What could he have possibly meant by the word *foam*? It was yet another question to stack on top of the millions of others.

"Is that why you changed your last name? You didn't want the kidnapper tracking you, Mom, and Aunt Sophie down if he ever did decide to come back?" I asked, already knowing the answer. Again, it all made sense. Why else would my grandfather change his last name?

"Yes, I changed our last names," my grandmother confirmed, looking down into the tissue box filled with used tissues. "I didn't want to take any chances, if that kidnapper did come back. He'd already taken my husband; I couldn't bare him stealing my daughter again."

"If you thought he was going to come back, why didn't you move, despite Grandpa's instructions?" Amber asked, practically entangling her index finger in her hair from twirling it throughout our grandmother's story.

"I should have," our grandmother sighed. "But I couldn't. It's as if your grandfather still lives here. Even though I can't see him, I can feel his presence. It's hard to stay now, but I do. I always will.

"I see so much of your grandfather in you both.

Cooper, you have his determination and spirit. Amber, not only do you look more like him than any member of this family, but you also have his tenacity."

Our grandmother got up from her seat and walked over to Amber and me. As she placed her hands on our cheeks, new tears formed in her eyes.

"And I know one of you has his abilities. I never thought to ask your mother," my grandmother said, looking from Amber to me. "Perhaps both of you have his abilities."

Amber bit her bottom lip, trying to stop herself from telling our grandmother the truth.

"It's me, Grandma. I have telekinesis, not Amber," I admitted.

My grandmother took a step back, looking me over.

After a couple of seconds, she leaned in and wrapped her arms around me, crying on my shoulder.

My grandmother deserved to know which of her grandchildren received her husband's curse. She'd pieced together quite a few clues for me. It was only right that I answered one of the questions that had probably been lingering in her mind for almost two decades.

"I thought you would never tell anyone," Amber said over our grandmother's shoulder.

"Yeah, well, things change. Plus, she is family," I stated, anticipating that more change would come.

17

AUNT SOPHIE

Amber and I managed to sneak back without our parents suspecting we had ever left the house.

I was still in disbelief over the fact that the kidnapper wanted my grandfather's powers. He was searching for telekinesis in his victims. At least I knew why he was kidnapping people, but I didn't understand how the blood types connected to having telekinesis. Was it possible that only people with AB blood had telekinesis? How would the kidnapper have come up with that theory?

Knowing the kidnapper wanted to find someone with telekinesis, I understood why the kidnapper took people from the hospital over forty years ago.

When my grandfather stopped the gurney, he assumed no one knew he was responsible for saving that person's life. Somehow, a doctor must have seen the incident and realized someone stopped that gurney with his mind. Maybe the kidnapper even suspected it was my grandfather but needed confirmation. It all added up. My grandfather saved a person, and then people started to mysteriously disappear from the hospital. When the doctor witnessed the telekinetic act, he didn't know who had the ability, so he kidnapped patients and staff who had AB blood because, somehow, having that blood type meant it was possible a person could have telekinesis.

That meant the present-day kidnapper must have witnessed a telekinetic incident. He must've seen the mugging incident, and that was why he was kidnapping students and staff from Erikson High School rather than taking people from the hospital.

I was to blame for the kidnappings. I used my powers, and now my girlfriend and others had become science experiments. I'd never imagined my nightmare could become someone else's.

Why couldn't the kidnapper have taken me instead?

If the blood type theory was right, I should have AB blood, too. What was he waiting for? How far down was I on his list of potential telekinetic protégés?

Guilt seared through every nerve of my body.

That idiot kidnapper should have taken me first. He would have found what he was looking for and everyone else would have been safe. However, as luck would have it, I was sitting comfortably in my room while those innocent people, including my girlfriend, were terrified, not knowing if they'd live to see the next day.

The kidnapper would puncture holes in their brains until he found what he was looking for. He could even kill them for all he cared. He murdered my grandfather, why would he flinch at taking another life? As long as he got this curse, this power, what did he care?

I jumped when I heard my mother come into my room.

"So, where were you tonight?" she asked, leaning against my dresser.

My eyes widened as I turned to face her. How could she have known?

"In here," I lied, quickly taking the medical records off my bed.

"Right," she said suspiciously. "What are those?" My mother nodded in the direction of the medical records I'd hastily stuffed into my grandfather's two manila folders and shoved under my bed.

"Nothing," I stated, lying on my sheets. Again, I used the ubiquitous code word. I really needed to come up with a better lie.

"Why so secretive?" my mother asked, sitting on the corner of my bed. "Want to talk about it?" she asked, patting my calf.

Sitting up, I brushed back pieces of hair that stuck to my damp forehead.

"Not really," I stated, getting up from my bed, preparing to take a shower.

Nodding, my mother got up from my bed and placed her hand gently on my shoulder.

"Well, if you ever need to talk, you know I'll always be here to listen," she said, smiling.

After thanking her, I jumped into the shower and let the icy cold water flow over my body. As the water began to warm, I felt as if the day was melting away. Everything disappeared in the water, except sleep. I could feel my eyelids slowly closing, and then the world turned into nothingness.

———————— ✦✦✦✦✦ ————————

The lilacs showered over the flood. I could feel the flowers dripping over my flesh, melding with my body.

Lying in the liquid, I relaxed every muscle of my body, allowing the petals flowing in the water to take over me.

"I'm yours," I breathed, giving into everything around me.

Even if the air ripped through my body and soul, I still wouldn't rise from the liquid that embraced me. Every part of me seemed to fit in the watery surface, as if it were longing to cradle my flesh.

"Get up!" the voice shouted, rippling through the refuge I created.

The sound of the voice froze the lilacs falling from the sky. The seabed I rested on shattered underneath my touch. I cried out in agony as my naked back slammed into the earth's hard, jagged surface.

"Why can't you just leave me alone!" I yelled, scowling at the empty air where I knew the voice hid. "Show yourself!"

Fiendish laughter split through the suspended lilacs. The voice formed them into tiny violet daggers that were aimed at my bare flesh.

"You can't see me because you're unwilling to accept me." The ominous voice ripped through the fabric of this sanctuary, revealing the darkness that hid underneath the surface.

"Why won't you let me seek refuge? Why won't you let me be?" I demanded, feeling the points of the lilac daggers nearing my skin.

"It's not time," the voice merely stated, pulling back the small daggers. "You have to find her first. Then, and only then, will you allow yourself to rest."

"Fine," I reluctantly muttered, closing my eyes.

I could no longer feel the voice's eerie presence. All that existed was the liquid, quickly making its way over my mouth. Breathing was no longer an option as the water pinned me to the earth's surface.

"Let me up!" I wanted to scream, but the water drowned out my senses. "Cooper, what the hell are you doing?" I heard a familiar voice shout.

———— ·+++++· ————

"Wake up!" my mother shouted, as I shot out of the water.

My mother turned off the shower before the water could spill out of the bathtub. I realized I'd been submerged in a sheet of water, and I probably would have drowned if not for my mother.

"Are you trying to drown yourself or something?" my mother asked with a serious mix of fear and anger in her tone, pulling me out of the water and handing me a towel.

"I—I must have fallen asleep in the shower," I said, wincing as I rubbed the back of my head, where I felt a fresh welt forming. "I'll clean up, I swear."

Shaking her head, my mother inadvertently parted my wet hair.

"It's okay, sweetie. The water will drain," she said, placing clean underwear and a pair of pajama pants in my hands. "Plus, I think you've had enough water for one night. You should get some sleep. You've had a long day."

Nodding, I thanked my mother and gave her a kiss goodnight. Sleep washed over me as soon as my wet head hit the pillow. But, even in sleep, I knew I couldn't relax until I found the kidnapper's victims, even if that meant dying like my grandfather.

For the first time in what felt like centuries, I woke up without feeling the residue of the sinister voice walking throughout my subconscious.

Looking over at my alarm clock, I realized I was up an hour before the alarm was set to ring. That's all I needed—to get up early for a day of school I wished I didn't have.

I knew that day of school was going to be the longest day I'd ever had. Every second would feel like a century as I longed for the bell to ring so I could visit Aunt Sophie and maybe discover other missing pieces to the puzzle.

As I'd predicted, the school day dragged out longer than any other day. Murdoch was still there with his team of police officers, who were vigorously checking IDs and making sure no one suspicious entered Erikson High School. Unfortunately, they didn't realize that everyone who had an ID was a possible suspect.

Only one more person, an art teacher, had been kidnapped. Now, the police were indeed confirming these *were* kidnappings. Security was baffled by her disappearance. None of the security cameras caught the kidnapper on tape. The officers claimed all of the cameras had been shifted to an odd angle to evade detection.

"So, let me get this straight. We're going to meet Mom at Burke Rehabilitation Center to see Aunt Sophie?" Amber asked, as we drove to the Bronx.

"I have to ask Aunt Sophie a few questions about Grandpa McEwin," I asserted, pressing the accelerator a little harder. "I almost have everything figured out. Aunt Sophie has another perspective; maybe Grandpa McEwin told her about the kidnappings as well."

"Yeah, but Aunt Sophie has Alzheimer's disease," Amber reminded me. "Even if he did tell her forty years ago, she probably forgot what he said."

"Well, it's a chance I'm willing to take."

Our mother was waiting for Amber and me near the entrance of the nursing home.

"Aunt Sophie will be so pleased to see you both," she said, wrapping her arms around our shoulders and taking us into Aunt Sophie's room.

Aunt Sophie was sitting by the open window, staring out at the sky. She looked as if her memories existed somewhere outside these walls and, as long as she watched them, they'd never leave her.

"Hello, Aunt Sophie. How are you today?" my mother greeted her.

Aunt Sophie didn't even bother to turn around and see who was in her room. Her eyes were glued to the clear sky.

"This is Amber, your great-niece. And this is Cooper, your great-nephew," our mother stated, nudging Amber and me forward.

"Hi, Aunt Sophie," Amber mumbled.

Aunt Sophie slowly turned her head at the sound of Amber's voice. Her wide green eyes looked confused, as if she were remembering something but she couldn't quite trust her own recollections.

"Hello, Aunt Sophie," I stated, contemplating where I should begin. I couldn't just come out and ask her questions. I didn't want to frighten her.

"Max?" Aunt Sophie asked, getting up from her chair. "Where have you been?"

Before I could tell her that she was mistaken, my great-aunt shuffled toward me with arms wide open. Wrapping her arms around me, Aunt Sophie began to cry on my shoulder.

"I thought you'd died!" she whimpered, squeezing me tighter. "Brian said you'd died."

"Brian? As in, Brian Vara?" I questioned, trying to make my way out of my great-aunt's bear hug.

"Yes. He said you were dead, but I knew you couldn't be," Aunt Sophie insisted, releasing me from her grasp. "You promised me everything would be okay, and I knew it would be."

I'd almost forgotten about Brian Vara's potential relative, who I'd seen at Parkway Hospital when I went to visit Michelle. Well, at least I knew who I would speak to next. Everyone who worked at that hospital during the kidnappings was a suspect. If this Brian Vara was related to the one in my grandfather's journal, then maybe Brian Vara knew which doctor was interested in paranormal abilities.

"No, Aunt Sophie," my mother corrected my great-aunt. "This is Cooper. He's Max's grandson. I'm Max's daughter, Anne. And Amber is Max's granddaughter."

Aunt Sophie studied my mother's face, as if she were trying to place her but didn't know where she belonged.

"Anne, I told you not to tell your mother about the tests," Aunt Sophie exclaimed, wagging her index finger at my mother. "She'll catch us and punish you.

Didn't I tell you that? You should listen to your aunt." "No, Aunt Sophie. I'm an adult now," my mother tried to explain. "I have children now. I have a husband. I'm no longer a little girl."

Unfortunately, my great-aunt wasn't aware that time had passed since she was a teenager. In Aunt Sophie's eyes, my mother would always be a little girl. I, on the other hand, was my grandfather before he died.

Even though she may not have meant to, my great-aunt was able to provide me with another clue, or at least a facsimile of one. Brian Vara had confirmed my grandfather was dead. His potential relative may be one of the few people who's connected to the kidnappings at Parkway Hospital.

"Sophie, did I say anything to you about the Parkway kidnappings while I was in the hospital?" I asked, playing the part of my grandfather.

"What are you doing?" Amber whispered, but I ignored her.

"Don't you remember?" my great-aunt laughed. "You said that even though you were gone, you'd always be around to care for me. But you're not gone, so it doesn't matter."

Aunt Sophie wrapped her arms around me once again, but this time, she pulled back right away. Her face was contorted in confusion. Familiarity escaped from her eyes. She didn't know who I was anymore. I wasn't her brother.

"Max has red hair. You're not him. You're an imposter!" Aunt Sophie screamed, aiming her index finger at me and backing away in fear.

"Aunt Sophie, this is Cooper, not Max. Max died," my mother stated, reaching out to touch my great-aunt on the shoulder.

"Get out, imposters!" my great-aunt yelled, as my mother, Amber, and I backed out of her room.

"Damn," I said under my breath, as a nurse rushed into my great-aunt's room to calm her down.

"Perhaps Aunt Sophie wasn't ready to see us yet," my mother admitted sadly.

"You can say that again," Amber mumbled, walking toward my car.

18

THE SECOND BRIAN VARA

Instead of driving straight home, as my mother instructed me to, I took a little detour to Parkway Hospital.

"What are you doing?" Amber asked, as I drove into the Parkway Hospital parking lot.

"I have to talk to someone," I said, parking my car. "Wait here."

"If you think I'm waiting, you're crazy," Amber exclaimed, getting out of my car.

Rolling my eyes, I didn't try to stop Amber from coming with me. I didn't have time to convince her to stay in the car. I needed to talk to Brian Vara as soon as possible.

I'd come up with a theory while I was driving toward the hospital. There was the outside chance the Brian Vara from the seventies was the Parkway Hospital kidnapper, and his relative, also Brian Vara, was completing what his elder relative had started. However, Brian Vara was not a doctor—though, by doctor, could my grandfather have meant an *aspiring* doctor?

The present-day Brian Vara had access to needles and knew enough about the medical profession to continue his relative's experiment. However, I still couldn't figure out how Brian Vara could get access to Erikson High School's medical records? Perhaps he had an accomplice.

When Amber and I entered the hospital, I didn't see Brian Vara at the nurses' desk.

"Excuse me," I said to a nurse behind the desk. "Do you know where Brian Vara is?"

"Vara? I think he's busy right now," the nurse stated, not looking up from the charts she was sorting through on the desk. "You can wait for him in the waiting room."

About ten minutes later, which seemed like a century, Brian Vara walked toward the nurses' desk.

The nurse who I'd talked to pointed out Amber and me to him.

"Can I help you?" Brian asked, nervously clutching his pager.

"Yes. My name is Max Fitzpatrick," I stated, wondering if the mention of my grandfather's name would hit a nerve.

Brian Vara looked over my head and squinted his eyes, as if he were trying to recall something.

"That name sounds so familiar," Brian said, taking a quick glance at his watch. "I think my grandfather mentioned that name before. Are you Max Fitzpatrick's grandson?"

So, he *was* related to the elder Brian Vara, and his grandfather still remembered my grandfather. That meant he probably still remembered the events of the Parkway Hospital kidnappings.

"As a matter of fact, I am," I stated, pride ringing in my tone. "Is there any way I could talk to your grandfather. I want to ask him a few questions about my grandfather. You know, about the old days."

"I'm sorry, but that's impossible," Brian said, lowering his head. "He died ten years ago."

Damn.

"I'm so sorry for your loss," I said, sincerity laced in my tone, along with involuntary anxiousness.

"It's okay. It happened a long time ago," Brian stated, shifting from side to side as he glanced at his watch again.

Why was he so uneasy? By the way he kept looking at his watch and clenching his pager, he obviously had to be somewhere. But where? Wait a minute. Maybe the signs of anxiety he showed were related to the present or past crime.

"Well then, maybe I could ask you a few questions about the past," I said, trying to stall him.

"I'm sorry, but I really don't know much about my grandfather's friends," Brian declared, trying to step around me. "Now, if you'll excuse me, I have to go somewhere."

"He was a victim in the Parkway Hospital kidnappings. I just need to ask you one thing. If you can't answer me, then I promise never to bring it up again," I promised, hoping he'd agree to my proposal. Glancing at his watch once again, Brian nodded and sat on one of the gray chairs in the waiting room.

"Thank you. Now, whoever this kidnapper was during the seventies was looking for something in the patients. Was there a doctor at the hospital who was studying or maybe wrote an article about the theoretical effects of a particular blood type relating to the activation of the brain?"

Brian had to take a second to ingest my question.

Even I was a little shocked by how I worded the question. I wasn't completely sure the blood type had anything to do with the brain, but it all seemed to add up.

The people who were kidnapped had puncture wounds in their forearms and head. The puncture wounds in the head passed through to the brain. Obviously, the kidnapper theorized that having AB blood somehow affected the brain, making it possible for a person to have telekinesis.

"There were many doctors who wrote various theories in medical journals on blood types," Brian stated.

For a second, I assumed he'd dismiss the question with that pithy answer. But surprisingly, there was a *however* lingering in his tone.

"There was one doctor my grandfather mentioned who wrote some crazy theories in his medical textbook. Some college students, who were premed, read it," Brian added.

"Which doctor?"

"I think it was Dr. David Leumas. He was a neurosurgeon here in the seventies, that is, before he was kidnapped." Brian glanced at his watch for the *millionth* time. "Now, if you'll excuse me, I really have to be somewhere."

"Of course," I said, reluctantly allowing him to run off.

Before I could look up whatever information I could find on David Leumas, I had to find out what Brian Vara was up to, and the only way I could do that was to follow him.

"Come on," I told Amber, pulling her out of her chair.

"Where are we going now?" Amber whispered, sensing that we were going to follow Brian Vara.

Brian walked at a quick pace; we tried to keep up, but we were less familiar with the hospital. We followed Brian down a series of multicolored hallways until he finally turned down what appeared to be the maternity ward. He raced over to one of the beds behind a green curtain.

Amber and I slowly inched toward the curtain, being careful to remain undetected.

Slinking up to the curtain, I pulled it back about a quarter of an inch to peek inside. Once I saw Brian Vara coaching a woman through breathing techniques while holding her hand, I had a feeling Brian wasn't going to be one of my lead suspects, for the time being.

19

REFLECTION IS THE KEY

When we got home, I immediately looked up everything I could find on Dr. David Leumas. I found several articles on Dr. Leumas's work as a neurosurgeon in the 1960s, as well as peer reviewed articles he published in the 1970s. Oddly enough, he only published one textbook, titled *Theoretical Medical Techniques*. In a denigrating critique of the text, the critic noted there was a section of the book that should have been disproven and removed from the text. The critic explained that this section focused on how certain blood types affect the brain; however, Dr. Leumas never provided persuasive evidence to prove his theory.

Cracking the textbook open, I didn't even have to read through the entire text to find what I was looking for; my grandfather left me a clue. A corner of one of the pages was folded over, and the second-to-last paragraph on that page was circled.

Engrossed, I carefully read and reread the paragraph.

> The somatosensory area of the brain controls the sensations coming in, such as the sense of touch. Already knowing that the parts of the brain do not work solely by themselves, it is possible to implicate the usages of the somatosensory area with the frontal, occipital, and temporal lobes. If a hereditary mutation occurred in the neurons near

> the somatosensory area, increasing the activity in that area, then the other lobes would be affected as well. The hereditary mutation would be carried throughout the AB blood type due to the lack of reaction to both the A antigen and the B antigen.

Flipping through the pages of the textbook, I expected to find more paragraphs my grandfather had circled, but to my dismay, which was the only clue he left me.

I'd read quite a few science journals, and not one of them stated such an odd theory without proper evidence. Critics must have written hundreds of articles condemning that one paragraph, so how and why was it published?

I was about to close the book when I thought to look under the folded corner of the page. While I was pulling it up, I assumed there'd be nothing under there. Fortunately, I was wrong.

To my surprise, my grandfather made tiny footnotes on the folded corner. Hopefully, he'd clue me in on why Dr. David Leumas would write a hypothesis that lacked reason.

The AB blood type reacts differently in telekinetic people, my grandfather wrote.

Thinking back to my grandfather's last journal entry, I remembered him writing that he asked my grandmother if she could bring him this textbook. He must have written this note here just before he died.

When my grandfather wrote that sentence in the textbook, he must have been trying to explain Dr. Leumas's theory. If by "hereditary mutation" he meant telekinetic powers, then Dr. Leumas must have been designing a theory to explain why people with telekinesis only had an AB blood type.

With the help of my grandfather, I finally found the last piece of the puzzle. Dr. David Leumas *had* to be the Parkway Hospital kidnapper. That explained why he wasn't discovered when the others were returned.

And, he was a neurosurgeon, so he would know how to thrust a needle through the somatosensory area of the brain and extract whatever he was looking for. Since my grandfather lost his powers before he died, Dr. Leumas must have taken them from him. That meant, somehow, Dr. Leumas had my grandfather's powers stored somewhere.

"That looks intense," Amber said. I jumped at the sound of her voice, not realizing she was standing in my doorway.

"Geez, don't you ever knock?" I asked, slamming the textbook shut.

"Not really," Amber stated, grinning. "You were studying that textbook like you were studying for a final exam. What is it?" After tucking the textbook under my bed and grabbing my jacket, I opened my window.

"The key," I simply said, climbing out the window. Halfway out, I turned to Amber. "Can you cover for me?"

"Where are you going?" Amber asked, following me out the window. She nudged me aside as we both stood on the roof.

"I'm going to the high school," I stated, concentrating on lifting myself off of the roof and lowering myself to the ground. Although I felt a light drumming in my head, my migraine had subsided enough for me to use my abilities without any pain. However, before I could lower myself, Amber grabbed my hand.

"Hey, you jump, I jump, Jack," Amber exclaimed, smirking. "I've been along for the ride so far; I want to see where this goes."

"This isn't a game, Amber," I snapped, pulling my hand back.

"I don't want you to get hurt."

Rolling her eyes, she exclaimed, "How cliché.

Look, like I said before, I don't need the 'big strong man' to save me. I can take care of myself. Plus, if whatever you are going to do is dangerous, then you need backup. I'm coming, whether you like it or not."

Knowing that fighting with Amber would be futile and would waste precious time, I reluctantly allowed her to come with me to the school.

When we finally reached the high school, only a few cars remained in the faculty parking lot, otherwise the area was pretty empty.

I figured Dr. Leumas must have somehow been involved in this new kidnapper's plot—or he *was* the Erikson High School kidnapper. But why would he come back to Parkway if he'd already taken my grandfather's ability? Why wait over forty years to come back? Before I knew the prior kidnapper was Dr. Leumas, I assumed the Erikson High School kidnapper worked on the inside or had an accomplice. Perhaps Dr. Leumas disguised himself as a janitor, teacher, or school security guard. Perhaps his accomplice worked in the school and staked out the people he needed.

Since Malcolm Felone also disappeared, then perhaps he was Dr Leumas's accomplice. Or, what if Felone tried to stop Dr. Leumas and, for that, Dr. Leumas killed Felone? At this point, anything was possible.

Although I was getting closer, there was still one clue that didn't make sense: the foam. Why did my grandfather say that word to my grandmother? What was he trying to tell her with that one, seemingly nonsensical word?

So far, whatever my grandfather wrote or said always had a purpose.

"What exactly are we looking for?" Amber asked, leaning against the entrance door.

"Something," I answered vaguely. Well, at least that was better than saying nothing.

I was hoping I'd see a van with an elderly man trying to shove a student inside, but I knew that was too easy. This guy was sneaky. How was he abducting these students and staff members? And, once he captured them, where did he take them?

Considering that the security cameras were moved when the kidnapper struck, I figured the kidnapper abducted people from inside the building.

Amber and I went around to the side entrance of the building and slipped inside, trying to evade the additional, newly installed security cameras. As we roamed the halls, I concentrated on turning the cameras away from us so we wouldn't be detected.

For the first time since I'd attended Erikson High School, the halls were completely empty. It was a relief not to squeeze through hordes of students, who were moving at the speed of snails, to get to my next class.

"So, what are we looking for?" Amber asked again.

"I'll know when I see it," I said, peering into each room as we walked down the hall. "This is where the kidnappings are taking place, so there has to be more clues here. There's something the police missed, I just know it."

Most of the lights in the classrooms were off, but that didn't mean no one was inside.

"The rooms are empty, Cooper," Amber stated, peeking into an art room.

Amber and I were about to climb the stairs to the second floor when we saw a light on in a classroom at the end of the hall.

"Hey, there's one," Amber pointed out, quickening her pace.

"Slow down," I whispered, hoping whoever was in the classroom wouldn't hear our footsteps.

When we reached the classroom, I recognized it right away; it was my physics class. Mr. Divad was inside, talking to one of Michelle's friends, writing something on the board. It looked like an after-school extra help session. Mr. Nelson used to hold those as well.

"Well, unless you're looking for an after-school tutor, we should check upstairs," Amber stated, heading for the stairwell. When we reached the second floor, I noticed one of the office doors was left open.

"I think this is the science department office," I said, peeking inside.

"Well, do you think whatever you're looking for is in there?" Amber asked, leaning against the wall beside the door. "Usually, these offices aren't open after school."

Although Mr. Divad was still in the building and probably left the door open for easy access, it was still a little strange that he would leave the office open.

"Stay here," I told Amber, as I snuck into the dim office.

"Yeah right," Amber whispered, following me. Rolling my eyes, I surveyed the office for any clues the kidnapper might have left. Unfortunately, everything looked pretty normal. There were five desks. Two were facing the door, one was randomly in the middle of the room, and the other two were in front of a large mirror that hung on the wall.

"What would a bunch of science teachers do with a huge mirror in their office?" Amber asked, walking toward the mirror.

"It may be for an experiment or a lesson, who knows," I stated, walking over to one of the desks.

Looking down at the contents on the desk, I noticed another nameplate was next to Mr. Frank Nelson's. A nameplate was already created for our physics substitute, Mr. Divad. The school board must have told him that if Mr. Nelson didn't return, he'd have a permanent job as our physics teacher.

"Who's that?" Amber asked, picking up Mr. Divad's nameplate.

"He's the substitute physics teacher," I said, glancing in the mirror.

I stared at the reflection I saw in the mirror for a few seconds, believing my eyes *must* have been playing tricks on me. What I saw in that mirror was too bewildering to comprehend, and yet it explained everything. There was no new or copycat kidnapper. The original kidnapper was walking among his victims, picking them with careful precision by pretending to be a trusted teacher.

"Damn!" I shouted, realizing who the kidnapper's next victim was going to be.

I practically slipped down the stairs as I ran toward my physics classroom.

"Wait! Where are we going?" Amber questioned, trying to keep up with me.

When I finally reached the classroom, the lights were already shut off and the door was locked.

"Damn!" I shouted again, banging my hand against the empty classroom's door.

"What is it? What's going on?" Amber demanded, turning me around to face her.

"I just let him go," I growled.

"Who? Who'd you let go?" Amber asked, her eyes filled with questions.

"David Leumas," I stated, casting my eyes downward in defeat.

"Everyone else knows him as Samuel Divad, our physics substitute."

CHAPTER

20

FOAM

Why would David Leumas disguise himself as a physics teacher by spelling his name backward? Why didn't he come up with a new name?

I practically flew up the stairs and back to the science teachers' office, but when I got there, the door was closed, and the lights had been shut off.

"Damn," I repeated, flicking my wrist and flinging the heavy door open as if it were a flimsy piece of paper.

"If he's gone, then what are we looking for?" Amber asked, following me into the office and turning on the lights.

"Shut the lights off," I snapped at her, flicking the lights off myself.

I should have run after him, but there was no point. He was long gone by now. He probably kidnapped one of Michelle's friends and ran to his hiding place with her.

If I was going to catch him, I had to have a plan.

Snaring him when he least expected it was the best way to go, but how could I do that? I could use myself as bait, but then again, I didn't know where I was on his telekinetic hit list.

I sifted through Mr. Nelson's desk, but all I found were a few lesson plans, some pencils held together by a rubber band, and a box of whiteboard markers. There was no clue in the drawer that would lead me to Dr. Leumas's hiding place.

"Damn," I muttered once again, sifting through his drawer one more time, hoping I'd missed something.

"Is that becoming your favorite word?" Amber asked, helping me rummage through the desk.

"It would be yours, too, if you'd just let a kidnapper go," I said, scowling at Amber.

"I kind of did," Amber admitted. "I am with you, after all. At least you figured it out."

I didn't respond to Amber's encouragement.

Figuring out the identity of the kidnapper was a step in the right direction, but that didn't save Sally, not yet anyway.

I didn't even know what I was looking for in that drawer. A map with a huge X marking the spot where he was holding his victims wasn't going to be folded neatly in his drawer. I was about to give up when I came across a piece of a clue that I desperately wanted. Pulling out the piece of paper from the bottom of his drawer, I immediately recognized it. Even with the mere moonlight that illuminated only a sliver of the desk, I would recognize the flyer anywhere. The large, vibrant, green letters against the white background was unmistakable.

"What'd you find?" Amber asked, looking from me to the flyer and back to me.

"It's one of the flyers from Mom's real estate agency," I said, folding the flyer and shoving it into my pocket. "We have to get out of here before someone catches us."

Since we hadn't driven to the high school, I spent the long walk home divulging what I had discovered. The full moon illuminated our walk home, as Amber asked clarifying questions, only some of which I was able to answer. When we finally made it back to our house, every light was off except for the one in my room.

"Do you think they know we snuck out?" Amber asked, staring up at my window.

"Oh yeah," I said, nervously watching our mother pace back and forth in front of my window.

Focusing on both Amber and I, I flew us up to my window.

"You might as well have come in through the front door," my mother stated, placing a hand on her hip. "I've known you were gone for about a half hour now."

"I'm sorry," I said, helping Amber through my window.

Balancing myself on the slippery roof, I grasped the windowpane and pulled myself in as my mother scowled at me. Disappointment practically burst through her retinas as she watched me brush off my pants and close my window.

"What am I going to do with you two?" my mother asked herself, running both of her hands through her hair. "You both chose now to sneak off, while these kidnappings are going on. Don't you care that I worry sick about you when you both just run off?"

Guilt rose in my throat as I listened to my mother's lecture. I wanted to tell her this sneaking out phase was only temporary, but I could not. I knew I was the only one who could help those innocent people who'd been kidnapped, which would mean sneaking out again.

"Mom, there's a good reason why we snuck out," Amber blurted out, nervously twisting her fingers through her red locks. "We're trying to stop the kidnapper. And, Cooper almost has it figured out."

My mom's eyes widened as she looked from Amber to me and back to Amber. As she closed her eyes, she rubbed her temples, as if she were trying to massage this information into her mind.

"You're doing what?" she exclaimed, opening her eyes. "Are you crazy? You could get killed!" Before Amber could interject, I firmly placed my hand on her arm to stop her.

"Mom, what place have you sold, or rented, recently to a Samuel Divad?" I asked, knowing I probably caught my mother off guard.

"What?" my mother questioned, her eyes filled with confusion. "Are you kidding me? You're going to change the subject by asking me if I sold or rented a space to someone named Samuel Divad?"

"Cooper found your flyer in Samuel Divad's desk," Amber stated, pulling the flyer out of my pocket.

Sighing, my mother looked at the flyer. She studied the flyer as if she were going to see more than what was on the surface, like she was a cryptologist and there was some type of hidden message in the piece of paper.

"Anyone could grab one of these flyers," my mother stated, folding the flyer as if it were a mere piece of paper and not evidence. "The agency puts one on every car and staples at least one to every telephone pole. He could have gotten this flyer from anyone; it doesn't mean he bought or rented a home from me."

"Try to remember. Samuel Divad," I urged, hoping the name would jog her memory. "He wears glasses with really thick, black, plastic frames. He's in his seventies. He's my physics teacher."

My mother tapped her cheek with her index finger and had a distant look in her eyes, as if the description sounded somewhat familiar. "I think he may be the one who bought an abandoned warehouse rather quickly. Also, he insisted on paying well over the sales price in cash."

"That's on the corner of Pershing and Trinity Avenue, right?" I asked, contemplating an escape plan so I could rescue Sally and the others.

"I don't like this. I don't like this at all, Cooper," my mother said, worry creeping in her tone. "You're putting yourself and your sister in danger. I'm going to the police station to tell Chief Murdoch what's going on."

"No!" Amber and I yelled simultaneously.

As our mother quizzically looked at us, I realized that, like my grandfather, I was now keeping secrets from my family.

"Mom, you just have to trust me. Murdoch can't help. This is something I have to do on my own. Please, trust me."

Our mother took a long pause, as if she were reasoning whether or not she could, or should, trust me.

"All right, I won't tell the police. But you both better be extremely careful," my mother warned, turning to walk out of my room. "Right now, you are both staying put, though."

I nodded, mentally crossing my fingers, trying to fight off the wave of exhaustion that was hitting me.

"Agreed," I lied, as my mother walked toward her room. I tried to keep my eyes open as I walked over to my bed and sat down on the corner. I just needed a moment to collect myself, and then I planned on sneaking out again.

Dr. Leumas might be expecting me to follow him, but I didn't care. I needed to rescue Sally before it was too late. I didn't know for certain it wasn't already too late.

"You look like you're about to pass out," Amber observed. "I'll let you sleep. Good night, Cooper."

"Right, good night," I mumbled, as Amber shut my door.

--------•••••••--------

"So, what are you going to do?" the voice asked, its tone shadowing the illuminated walls.

Lying in the darkness, I could only feel the reverberation of the voice against my humming heart. The faint memory of the light that once existed in this room dimmed with each passing moment.

The expanse of shadow over my body made me question my existence. Who was I? What was I doing here? Why was I lying here? What was I lying on?

I couldn't feel anything holding me up, and yet I knew something must be underneath me. Otherwise, how could I be lying down?

No, nothing can hold me up. I can hold me up. My mind can hold me up. I have powers that defy logic and reason, and yet I choose logic and reason above everything else. I am a paradox, living in a world where my entire existence is a lie to the one person I'm trying to save.

When did it come to this? How could my life have been driven this far down a spiral of lies? "I'm going to save her," I insisted.

My voice could be heard. For the first time, I could hear myself speaking. I was able to breathe and speak!

How? I always had to suffer; it was the voice's will. I could never talk without a struggle because the voice wished to cause me pain. Why had it changed its mind? Why did the voice allow me to be heard?

"You've said that before," the voice countered.

In the darkness, I felt a figure slowly moving forward. With each step it took, my heart pounded through my chest. Forcing my eyes open, I refused to blink, knowing that, in a flash, the mysterious figure might disappear.

"And you've always told me that actions are louder than words," I retorted, feeling as if my voice had a mind of its own.

My words were willing to challenge the voice, and yet my body was terrified. The voice had more power than I could ever control. It could easily slice through worlds that took every ounce of power I had to create.

How could I ever live up to the challenge? I was inferior to this voice; it couldn't respect me enough not to rip through my being right now in order to take over my humble abode.

"That's true, but you are taking action," the voice stated, as I felt it coming closer.

I could make out the blackened silhouette of the figure as it neared my levitating body. Familiarity seeped through my mind as I gawked at the body from which the voice spoke.

"It can't be," I muttered, knowing full well that the truth stood in front of me.

Wisps of dirty blonde hair fell in front of his piercing green eyes. His body was stiff with confidence. His feet were firmly planted on the nonexistent ground. If an earthquake split the darkness at that moment, his stance would remain firm.

"Yes, Cooper," the voice stated, me to my feet just by staring at me. "You were never able to accept that this part of you existed. You've been filled with so much doubt that you have never been able to let me in."

Even though this other me allowed me to speak, I couldn't. The realization that this other me existed froze my voice. But my thoughts could not be silenced. *How could I not have known? Why did he hide behind sound? Was he really an extension of myself that I couldn't accept until now?*

"You know you're going to face Leumas soon. All the pieces have fallen into place. Almost everything makes sense now," the other me stated, crossing his arms over his chest and waiting patiently for me to take it all in.

"Yes," I blurted out.

Feeling as if my knees had suddenly turned into jelly, I sunk into the darkness. Instead of feeling the hard surface on my back, I just kept falling.

With the flick of the wrist, the other me quickly pulled me up.

"You need to think, Cooper," the other me insisted, still holding me up with his gaze.

"Yes, I need to think," I agreed, trying to hold up my own body.

I nodded toward the other me when I got a grip on my powers. Holding myself up so I was at eye level with the other me, I tried to think of the piece that didn't quite fit into the puzzle.

"Foam!" I yelled, the word jumping off the tip of my tongue. "What does foam have to do with the mystery? Why would my grandfather say foam? He wouldn't say that word if it didn't have a purpose.

Perhaps foam had something to do with the experiment? No, that didn't make sense. What would foam have to do with trying to extract telekinesis out of people with an AB blood type? I shoved that theory aside for a second, just in case I couldn't come up with anything better.

"Do you know?" *I questioned my other self, hoping he'd have the answer.*

"If I did know, I couldn't tell you. It's in you. The answer lies right there. You just need to realize it," *the other me stated, eyes cast down at the black abyss we were floating over.* "I'm not here to just give you the answer. If it were that easy, you'd have it already."

"That's ridiculous," *I argued, grimacing.* "If you're here to help me, then do so."

"I am," *the other me laughed.* "I'm trying my best to help you through this dilemma. You just have to think harder. The missing piece of the puzzle is* foam. *You need to ask yourself why that is."

Foam. Foam forms on wet soap. A thick, frothy substance, like whipped cream, could be foam. There's foam rubber. There's Styrofoam. There are foam mattresses and cushions. So, what did my grandfather want my grandmother to know about foam?

"There's no reason why* foam *should be a piece of the puzzle!" I shouted, aggravation washing over me.* "Maybe he said it because he was delirious. Maybe he was trying to tell my grandmother that the experiment the kidnapper was conducting had something to do with foam. Maybe he didn't even mean to say foam!"

The other me's smile grew when he heard my last statement.

It was there all along, and I hadn't been able to see it. Of course, my grandfather didn't mean to say foam! His Broca's area, the part of the brain that controls speech, was damaged. He meant to say something that sounded like foam!

What sounded like foam *and made the puzzle complete? The other me said it was right in front of me.*

Clearing my mind, I relaxed every bone in my body and stood with the same confident stance as the other me. Determination rang throughout my body as I closed my eyes and focused on every piece of the puzzle I had.

My brain began to break down the clues. One clue. Foam. It meant something I'd been overlooking. The journal. The kidnapper. The kidnapped. The missing. David Leumas. Samuel Divad. Max Fitzpatrick. Max McEwin.

Malcolm Felone.

"Felone!" I screamed, excitement and relief bursting through my elated voice. "Foam! Felone! Malcolm Felone!"

The other me smiled and nodded as he disappeared into the dissolving shadows.

"Felone!" I screamed, waking myself up a couple of minutes before the alarm would have. Shaking my head, I realized I must have drifted off. At least the night's sleep wasn't a waste. My incessant nightmares finally became useful.

My grandfather was trying to tell my grandmother something about Malcolm Felone, but what? Was it possible Malcolm Felone was the Erikson High School kidnapper, not David Leumas? But then, why would Malcolm Felone spell David Leumas's name backward to disguise himself?

If Malcolm Felone was the Erikson High School kidnapper, he probably spelled David Leumas's name backward in order to frame David Leumas! But why was he framing David Leumas?

Maybe he wanted extra security, in case someone figured out his lame excuse was a disguise. Why wouldn't he use an anagram to disguise the name David Leumas? That is, unless he *wanted* someone to figure out Samuel Divad was really David Leumas!

But why would he want someone to find out that Samuel Divad stood for David Leumas? That is, unless he wanted the *right* person to find out that his name was David Leumas.

"My mother!" I blurted out, quickly placing my hand over my mouth.

Malcolm Felone kidnapped my mother. He probably wanted Anne Fitzpatrick, or one of her kids, to find him because he couldn't find her. He might think she was the one at Erikson High School who stopped that mugger, so he kidnapped teenagers believing that her offspring could have stopped the mugger with or instead of her.

The mugging was a test! It made sense. Why else would a mugger take a woman's purse in front of Erikson High School in broad daylight?

Malcolm Felone must have assumed Anne Fitzpatrick, or her teenage son or daughter, would stop the mugging. Unfortunately, I proved him right.

So, why didn't he come after me? That is, unless he didn't know it was me. I was the one who chased the mugger. Obviously, he wasn't positive it was me. However, he did know someone at the school stopped that mugger using telekinesis. And, since I probably had an AB blood type, I was somewhere on his list of suspects.

Since I knew his true identity, and soon I'd know where he was staying, I'd be able to get him before he got me.

Before heading to the warehouse, I needed to make sure my mother didn't contact Chief Murdoch, not yet anyway. Of course, I wanted Felone locked away so he couldn't hurt anyone ever again, but if the police discovered what Felone was really up to, then sooner or later, his experiment would be traced to my family. I couldn't risk discovery. I needed to rescue those people on my own to keep my secret and to prevent anyone else from getting hurt. However, in order to do so, I would need Amber's help.

Without knocking, I entered Amber's bedroom and locked the door behind me. Looking over at the lumpy comforter, I knew Amber was still asleep.

"Amber," I hissed, "Amber, wake up!"

As I saw the lump under the comforter stir, I knew she heard me. In a moment, Amber poked her head out and looked toward her bedroom door.

"Cooper, don't you knock?" she asked, rubbing her eyes.

"Amber, I need you to keep Mom from calling the police for a while. I need to face Divad on my own. He's crafty. If he's dodged them for four decades, there's no way they're easily going to catch him. I have to stop him," I declared.

"All right," Amber said, without an argument.

I placed my hand on her doorknob, dumbstruck.

Was I delirious or did Amber just agree to stall our mother without wanting to come with me to stop the kidnapper? If someone would have shown me a replay of what I just experienced, I would have accused them of brainwashing Amber before setting up that scenario.

Shaking Amber's reaction off, I left her room, snuck out through my bedroom window, and ran toward the abandoned warehouse. Finally, I would find and save Sally and the other innocent people who were kidnapped. And I would not be facing the substitute physics teacher, Samuel Divad; I would be facing the sinister kidnapper who abducted people due to his never-ending hunt for telekinesis, Malcolm Felone.

CHAPTER
21
FINAL SHOWDOWN

The warehouse was about three stories tall, and yet it appeared to be one hundred stories taller. Thin sheets of translucent plastic blew into the building, masquerading as curtains that tried to hide the innocent people trapped within its walls. The windows that weren't covered in plastic were boarded over by fresh, thick, rectangular pieces of wood. Adorned in chipped red paint, the warehouse seemed distorted, as if it was the typical place to store the bodies of those who disobeyed the wicked kidnapper within the ominous walls.

Taking a deep breath, I slowed my heart rate down to a steady buzz and walked up to the warehouse.

Surveying the perimeter, just to make sure the coast was clear, I lifted myself up onto windowpane.

As quietly as I could, I placed my feet on the floor inside the warehouse and lowered my body to the ground. If not for the rays of light that seeped in through the translucent plastic covering the window, the warehouse would have been pitch-black.

Crawling close to the walls, I tried not to sneeze from the years of dust that had been unearthed by my movement. If Felone was keeping his victims in this warehouse, he definitely wasn't keeping them on this floor.

I stopped for a second, trying to adapt to my surroundings. I needed to know everything that was in this warehouse, so I could use it to my advantage, just in case Felone showed up and I needed to evade an attack.

It took me a couple of minutes to acclimate myself to my surroundings. On the floor I explored, there were no rooms. A huge expanse of wooden floors and walls covered the first floor. An assembly line table and a couple of dusty, ancient chairs were the only pieces of furniture I came in contact with, and they'd probably been here since the warehouse was built.

The air was filled with specks of dirt. I couldn't inhale without flinching from the dirt making its way into my lungs. I tried to only breathe through my mouth so the dust wouldn't make its way up my nostrils.

I promised myself that when I made it out of the warehouse, I'd take one hundred showers each day just to remove the dirt that clung to my flesh and clothes.

When I finally familiarized myself with the first floor, I found the stairs and carefully walked up to the second floor. I had to test each step, so my feet wouldn't land on a creaky step and give away my position.

After a couple of minutes, I finally reached the second floor. I expected to find the second floor in the same condition as the first; however, to my surprise, my assumptions were wrong.

The second floor was covered in a thick sheet of canvas. The sunlight illuminating slivers of the air revealed that there was less than half the amount of dust particles in the atmosphere than there was on the first floor. Taking in a few breaths of cleaner air, I carefully walked around the second floor, making sure my footsteps didn't make a sound.

Every few seconds, I would stop to see if I could hear any other life on this floor. The entire floor felt hollow. I kept wishing I heard a muffled voice or the sound of someone trying to untie the ropes, or chains, I assumed were wrapped around the kidnapped victims. Unfortunately, the only sound I heard was my own heart trying to beat its way out of my chest.

Adapting to my surroundings on the second floor, like I had on the first, I found a few interesting items.

Similar to the first floor, there were no rooms. However, I did find a large, rectangular table next to a smaller replica in the corner. On the smaller table lay a vast array of syringes, no two were alike. The largest was almost half the size of my arm.

Each syringe had been pristinely polished to the point that I could see my tiny reflection in the glimmering, deadly, metal tip. Cringing at the thought of the syringe's needle being thrust into a human's head, I searched for anything else Felone kept on the second floor.

Unfortunately, the syringes and the tables were the only objects there.

Before I left the second floor, I took a closer look at the two tables. The smaller table was perfectly cleaned, as if it had just been polished.

The bigger table, on the other hand, was anything but clean. Pieces of fingernails and dried blood were strewn across the rough surface of the table. Strips of hair were mixed into the dried blood, which crusted over the top. Wincing, I walked away from the table before I could see if there were any pieces of human flesh that had melded with the ridged exterior.

Quietly walking toward the stairs, I made my way up to the third floor, avoiding the creaky steps once again. I yearned to float up the steps so I wouldn't have to be so careful, but I couldn't risk it.

The third floor was caked with a little less dirt than the first floor but definitely more than the second.

Unlike the other floors, the third flood was divided into sections. Adapting myself once again to my surroundings, I cautiously went into the first room I found.

With spider webs adorning the dirt-encrusted walls and floor, I slowly closed the door, seeing that the first room hadn't been touched in decades. No windows were ever built in this room, so the only light those spiders ever saw was the sliver I let in when I left the door ajar for a couple of seconds.

As I crept through the third floor, I found yet another tiny room crawling with spiders that had probably lived there for three generations. However, unlike the first room, there was one boarded up window in the corner, where hundreds of spiders made a web condominium for themselves.

Gently closing the door, I moved throughout the third floor again, hoping to find something other than spiders and dirt.

Taking a couple of steps forward, I came across a third room. As my hand reached for the doorknob, I noticed it wasn't covered in dust, unlike the others. As hope rose in my throat, I gingerly opened the door, praying I wouldn't find Felone on the other side.

I cracked open the door as I prepared myself for the worst. If Felone was in the room, I'd have to lock him inside until I rescued the people he kidnapped. Taking a deep breath, I opened the door the rest of the way to find a large room filled with layers of thick, brown, wool blankets.

Sighing, I was about to close the door when I saw one of the blankets move. I tentatively lifted up the wool blanket to find thick strands of brown hair peeping out from another blanket underneath the first one. I quickly ripped off the layers of blankets covering Felone's victims. Checking each one of their pulses, relief washed over me when I felt slow and steady beats.

Every person underneath the wool blankets was unconscious. Their hands were bound behind their backs with rusty chains digging into their wrists. Then I saw Sally among the victims. I practically jumped over the comatose kidnapped to get to her.

Gently pulling her out from the pile, I sat on the dusty floor and laid Sally's head in my lap. Tears streamed down my cheeks as I brushed back the flaxen hair that covered her closed eyelids. As I brushed my fingers through her tangled hair, I felt dry scabs along her scalp.

Turning over her arms, I saw puncture wounds on her tan forearm, where Felone must have extracted her blood.

"Sally," I whispered, wrapping my arms around her body. "I've found you. I *finally* found you."

I could have sat in that warehouse with Sally in my arms for the rest of my life, if not for the footstep I heard falling on the dirt-coated ground outside the door.

My eyes widened as the door gradually opened. Cautiously laying Sally down on the floor, I stiffened, preparing myself to use whatever amount of power I had to in order to stop Felone.

"You're not hurting her," I grumbled, malice washing any reason from my tone. "You're not hurting any of them. You'll never kidnap another person ever again."

"Cooper is that you?" a familiar voice questioned, as the door was flung open.

My jaw dropped when I saw Amber standing in the doorway, brushing layers of dirt off her arms.

"What the hell are you doing here?" I whispered, pulling her into the room.

"Did you actually think I'd stay away? I followed you," Amber stated, taking in the expanse of unconscious people lining the room. "Oh my God, he just stuffed them all in here. What the hell is wrong with that man?"

"He's a kidnapper, what did you expect?" I whispered. "Now, help me wake them."

How could Amber have risked her life by following me?

How could I not have known she was tracking me to the warehouse? I should have suspected she would follow me.

"They're not waking up," Amber whispered, poking one of Felone's victims with her index finger.

Amber and I tried shaking people's shoulders, but it was no use. Everyone remained unconscious. Remembering the syringes downstairs, I realized it was very likely everyone had been injected with a strong sedative. Looking at the chains on the victims' wrists, I at least knew I could break those off. I concentrated on the rusted metal, ripping it with enough intangible force to snap the chains in half.

"Better than pliers," Amber hummed, easily pulling the broken chains off the rest of the unconscious people.

"Look, we have to get them out of here before …" my voice trailed off when I heard an unfamiliar footstep fall near the room.

Amber gasped when she saw the dark silhouette of a man standing in the doorway. My heart betrayed me by stopping in midbeat as a man with thick, black, plastic glasses stepped out from the shadows.

"Cooper O'Neil," the kidnapper purred, grinning. It was almost like he'd expected me to come. Last night, he must have been hiding in the shadows, watching me sift through his office drawers. He must have figured out I was the one he'd really been looking for. Perhaps he didn't know when he'd kidnapped these people, but he definitely knew it now by the way his dark eyes glimmered with satisfaction.

"Let them go," I demanded.

"And what do I get in return?" the kidnapper questioned, leaning against the doorway, peering down at my pale face.

"Nothing, *Felone*," I responded, emphasizing his real name.

I had him; I knew his secret. I thought this knowledge would get a rise out of him, but his reaction was unexpected. His grin grew wider and more malicious. It was as if he was humoring me. I still wasn't sure how much he knew; I knew he was looking for my abilities, but I could not be entirely certain he knew I was the one who possessed them.

Without me, his experiment would fail. I was the one he was looking for all along, and he knew he'd have to let his victims go in order to get his hands on me. For Sally, I was willing to make that sacrifice.

"So, you figured me out, did you?" Felone laughed, as his sinister eyes took in the bodies he'd collected for his experiment. "I was hoping to pin everything on David Leumas."

"Where's Leumas? Is he your accomplice?" I questioned, rising from the floor and pulling my sister with me.

Adjusting his glasses, Felone cast his eyes downward and smiled as if he were remembering an old friend.

"I was *his* accomplice over forty years ago, Mr. O'Neil," Felone stated, taking a step into the room. My entire body stiffened. "That is, until someone died. He quit then and retired. He's probably dead by now. Pity, we could have kept going, but Leumas didn't have a scientific mind. His conscience got the better of him."

"Max Fitzpatrick," I declared. "Who killed him?" He gave a curt laugh, and I had my answer.

So, I was partly right, in a sense. Dr. Leumas may have been the original kidnapper, but Felone was the one who murdered my grandfather. I had more than enough evidence and witnesses to hand him over to the police. The discussion had to end there; he had no power over me. I could hold him with a glare, so Amber could help the others out of the warehouse and call the police.

Before Felone could take another step, I concentrated on his legs, feeling every atom in him awaken as I rose him off the floor. He should have been terrified, or at least mesmerized, but his expression was one of slight interest.

Raising one eyebrow, his smirk grew at my display of telekinetic prowess. Instead of begging me to let him down, his eyes were filled with the fire of a challenge.

"Get everyone out while I hold him," I ordered Amber, still focusing on the grinning kidnapper.

"Mr. O'Neil, do you really think I'd find potentially telekinetic individuals without being prepared for an attack?" he exclaimed, thrusting his palm into the air.

Before I could even blink, without laying a finger on me, he drove my body into the wall behind the unconscious bodies on the floor. Amber's scream drove out the silence that once encompassed this warehouse.

So, Malcolm Felone wasn't just a doctor searching for telekinesis; he had the same power he was searching for. If he already possessed the ability, why was he trying to extract it from others?

Pushing all of my questions aside for the moment, I concentrated on my body, struggling to lower myself to the ground and away from the wall. It was as if an invisible hand was holding me to that wall as I tried to fight against it.

Felone held out both of his palms, feeling that I was breaking free from his telekinetic grasp. Beads of sweat formed on my brow as I began to pull away from the wall. Breathing became difficult with each step I took.

"You can't hold me," I managed to say, as I finally fell forward, escaping the telekinetic hold Felone had over me.

"Your grandfather was easier, I must say," Felone stated, backing out of the room while still keeping that infuriating smirk on his face. "I didn't realize Max was your grandfather, that is, until your little display."

Turning toward Amber, I pointed to the unconscious people lining the room.

"Amber, help these people. Get them out as fast as you can," I commanded her, breaking her out of her shock.

"S-sure. But, what about you?" Amber asked, pulling one of the victims, Samuel Murdoch, to his feet.

Shaking my head slightly, I couldn't even believe what I was going tell my sister. In my worst nightmares, I never imagined we'd be having this conversation. But here we were, trying to save people who had been kidnapped by a demented scientist.

"I need to stop him," I said, stepping out of the room and into the shadows of the third-floor hall, where I knew I'd have to stop the Parkway kidnapper from experimenting on anyone else ever again.

When I entered the hall, the former doctor was staring at the wood boarding up the windows. Then, as if it was glass, the wood shattered into tiny daggers, falling to the dirt-coated floor. Rays of light poured into the warehouse.

"Turn yourself in, and there will be no fight," I said, keeping my hands firmly planted to my sides.

"Now, now. If I turned myself in, how would I take your powers?" he asserted, pulling out a large syringe from his sleeve.

"Why did you kidnap people when you already have powers?" I inquired.

"When I was younger, I hardly had any powers," he stated, holding the syringe at his side.

I could tell he was itching to thrust the needle into me by the way his eyes kept shifting toward the device he grasped tightly in his right hand. Nervously clenching and unclenching my fists, I anticipated an attack, especially an invisible one.

"But you did have powers?" I asked, stalling for time until I thought of a tactic that would lead him into a trap.

"If you must know, yes, I did," Felone exclaimed, glancing down at the syringe for the hundredth time in a couple of agonizing minutes. "I'm assuming you've read Leumas's textbook. Knowing Max, he probably kept it around. He wanted so badly to become a doctor. It's such a shame I had to take away his powers to complete my serum."

"Serum, what serum?" I asked, quickly glancing at the shards of wood lying on the floor.

"In the textbook, Leumas suggested that if there was a hereditary mutation in the genes, then there was a possibility an ABO blood type group wouldn't react the same to the proteins—the A antigen and B antigen— which determine what blood type you are," Felone lectured, caressing his precious syringe as he spoke. "I told him that if the A antigen and B antigen were applied to a person with an AB blood type, who had a 'hereditary mutation,' then the antigens wouldn't react to the blood, at first. If the A antigen and B antigen don't react to a blood type, then that blood is an AB blood type. However, if a person with an AB blood type has telekinesis, then the A antigen and B antigen will react to the blood in a way it wouldn't normally react. The blood will begin to move on its own.

"Although this was Leumas's theory, I was the one who figured out how to create a serum that could replicate the mutation in the blood that caused telekinesis. However, in order to do that, I needed to extract AB blood from the brain, especially from the somatosensory area, of people who had telekinesis. In a telekinetic person, the somatosensory area acts like an invisible hand that can grasp or move anything based on the power of the mind.

Leumas didn't have the courage to see this through. I won't make that mistake."

As Felone continued his monologue, I calculated the angle at which I could pin him down with the tiny wooden stakes he created when he shattered the wood boarding up the windows.

While I concentrated on Felone's tale, my sister was quietly trying to wake his victims. I heard a few of them stirring in the room. Hopefully, Felone was too engrossed in his own story to hear anything.

"I created a serum that can give a normal person, with any blood type, telekinesis," Felone continued, grinning at his devious accomplishments. "Over forty years ago, I saw a gurney stop without anyone touching it. I immediately knew someone in that hospital had telekinesis, so I began collecting people who had an AB blood type, with the help of their medical records, at Parkway Hospital.

"When not one person I kidnapped showed any results, I almost gave up, that is, until I saw a baby staring at pencils that seemed to be moving on their own. That's when I figured out Max Fitzpatrick's little girl was exactly who I was looking for. His daughter was the key to the greatest scientific discovery."

"So, you extracted her powers," I concluded, realizing that was why my mother didn't have telekinesis.

"Yes, the baby was fine without hers, but extracting them from Max proved to be fatal. It's too bad he fought back. If he hadn't, maybe he would have survived the extraction. However, even with their powers combined, the serum was only strong enough to test on one person. Since I had the weakest telekinetic powers to begin with, I tested the serum on myself. As you can see, it proved to be a success. My powers have quadrupled in strength since then."

"If you have what you want, why come back?" I asked, hoping my questions would distract Felone long enough for Amber to wake his victims and get them to safety.

"It wasn't enough," Felone stated, walking closer to me. "This discovery should be shared with the world. Why should you and I be the only ones with this gift?"

Greed, a typical mad scientist motive. "Can't you just extract what you need from yourself? Why do you need anyone else," I asked, ensuring Felone's attention was on me. As I stared into his eyes, I could hear the soft steps of Amber leading Felone's victims out of the room and down the stairs.

"Why would I do that?" Felone countered, narrowing his eyes. "Actually, I was going to look elsewhere for others with telekinesis. I figured Max

Fitzpatrick's family probably left Parkway. In fact, I assumed that for over forty years while I traveled around the nation, trying to find homeless people to experiment on. However, about a year ago, I was in the Bronx when I felt the ground rumble beneath my feet. It felt almost like an earthquake. When I turned on the news later that day, the broadcast said it was a minor earthquake that, according to the Richter Scale, originated from the small town of Parkway. Now, it was possible there was an earthquake in Parkway, but it was also possible I was wrong about the Fitzpatrick family leaving Parkway."

Groaning to myself, I realized my telekinetic outburst that morning, when Sally and I were getting intimate, tipped him off to the fact that someone with telekinesis resided in Parkway. I unintentionally led him here, and, in turn, he kidnapped the girl I loved.

"It took me about a year to set up," Felone continued. "I had to find pawns who would do my bidding, and I had to find a place where I could set up a lab to experiment on my subjects. I set up tests all over town—runaway cars, pickpocketing, and such—to see if anyone would use their powers to stop one of them. I'd almost given up hope when no one stopped the attacks and crimes using telekinesis. That is, until the mugger I hired hit the ground and was pulled backward by an invisible force near Erikson High School. That's when I assumed the telekinetic person either worked at or attended the high school. So, I became a substitute. I was invisible enough to observe. After I'd had little success with the few people I'd kidnapped, I set up another test with that car I'd flipped and detonated. When the door was so easily ripped off, I knew the telekinetic person was still at Erikson High School.

"However, I didn't expect the person with telekinesis to be Max Fitzpatrick's grandchild. I should have known. You're smart, just like he was." Felone sighed, thrusting out his palm at the wall behind me.

"Unfortunately, your sister is not."

Spinning around, I saw Amber trying to struggle against Felone's telekinetic grasp as she was pinned to the wall.

"Let her go!" I shouted.

Concentrating on the shards of wood lying underneath the windows, they rose at my will. Aiming each wooden dagger at Felone's body, I released the stakes, making sure they plunged into his flesh.

Screaming out in agony, Felone released his hold on my sister in order to thrust the wooden stakes digging into his sides back at me.

Instinctively, I closed my eyes and held out my hands in front of my face, focusing on Felone's weapons. Time seemed to slow to a halt as I heard Amber's scream over the whiz of the wooden daggers flying toward me.

I couldn't understand why I wasn't crying out in pain. The daggers should have pierced my flesh. I should have been falling to the ground as blood oozed out of my body. Gingerly, I opened my eyes to see the stakes stopped in mid-flight. Each one was aimed at my head, and yet none were willing to budge.

Throwing down my hands, I watched as the wooden daggers simultaneously fell to the floor. A second ago, they had been filled with a murderous purpose. Now, they were mere pieces of sharp wood lying at my feet. I must have instinctively used my telekinesis to stop them.

"Amber, run!" I commanded my sister, not having to turn around to know she hadn't left me.

"He'll hurt you. I won't leave you," Amber whimpered, running to my side.

"Loyalty. How refreshing," Felone mocked, watching as Amber clung to me. "However, in your case, your sister's loyalty will be your downfall."

Before I could take control of his weapons, Felone aimed the stakes at my sister.

"Move even an inch, and she dies," Felone warned.

The wooden daggers circled Amber's head, as if they were vultures waiting for death to come. Amber's eyes were filled with terror as she watched the stakes inch closer to her face. Refusing to blink, tears streamed down her large, emerald eyes as she waited for the wooden shards to pierce her vulnerable flesh.

"Get him," Amber demanded, slightly separating her dried lips to speak. "He kidnapped Sally. He kidnapped others. Get him."

I nodded but stood still, calculating my next move. Even if I moved quicker than I ever had, all Felone had to do was blink, and the wooden daggers would thrust themselves through my sister's flesh. I wouldn't allow Amber to get hurt; there had to be another way I could stop him. There was always a plan B beneath the surface, there just had to be.

"All right," I stated, surrender laced in my tone. "You can have me. Just let my sister go."

Felone's malicious grin appeared once again on his sinister face as he moved the stakes about a centimeter away from Amber's head.

"Come forward," Felone commanded, gripping the syringe tighter in his grasp. "I'll let her go once I have what I need."

"Don't do it, Cooper!" Amber screamed, momentarily forgetting about the wooden daggers.

"I have to," I told her, stiffening with each step I took. "You may be able to take care of yourself, but that doesn't mean I won't fight to protect you."

As I walked toward the enemy, I felt as if I were floating over my body. I couldn't be walking toward a person who was threatening my sister with stakes. I couldn't possibly be walking toward a man who had the skill to extract my powers from me. I couldn't be walking into death when I was only seventeen years old. And yet, I was. As unbelievable as this scenario was, it was my life. There was no denying what I was doing.

I couldn't walk into the beast's trap so easily. He had my sister at stake-point, but there had to be a way I could get her out before I reached Felone.

Malcolm Felone's grin grew wider with each step I took. He was probably already patting himself on the back. Fortunately for me, he was congratulating himself a little too early.

As quickly as I could, I flicked my wrist and sent his glasses flying off the bridge of his nose. Felone immediately fell to the ground, trying to find them. By the thickness of the lenses, I could tell he was practically blind without them. The minute he began to search for his spectacles, he released his telekinetic hold on the stakes and the sharp pieces of wood fell to the floor.

Focusing on the shards of wood, I flew them out the window before Felone could try to use them against my sister or me once again.

"Watch out!" Amber screamed, pointing toward the ground.

Felone had found his glasses quicker than I thought he would. With his glasses back in place on the bridge of his nose, he lunged at me, trying to shove the syringe into my scalp.

I jumped back just in time for the syringe's needle to catch the air and plunge into the dirt-coated floor.

Scowling, Felone pulled the syringe out of the floor and made a second attempt.

"Not so fast," I said, jumping into the air, levitating about ten feet over Felone.

Imitating my jump, Felone leapt, and we were face-to-face in midair.

"You're different than your grandfather," Felone exclaimed, his knuckles turning paler by the second as he gripped the ominous syringe. "There were no tricks up his sleeve. He gave into my demands when I had his daughter in my grasp. But not you. You're not as willing to give up your powers as he was."

At that moment, the fairy tale my mother told me when I was little came to life. Felone was the dragon, and my grandfather was the knight in shining armor who saved her.

Felone released the syringe, sending it flying at my head. Focusing on the speeding weapon, I turned its direction south and sent it diving into the floorboards once more.

"Over the years, I've gotten used to my powers," I countered, as I thrust my palm forward and sent Felone flying into the wall behind him. "They're a part of me. I'm not going to give them up without a fight."

A shower of dirt rained down from the walls from the impact of Felone's body. Shaking off the dirt sprinkled over his clothes, Felone countered my attack by releasing the syringe from the floor and aiming it upward. I stopped it in midflight. Feeling its metallic surface in my mind, I focused on the tip of the weapon.

Before Felone could call back the syringe, I dulled the tip and sent it flying out of one of the windows.

"It's over, Felone," I avowed, still keeping my guard up. "You either turn yourself in peacefully, or we'll take a more painful route. It's your choice."

Smirking, Felone shoved his hand in his pocket and pulled out about five syringes half the size of the one I banished from the warehouse.

Before I could even blink, he sent them flying at my head. Again, I flicked my wrists in the direction of the syringes, but they refused to stop. Felone thrust both of his palms in the air, using all of the strength he had left to send them flying toward me.

"Cooper, watch out!" I heard Amber scream from the ground.

Again, I tried to stop them in midair, but to no avail.

Felone wasn't going to give up so easily.

Concentrating on the tiny weapons aimed at my head, I put all of my strength into trying to slow them down. I only managed to decrease their speed by a couple of seconds. If those syringes made their way into my flesh, they'd pierce right through my brain. Felone would get exactly what he wanted, and my grandfather's fate would be mine.

Holding out my hands, I roared as the syringes continued to fly toward me. The seconds seemed to slow down to minutes as I put all of my will into trying to stop their trajectory.

I imagined myself stopping everything around me. Reaching beyond these walls, beyond this town, I willed everything to stand still. My limitations were withering away as I felt the energy of every atom, even those past my normal reach, tingling in my mind. Every molecule vibrated in my hold, fighting to move once again.

Tears streamed down my cheeks as I focused on every living thing, stopping them in their path. Even time itself seemed to stop as I thrust my hands outward, feeling the stored energy of every moving being in my mind.

"No!" I commanded the syringes, closing my eyes.

Wincing, I expected to feel the deadly points of the syringes' needles through my flesh. It seemed as if I hung in the air forever, waiting for Felone's weapons to drive themselves into my brain. However, nothing happened.

They never made their way to my head.

Opening my eyes, I couldn't believe what I saw in front of me. I thought my eyes had betrayed me, but what I saw in front of me wasn't a fantasy my mind had created to help me deal with the pain. In front of my eyes, a thick, translucent film circled my body. It was as if I'd created a protective bubble with my mind.

"How did you do that? How could you do that? Is that possible?" Amber screeched in a mixture of fear and surprise.

Shaking off Amber's questions, I focused on the levitating syringes, easily willing them to the ground.

Felone couldn't stop staring at the transparent shield I'd created with my mind.

"How *did* you do that?" Felone asked, unable to hold himself in midair for another second.

Felone was completely drained; he could hardly hold up his own body with or without using his powers. I, too, was practically depleted, but I had enough power to hold him to the ground.

"Amber, get the chains and tie him up," I breathed, hardly able to speak as my translucent shield dissolved back into my mind.

Amber quickly wrapped the chains, leftover from Felone's victims, around his wrists and ankles. Before Amber finished tying him up, Felone's eyes closed, and he slumped over in exhaustion.

"Done," Amber stated, brushing the rust off her palms.

"Good," I exhaled, releasing my grip.

I could hardly hold myself up. My mind-numbing migraine returned for a reunion and brought friends.

Leaning on my sister's shoulder, Amber led me near the stairs and leaned me up against the wall so she could call the police.

22

ACCEPTANCE

Murdoch, and almost every police officer who worked in Parkway, surrounded the warehouse. Before Murdoch even thought of arresting the kidnapper, he wrapped his arms around his son.

About ten police officers followed Amber inside the warehouse. Smiling to myself, I held my palm to my forehead, feeling as if someone had beaten me over the head with about a hundred buildings.

"He hit you pretty hard, didn't he?" Murdoch asked, placing his hand on my shoulder as I lay on the gurney outside of an ambulance.

"Yes," I said, straining my voice just to say that one syllable.

I could hardly see straight from the constant buzzing distorting my vision, but it was worth it. I'd stopped a psychopathic doctor who would stop at nothing to obtain more power. While, as an aspiring physicist, I found his and Leumas's theory intriguing, it should not come at the cost of human life.

Before Murdoch left my side, I had one question I had to ask him.

"Chief Murdoch, how is it that Felone's victims couldn't remember him?" I asked, practically wearing out my vocal cords to ask that one question.

"You'll just have to hear about it on the news. My guess, with all toxins we found in that warehouse, he injected his victims with something to make them forget," Murdoch declared. Before he left, he patted me on the shoulder. "Good work finding him, O'Neil."

Nodding, I smiled to myself, knowing that I'd finally rescued Felone's victims, especially Sally. Lying down on the grass, I closed my eyes, hoping sleep would deaden my throbbing forehead and wash over my raw, living nightmares.

"You know you can never really relax," the other me stated, floating over moving needles.

Smiling, I lay back on the dull tips and let my body float over the harmless weapons.

"Yeah, I know," I responded, closing my eyes. "But I can at least relax for now."

Nodding, the other me faded into the back of my mind, finally leaving me in peace.

"Wake up, sweetie," my mother said, gently shaking me awake. "You've been asleep since yesterday."

"What?" I said, shooting up from bed.

My headache caught up with me a second after my eyes opened. I couldn't help but wonder if the day before had just been a dream. My intense migraine reminded me that what happened was not a fantasy.

"Sally!" I shouted, suddenly realizing I did not check to see if she got out of the warehouse safely; after all, I risked my life to save her. "Is she okay? Where is she?"

"Calm down, sweetie," my mother said, pushing me back down onto the hospital bed. "She's visiting Michelle right now. She was sitting by your bedside all night."

Sighing, I laid my head back on my cool pillow. "Any other visitors?" I asked, wincing from my throbbing headache.

"Well, your father and sister are sitting in the waiting room. Amber wants to know if you considered being the next Sherlock Holmes," my mother laughed, fixing my sheets. "Chief Murdoch came to visit just a little while ago. He hopes Malcolm Felone gets life imprisonment. With kidnapping and a murder charge, he probably will. Oh, and he told me that you wanted to know why the people Felone kidnapped didn't remember him."

"He figured it out?" I inquired, knowing Felone must have confessed.

"Malcolm Felone told Chief Murdoch that he slightly damaged the hippocampus. It's a part of the brain that controls memories. He obviously knows his neurology," my mother exclaimed, inadvertently parting my hair.

"Wait, what about Felone's powers?" I asked, knowing that a prison couldn't hold a person with telekinesis.

"Apparently, Felone kept screaming that he didn't have power," my mother stated, smiling. "Chief Murdoch thought he was screaming about a different type of power. However, Amber explained the whole ordeal to me. The fight he had with you must have depleted his powers permanently, since most of it was artificial."

"Good," I said, smiling to myself.

I was thankful I survived my encounter with Felone. If not, my mother couldn't have kept fixing my hair.

"I'm so proud of you, sweetie. I feel like I don't tell you that enough," she stated, tears filling her eyes as she hugged me.

"Yes, you do. I love you, too," I said, hugging my mother back.

After I'd spoken with my mother for a couple of minutes, Sally entered my hospital room.

Seeing Sally in the doorway, my mother turned to me and smiled.

"I'll leave you two alone," my mother said, giving me a kiss on my forehead before she left.

Sally pulled a chair up to my hospital bed and laid her warm fingertips on top of my hand. Her glimmering smile illuminated the dim hospital room. All I wanted to do was wrap my arms around her and sink into those shimmering blue eyes for the rest of my life.

"Hey," Sally said, unable to hide her luminous smile.

"Hey," I responded, placing my left hand on top of hers. "How are you?"

Brushing her hand through her flaxen hair, Sally laughed.

"Well, for a person who's just been kidnapped, I'm doing pretty well," she stated, casting her eyes downward. "I can't believe you saved my life, so many lives. That was so brave, Cooper."

"You remember?" I asked, wondering if Felone forgot to damage Sally's hippocampus.

"Actually, it's all just a blur. Chief Murdoch and your sister filled me in on the details I couldn't remember."

Hopefully, Felone didn't cause Sally to have early-onset Alzheimer's disease with his telekinetic science experiment.

"How's Michelle?" I asked.

"Well, she'll be out of the hospital soon," Sally said, caressing my forearm. "Actually, she gave me a message for you. She told me to tell you, 'Nice going, hero.'"

Smiling to myself, I realized it taken almost dying to save Sally to earn Michelle's respect. She was quite a hard person to please. I just hoped her suspicions about my telekinesis would subside with time.

"I love you, Sally. I don't know what I'd do without you," I said, gently stroking her cheek with my fingertips.

"I love you more than anything," Sally stated, tears running down from her iridescent, sapphire eyes. "And I always will, no matter what."

"Well then, I have something to tell you something I should have told you a long time ago," I began, knowing I needed to trust her. If I were willing to sacrifice myself to save her, I had to believe she would accept me—all of me—for who I was. I knew she would love me, even with my unusual talent.

ABOUT THE AUTHOR

 Jenna Marcus is an academic leader. She has a fervent passion for leveraging her decade of expertise to robustly enhance and redefine the quality of teaching and learning. As an avid reader, she believes every child should find a book to love. In her current position as a Literacy Coordinator, she seeks to imbue a passion for reading in students. This is one of the primary reasons she writes young adult fiction, so our young people can discover stories they relate to and inspire them to read.

Until June 2020, she held the combined roles of Director of Student Achievement and IGCSE Coordinator at the private international boarding school EF Academy in New York. In addition to her professional experience, she holds a MS. ED in Educational Leadership, a MS. ED in Middle Childhood and Adolescent English Education, and a BA in Literature. She is also certified in School Building Leadership and ELA. Currently, she lives in New Rochelle, NY.

www.ingramcontent.com/pod-product-compliance
Lightning Source LLC
Chambersburg PA
CBHW020633110726
47899CB00002B/753